Skid: Death Hounds MC #2

Copyright

Cover Designer: Traci Douglas- Black Water Covers & Formatting

Editor: Jackie Ziegler

Proofreading: Rebecca Vasquez

Warning:

This book contains scenes that describe abuse, assault, and dubious consent in a generalized manner and should not be read if these subject matters bother or offend you.

Dedication

To the countless souls who've survived what no one should endure. Lift your face to the sun and know you are loved.

Synopsis

From a young age, I followed the rules set for me, being the good girl and never wanting to feel the painful sting of rejection. I thought all my wishes had come true, but everything changed in an instant, and I was forced to see the harsh and ugly realities of life. I ran from everything I knew, vowing a life alone was better than living under the control of others.

My new life wasn't perfect, but it was mine. Forged with sweat and tears, I built something I could be proud of, but I still kept people at a distance. I existed but never truly lived. The moment I saw him, I knew he was different. His haunting eyes told me he wasn't scared of the darkness that resided within me.

He pushed through the walls I built around myself and taught me that love was real, giving me the strength to face my nightmares and step out of the darkness. The Death Hounds showed me what family was and that loyalty was valued above everything. When I decided to stop running and fight, they stood beside me, proving that family was who you chose.

But then he betrayed me and sent me back down a path of dark nightmares and into a life of silence. Now, he's fighting for both of us, showing me that his words of devotion were true. When he discovers the secrets I've been carrying, will he still see me the same, or will he push me away and force me back into solitude?

Never again will I make a wish.

It may come true, but at what cost?

Author's Note

While this is the second book in the Death Hounds MC series, it is the final piece of the storyline in the Embattled Dream Series. It's not necessary to read the series before reading Skid, but it will give you a better understanding of the events that led up to this book. You can start with Embracing My Nightmare if you want to know where the Dark Nightmare began. Welcome to Portstill, Tennessee, where a madman once ruled the streets and, in his absence, gave rise to the Death Hounds.

Prologue

Grace

When trust is destroyed, there is no rebuilding it. You can only learn from the painful lessons and move on. I thought losing my dad at four was the hardest thing I would have to survive, but my mother giving me up the following year was a blow to my self-worth. How could she throw me away like I never mattered?

The foster system was designed to help kids in need by placing them with families who wanted to help give them a better life. For years, I had it pretty good. Besides dodging judgment and scorn, I was treated fairly well.

The moment it changed, I realized I could no longer trust myself or how I perceived things. What I was taught, and how good things were twisted into depravity, made me untrusting and unsettled.

Never again will I make a wish.

It may come true, but at what cost?

Chapter 1

Skid

The night I patched into the Death Hounds, all my dreams came true. I was finally part of the brotherhood I longed for, but in an instant, everything changed. My younger brother was saved by a madman, and I vowed a debt to him. A life for a life.

For ten years, I lived a dual existence. Half of it was spent with the Death Hounds, fulfilling the dream I had since the first time Uncle Mick took me for a ride on his motorcycle. The other half was spent in the employment of Devlin Callahan, the madman of the Flats. Or at least he used to be. I first pledged my loyalty to him for saving my little brother Jacob's life and was thrust into a different dark and dangerous world.

Everyone assumed he was a killer without remorse, looking to grab power and money for his own benefit. His motivations were much deeper and profound than anyone, other than his brother James, could understand. The two men met as boys and were pulled into a world so twisted and sick, I'm shocked they had any sanity between the two of them. They survived, like most people in the Flats, by using their cunning and taking opportunities as they arose.

When Devlin took control of the area from Marco, a completely demented human being, everyone assumed it would be business as usual. Slowly, Devlin changed the Flats, running the pimps and drug dealers out of town, shutting down the rampant assaults and rapes that were commonplace, and showing the citizens compassion. He was still feared and spilled blood in the streets without remorse, but his reasons only became known years later, and only to a select few people.

He worked hard throughout the years, and I learned everything I could from him. Soaking up as much knowledge as he and James would give me, I became proficient in hacking, code writing, and cyber security. It was a far cry from the life I thought I'd lead, and the more I learned, the more their trust and loyalty in me grew. When the programs we had been working on for years to enhance facial recognition and voice print analysis were sold to the government for millions of dollars, suddenly, the madman was respectable, and he started his master plan.

It wasn't world domination, illegal activities, or anything for personal gain. Devlin's motivation for everything was a beautiful woman named Elise, who had become his obsession years before I met him. Every move he made and every deal he brokered was done with her in mind, even if she wasn't aware of it for years.

The afternoon he sat me down and handed me an envelope with a check for over three million dollars was the most surreal day of my life. I grew up in the Flats with my big sister, Sadie, and my younger brother, Jacob. Our mother was a useless bitch who neglected Sadie from an early age, left me alone as a little boy with my sister to look after me, and when Jacob was born, she practically disappeared. If it wasn't for Uncle Mick, we would have been sucked up into the darkness. He helped as much as he could, and Sadie gave everything she had to raise us into semi-descent citizens. After experiencing firsthand the destruction and immorality of living in the Flats, I vowed never to let anyone experience what my sister lived through.

A few years ago, my brother-in-law and club President, Gunner, and I found out one of my sister's rapists was still alive, and we carved him like a turkey, leaving him for the vultures to eat. It felt good to dole out justice, and soon after, I took on more personal business for Devlin. A part of me craved the rush of hurting men who thought it was okay to force women into depraved, life-altering situations. I learned to foster the darkness but never allowed it to overtake me.

James discovered he had a sister named Aubrey a few months ago, and when she was able to finally tell her story, my heart broke for her, and the monster inside of me yearned for blood. She fell for one of my good friends, Hayden, and it took time for her to be able to speak her truth. It was darker and more painful than any single person should have to live through, and I saw the same murderous look in Devlin's and James's eyes that I felt in mine. She not only survived but thrived after being dealt not one but two horrific blows.

We discovered what three selfish assholes had done to Aubrey when she was a teenager and killing them became a top priority. Feeding one of the rapist assholes to the alligator was a start, but there was something more I could do. One last thing before I left the employment of Callahan once and for all . . .

Finding the man who took from Aubrey when she was a child and end him.

She had given James a thumb drive that documented something so vile that I told Devlin I would watch it and gather information. He insisted he could do it, but I didn't want him to have that vision in his head. He, his brother, and newfound sister deserved that much. Besides, it would put him in a dark place that Elise would struggle to bring him back from, so I took the thumb drive from him.

It sat on the desk in my cabin for over two weeks before I could bring myself to watch it, then I threw up twice while viewing it. My anger was deeper than anything I'd ever experienced before, and after capturing screenshots, I secured the thumb drive in my desk. For the next week, I ran every picture through our facial recognition programs and let the system analyze the data.

Aubrey deserved justice, and while we were able to give her some measure of vengeance, there was still someone out there who deserved to die.

It was an old newspaper article that sent me down the path I'm walking, hoping to chase down any other victims of that sick fucker's degeneracy. The man who hurt Aubrey in unimaginable ways had died four years ago, along with his wife, in a car accident in Atlanta while on their way home from vacation.

With the contacts Devlin fostered through the years, we used back doors to track people the government needed to disappear without getting their hands dirty. Those same contacts turned their heads when we needed to find someone, so I began digging through the dead man's life. From all outward appearances, he and his wife were good people, but I knew his revolting truth. Aubrey may not have been his first victim, or his last.

The newspaper article I found in their local small-town Missouri newspaper praised how they fostered children who needed homes until they could be reunited with their families, and they were touted as gracious, giving, and loving. I scoffed as I read it, knowing what kind of a sick freak he really was.

Questions began to swirl around my mind, and I used a back door into the state foster system, gaining a list of kids placed with them through the years. The state of Missouri closed their files since they didn't have any foster kids under their care when they passed. The list wasn't long, and I accessed every back door Devlin placed in his security systems to get the information I needed on every child placed in their *care*.

They were both in their mid-forties when they died and had fostered eleven kids over sixteen years, five boys and six girls. Running background checks on eleven foster kids was harder than I anticipated. Some kids aged out of the system or were returned to their families, leaving little to no information for me to find. During my search, I questioned why they fostered instead of adopting but knew I'd never get an answer to that question.

After finding what information I could, I began to condense the list, removing the boys and praying they weren't affected by him. The girls were all ages during their time with them, and I went one by one, either removing them due to age, how long they were with them, records from the state on their next placement, or a gut feeling.

That left one girl who spent twelve years with them and was listed as a runaway with the state. She was their longest placement, and they never made a move to adopt her.

Grace Palmer.

I read how she ended up in foster care, and my heart broke for the girl. She was another casualty of the rampant drug problems destroying communities, yet from every indication, her early life wasn't all that bad. She lost her father to a sudden heart attack, and within a year, her mother lost her to foster care due to addiction.

Grace was placed with the Ringmans when she was four years old, long before Aubrey's nightmare, and seemed to have a normal life until she was almost sixteen. Her state record said she had been a mild-mannered young woman, even with her past trauma. Shortly before she disappeared, her social media took a depressive turn and then it just ended. Her pages weren't closed, but there hadn't been any activity in years. Not even secret logins, which I looked for.

Without access to social security records, which were locked up tight within the government, it made finding her harder. There were no marriage or death records that I could find, no criminal background, no employment records, and after exhausting all available avenues, I called in the experts.

Devlin, James, and I began accessing the cameras and security systems that had been installed all over the country. Private homes, small businesses, traffic lights, ATMs, and major corporations all had Callahan Security systems installed.

For months, the system scanned every face captured on its cameras, and I continued to use the back door we had with the government programs, hoping to catch a glimpse of what our computers predicted she looked like. Without a current picture, we were flying blind, and with every passing day, my obsession to find Grace grew. The last photo of her was taken ten years ago, before she ran away, and the likelihood she had altered her appearance was high.

I was sound asleep in my comfy bed, the fireplace blazing in the corner, when my phone chimed from the end table. It was dark outside, and I stretched under the warm covers before reaching over to grab my phone from the charging dock. I was used to late night calls from club brothers in need or one of the Callahans. Reading the report, I shot up in bed and turned the lamp on as I quickly scanned the information.

"Fucking finally," I spoke into the empty room as I slid from the bed and walked into the bathroom.

It was chilly for an early spring morning, so I slipped on a pair of gray sweatpants and a long-sleeved T-shirt before sliding my feet into my new house shoes. My laptop was on the coffee table from my search last night, and I needed to pull up the full report before getting my hopes up. We've had eight false reports, and I feared this might be another one.

Turning my computer on, I started a pot of coffee and tossed fresh wood into the living room fireplace, feeling the warmth across the open living room into the kitchen. My computer pinged, letting me know I was on a secure network, and I sat down. Reading the report, I flipped through the attached photos and felt my heart racing as each one downloaded.

After months of dead ends and false hope, Grace Palmer was staring at me through the screen. She had a small smile on her beautiful face as she made a withdrawal from an ATM. After finding the location of the machine, I realized it was installed last week in Alabama, along with a few hundred more across the southern United States.

Headlights flashed across the large windows along the front of my cabin, and I unlocked the door, knowing who was about to walk in. The coffee pot finished bubbling as James walked inside, shaking the water droplets off his jacket. I lifted my chin to him and turned the corner into my kitchen, reaching up and pulling down two cups.

"I was wondering how long it would take you to show up after the system sent the report," I stated as he walked into the kitchen and accepted a cup from me.

"I got the notification about an hour ago and jumped in the car. I know we agreed to let you take the lead on this, but I feel like I need to do something." His voice was filled with rage, and I sat down at the small kitchen table, waiting for him to join me.

James was a killer unlike any other. From outward appearances, he looked like a bored frat boy who wouldn't hurt a fly. In reality, James has a higher body count than anyone I know. He was ruthless when he was younger, and it's only been since he met Amaya that he found any part of a soul. Knowing, without exactly knowing, what his sister endured when she was only twelve years old had brought James's monster to the surface.

"How are you going to handle this?" he asked, and I shrugged.

We didn't know if Grace had to endure what Aubrey did, but my gut said something happened to that beautiful girl to make her run. She was a good student, active in her school activities, had friends who she spent time with, posting pictures of their infectious youth, but slowly, her outward life seemed to dim. Then she was gone . . . until now.

"I need to know if she's okay. Sadie and Aubrey kept everything hidden for years, and I . . . I just need to know."

James ran his hands through his brown hair and sighed deeply. "Do you think he hurt her too?"

Pursing my lips, I gave him a quick nod. "Something happened to that sweet little girl. It was either him or something else, but there must be a reason her life went from what looked to be happy to solemn. Then she disappeared into thin air, and no one gave a damn. If I'm wrong, then I'll be content knowing his sickness didn't touch another young girl."

"What are you going to do once you find her?" he asked, leaning his forearms onto the table. "If she's like my sister, she's going to have a false protective shell around her, telling everyone she's happy when deep down inside, she's miserable and haunted."

"I saw the look in Aubrey's eyes the night she and Hayden got together, and I've seen it in my sister's since I was eight. It's something that can't be hidden behind a false smile." My response was gruff, but it wasn't directed at him.

It was directed at piece of shit men who forced themselves onto women and girls. I wasn't a saint when it came to women, but consent was always required. Too much alcohol was a deal-breaker, along with drugs, tears, or any outward sign she wasn't digging what was happening. I'd fuck a willing woman until she couldn't walk straight, and I had, many times, but I would never take advantage or force myself on anyone who didn't want me.

James left shortly after we spoke, and I watched the sun rise through the trees. My mind drifted to the beautiful woman I'd spent six months searching for, and I debated on just letting the past stay buried, fearful I would rip the scabs off old wounds.

I should leave her alone, but I'm not going to. I knew, no matter what, I was going to protect this woman. She's been alone in the world for too long, and I prayed that I could at least give her the peace of mind that someone in the world cared about what happened to her.

After I spoke with Gunner, I packed a few changes of clothes and climbed on my bike. The trip to Alabama would give me a chance to clear my head before I found Grace. The last thing I wanted to do was cause her any more pain.

Chapter 2

Skid

For three weeks, I frequented a bar on the backwaters of Alabama, sweating my ass off, swatting mosquitos the size of a dinner plate, and trying to catch glimpses of Grace. After arriving in town and securing a trailer to rent for a few months, I set out to find her but was taken aback when I discovered she was slinging drinks at a bar tucked against the river, hiding in plain sight.

She always had a smile on her beautiful face as she served the patrons, a mix of military, bikers, locals, and the occasional tourist looking for trouble. I kept my back to the wall when I was here, not knowing who was going to take a swing at whom next. The bar wasn't a dive, but it was far from upscale. Sawdust on the floor, smoke lingering in the air, the smell of stale beer and cheap whiskey overpowered the room, and a band playing classic rock covers too loudly gave it a unique vibe.

My usual waitress walked up to the small table, leaning over and giving me a clear shot of her thick cleavage as she shouted over the band, "Do you want another, or is there something else you want?"

Her dull brown eyes ran up my chest before tracking to my eyes. She licked her lips and raised her eyebrows with a smirk on her face. She wasn't unattractive, but I wasn't in the mood for a random hook-up.

"Another whiskey." I swallowed the last measure in my glass and went to place it on the table.

She took the glass from my hand and let her red painted nail run across my fingers. I pulled my hand back and leaned into the chair, crossing my arms over my chest and looking her directly in the eyes. "Not going to happen, darlin'. Save yourself the trouble."

She stood straight, her face twisted into a scowl as she turned and walked away. I could see her lips moving, but the patrons and band made her words inaudible. Sighing, I turned my eyes back to Grace, who was pulling another beer from the cooler with a pep in her step. She smiled as a tall man slid money across the bar to her, then she quickly turned her attention to another person wanting a drink.

He looked crestfallen as he turned away from the bar with his beer and made his way to the table filled with his friends. He sat down, and they started loudly ripping into him while one of them pocketed a few dollar bills from the table with a raucous laugh. They looked to be in college, and from their clothes, I'd say they're fraternity assholes who were drinking away their parents' money. I'd seen them in Knoxville for years when the Death Hounds would go on poker runs.

They were used to getting what they wanted, and most of them loved to look down on people of lesser monetary status. It pissed me off seeing them ogling Grace. My fists clenched as they slapped more money on the table and a different asshole stood to approach the bar. He smirked over his shoulder to the table before stepping up to the bar and leaning over, invading Grace's personal space.

She was around five-foot-three and petite, so this asshole loomed over her like he was trying to climb over the bar and wrap himself around her. She lifted her head and tilted it to the side as he said something to her, then she smiled with a nod before putting her hand out for money. He handed it to her and turned away, sauntering to the table and lifting one finger to his douchey friends, encouraging them to remain calm.

I watched the whole scene unfold with a bad feeling in the pit of my stomach. They kept watching her as she poured a tray of shots, and I could see her visibly exhale as she grabbed the tray and walked from behind the bar. Asshole licked his lips, and I leaned forward to get a better view as she approached the table.

The band announced, "We're going to take a fifteen-minute break," and the loud music ended, making the conversations in the bar easier to hear.

Grace approached the table and placed the tray down, sliding a shot in front of each dumbass while the one who ordered them began to reach his hand out. When the last glass was off the tray, she went to stand just as he palmed her juicy ass with his scrawny hand, causing her to shoot straight up, her back rigid and her face filled with rage.

"Is there a reason your hand is on my ass?" she asked, her eyes cast down at him.

"I wanted to feel what I would be gripping into later tonight as I ride you," he replied, and all his friends laughed.

He had an eat-shit smile on his pimply face, and just as I went to stand to get him away from her, I heard a voice yell from behind the bar, "Don't do it, Grace."

Her lips pressed up and her eyes hooded as she turned her head over her shoulder to see the guy squeezing her ass. Lifting her head, she bit her lip and warned calmly, "I'll give you three seconds to take your hand off me, and there won't be a problem."

Grabbing her with his other hand, he tugged her closer to him, and that was the last second he was sitting in the chair. Grace still had her hand on the drink tray, and with lightning speed, she swung it sideways, catching him against the side of his head, knocking him onto the floor. His hands fell from her body, and she stepped over him as the bar went silent.

Leaning over him with the tray in her hand, she spoke in a deadly tone. "If you ever put your hands on me again, God himself won't know where to find you during the rapture." She looked at each guy at the table, all stunned that a tiny woman knocked their friend out. "If you assholes think it's okay to treat women like this, I feel sorry for you. When a woman says no, she fucking means no. Leave this bar and do not come back, or I swear to everything that is decent and holy, I'll feed you to the gators in the river."

Fuck, I think I'm in love.

I couldn't keep the grin off my face as the tiny woman corralled the men out of the bar, dragging their groggy friend with them. Their shots sat untouched on the table, and she lifted one, drinking it in one swallow before slamming the glass to the table.

"Anyone else?" She swung her eyes across the bar, and you could see heads shaking as she nodded. "Drink up."

She walked away from the table, and a few people reached over, snagging the free drinks and laughing. I could see Grace duck behind the bar and reach into her small bag before motioning to the older man who owned the bar that she was stepping outside. This may be my chance to speak with her, seeing a real piece of her for the first time since I walked into the bar.

I stood from my spot in the corner and walked toward the bar, only to be stopped by the old man who worked alongside Grace.

"Hey, slick," he said to me, and I turned my head and lifted my eyebrows at him. "Let me talk to you for a few minutes."

He was in his mid to late forties and his eyes were filled with wisdom. He appraised me with some level of understanding as I turned toward him. Approaching the old wooden bar, I sat down on one of the stools near the door where Grace exited as the man slid a glass of whiskey across to me.

"I've seen you in here for the last few weeks. And from the way you can't keep your eyes off Grace, you're interested in her." I shrugged before taking a sip of the drink and placing the glass onto the bar. He leaned over and spoke quietly. "I don't know what you think you'll achieve by making a move on her, but you see what happens when someone gets too friendly with her. Do I have to worry about that with you, son?"

His eyes fell to my Death Hounds cut and he hardened his stance behind the bar. Smirking at the old man, I finished the glass of whiskey in one swallow and stood. Leaning over to yell in his ear as the sound of the band filled the room, I replied, "I wish she would have broken his nose with that shot, but I'm assuming she was being . . . nice?"

He chuckled and yelled back to me, "Nice may be a bit of an understatement when it comes to Grace and her personal space. Good luck, and remember to duck if something comes flying at your head."

Shaking my head with a smile, I pushed away from the bar as the old man turned to pull a beer from the cooler for another customer. The door to the right was marked 'Employees Only', and I opened it, expecting to find a small break room. I was pleasantly surprised to find a large, enclosed area surrounded by a tall wooden fence with a table and chairs under a small pavilion.

The sound of the bar filtered to barely audible as the door closed behind me and I stepped into the night air. The smell of damp earth hit my senses first, followed by the stinky smell of weed. I followed the smell to the side fence and saw Grace leaning back in a chair with her face tilted to the night sky. She had a joint in her hand and blew a plume of smoke into the air. I stood silently and watched her for a moment, wishing I could see inside her beautiful mind to get the answers to my questions. Clearing my throat to alert her to my presence, I walked closer to her as she turned and looked over her shoulder at me.

She sighed heavily and snubbed the joint out in an ashtray next to her chair before turning her full attention to me. There was little light filtering to this side of the enclosure, so I halted my steps, leaving ten feet between us.

"Can I help you?" she asked and stood from her seat, crossing her arms over her chest and tilting her head to the side, waiting for my response. She was defensive and her body was full of thinly-veiled anger.

"I was hoping we could talk?" It was lame, but those were the first words that popped into my brain.

The next was *mine*, but I pushed that urge down and waited for her to answer.

She looked me up and down with curiosity before she shrugged and walked to the pavilion. Taking a seat, I followed behind her and sat down across from her, wishing she was in my lap. I had to will myself to stay on track and not go caveman on her. I'd never felt the tug to a woman like I felt the first time I saw Grace standing behind the old bar, pouring beers with a smile, and now I was at a loss for words.

"Are you going to talk or just stare at me?" she inquired as she leaned back in her seat.

Clearing my throat, I picked a jumping off spot, hoping to break what appeared to be a layer of ice around her, freezing anyone who got close and keeping them at a distance. "That was pretty impressive back there. Does stuff like that happen a lot?"

"The asshole frat boys?" she asked, and I nodded. "From time-to-time, guys from the next town over come in, and mostly, they aren't a problem."

"I can see why. Damn, you wield a tray with force."

She stood from the table and pushed her chair back under as she explained, "No one has the right to touch me without permission." Turning, she walked to the back door of the bar, but before she opened it to enter, she looked over her shoulder at me and reasoned, "I've seen you watching me. You're barking up the wrong tree. I'm not on the menu."

I stood just as she opened the door, letting the loud music flood the quiet space. "I'm not looking at a menu, Grace. I'm looking at you."

"Don't bother. I'm not worth the effort."

With those sad words, she walked inside and the door closed behind her, leaving me in stunned silence. I could see deep pain in her eyes behind the fake smile she gave everyone, and all I wanted to do was pull her into my arms. She needed to know she was special and worth any effort it took to win her heart.

Chapter 3

Grace

I tried to keep the past where it belonged, but some days, it was harder than others. I'd been gone for ten years, and no one had come looking for me, so I assumed they wrote me off like so many others. I would say I prayed for them to forget me, but prayers didn't pass my lips. Not after them.

Returning to my usual spot next to Eddie behind the bar, I jumped back into work, refilling drinks for the regulars and trying to keep the angry tremors from overtaking me. It was the memories that threatened to break through my skin that were keeping me on edge. I knew those frat boys were going to be trouble the second they walked through the door. They all dressed similarly, with faded blue jeans, a douche slogan T-shirt, and boots that cost what most of the customers made in a week.

Eddie watched while I gave another fake smile to a customer as I handed them their drink, and he shook his head, his disappointment in me palpable. Since he helped me all those years ago, he'd encouraged me to live my life, to experience the joys and heartbreaks that came with it, but I never stepped out of my bubble to give anyone a chance. I still was afraid deep inside me, and no matter how hard I tried, I couldn't shake it.

"You've got to let all that shit go, Grace. It's an anchor around your neck, dragging you down." I snapped my head to Eddie as he slid a beer across the bar and turned back to me.

"I have let it go," I responded, hearing the lie fall from my lips.

"Bullshit," he muttered and slipped out from the side of the bar to grab another case of beer stacked in the hallway.

Looking across the room, I could see the guy from earlier in his usual spot, slowly sipping on a whiskey, and watching me with heat in his eyes. The first time he walked into the bar, my heart leaped into my throat, and I felt desire coursing through my veins as he silently watched me. It was a strange occurrence, and I feared my reaction to him. I asked one of the waitresses to put the moves on him, to see if he would take the bait, but he turned her down every time.

Each time he returned, I smiled a little more inside. Of course, I wouldn't tell him that I thought his black hair and thick beard were sexy, or that his blue eyes pierced through me the first time our gazes locked across the room. Just knowing he kept coming back, for what I assumed was me, was flattering, even if I never allowed it to go any further than the conversation we had.

His deep voice curled around me like smoke, and I wanted to fall at his feet. That had never happened before, so when he walked outside to talk to me, I kept the hard persona firmly in place, hoping to push him away before I made a fool of myself.

"You should go have a drink with the man since he can't keep his eyes off you," Eddie commented as the bar started to empty shortly after midnight.

Last call was in thirty minutes, and I'd completed all my prep work for closing. The band was packing up their equipment, so the jukebox was turned on, its volume much lower than the live music we had whenever they decided to show up. I looked at my boss, my friend, and shook my head as I wiped down the wooden bar with a towel.

"That's not a good idea, Eddie. I don't know anything about him. He could be a serial killer for all I know."

"Then having a drink will give you a chance to learn a few things. You deserve to have a little fun, Grace. And I seriously doubt he's a serial killer. Looks more like a guy who enjoys a little freedom in his life."

My eyes met his, and he smiled sadly down at me as I chewed on my lip with worry. I met Eddie when I was at my lowest, and he gave me a safe place to land when I needed help the most. It took over a year for me to open up to him, and I only told him a fraction of what caused me to run away at sixteen years old.

He never looked at me with pity or disgust, and I never told him the whole story, even though he could probably guess. He helped me get my GED online and has been the closest thing to family I've had since my father died when I was four. I don't have any real memories of my father, just the feeling of him that I still experience from time to time.

Shaking off the painful memories, I glanced over at the bearded man and back to Eddie. "I guess you're right. Just don't make a habit out of it."

He raised his hands in mock surrender, and I chuckled at him as he handed me two clean glasses and a bottle of whiskey. Shaking my head, I took

them from him and walked around the front of the bar, stepping around customers standing in the walkway and slowly approaching the mystery man.

He smiled up at me as I grew closer and pushed the chair across from him
out with his boot, giving me a place to sit down. Placing the two glasses and
bottle on the table, I took my seat as he poured us two fingers of whiskey in
each glass. Seeing him so close with the light hanging over the table, I noticed
how deep blue his eyes were, and I swallowed down my nerves.

He slid the glass to me, and my fingers brushed his as I took it. An elec-
tric shock shot through me, and I drank the glass in one swallow, needing to
take the edge off. A strong, tattooed hand came across the table as he spoke,
his smooth voice like honey as he said, "Dalton, but you can call me Skid."

I shook his hand, and the tingles from his contact warmed me, starting
a slow simmer deep inside me that I feared would never leave. "Grace. And
you can call me Grace."

A beautiful smile filled his handsome face as he withdrew his hand and
tipped a splash of liquor into my empty glass. I'd noticed over the last few visits that he always wore a leather jacket covered in patches, even when it was
getting hot outside, so I leaned in to inspect what the patches said.

Death Hounds MC Portstill Chapter.

"What's a Death Hound?' I asked as the buzz from the alcohol began to
course through my blood.

He leaned back and glanced down at his jacket before answering, "The
Death Hounds are my club, my brothers, my family."

"Where's Portstill? I've never heard of it."

"Tennessee, between Nashville and Memphis."

His responses were clipped, and I wondered if either of us could open up
or if this was going to be a tug of war to give the smallest answer possible. Sitting back, I heard Eddie ring the bell for last call and glanced over my shoulder to see only two orders being placed. Knowing he could handle it, I decided to sit with Dalton for a few more minutes.

"What brings you to Alabama?" I asked, finishing the small amount of
liquor and placing the empty glass back on the table.

He went to lift the bottle, and I placed my hand over the top of the glass,
stopping him from pouring any more. I had to drive home, and I didn't need
any more of a buzz. Drinking wasn't something I often did, preferring to get

my relaxation from the occasional joint and daily yoga. He set the bottle down before he answered.

"I had some business to take care of in the area and decided to stay for a while. It's a cute community."

I shook my head with laughter. "It's as backwoods as you can get, but it's home."

"Are you from around here? You don't have much of an accent," he remarked, and I pushed back from the table slightly.

"Midwest girl," I answered vaguely and deflected back to him. "Tell me about yourself, Dalton."

"Not much to tell. Older sister is my club President's old lady, younger brother is in college for computers. Tennessee is home, and I'll be headed back that way . . . eventually." His heated gaze never left my face, and I could feel his caress across the table.

"Do you have any siblings?" he asked, and I shook my head.

"Just me and Eddie." I looked over my shoulder to see him returning bottles to the shelves and locking the coolers behind the bar.

A voice from the next table caught me off guard as the music from the jukebox faded. The words were whispered and they ran across my spine, pushing me closer to the bleak darkness that I couldn't shake, no matter how hard I tried.

"Come to Daddy . . ."

I stood from my chair and grabbed the empty glasses and bottle on autopilot. He looked up at me with confusion, and just as I went to leave, his voice broke through the painful memories overpowering me. "Grace, are you okay?"

Everything was happening in slow motion as I tried to capture his gaze with mine, only to feel myself tumbling into darkness. I made it one step before my feet failed me and I started to fall. My hands were filled with glass, and I threw them out, trying to break my fall as my vision grew to a pinpoint, casting me in blackness.

"Grace!" Dalton yelled as he jumped from the table and grabbed onto me, stopping me from hitting the dirty floor.

I could hear Eddie yelling my name as strong arms held me close to a warm chest. An intoxicating scent surrounded me as I fought to pull away from the years of pain and regret flashing before my eyes. The feeling of being lifted into the air brought a wave of nausea, and I struggled not to be sick as I was carried into Eddie's office and placed on the couch along the side wall.

A warm hand caressed my face as my vision slowly came back, and the memories receded into the vault I locked them away in. It had been years since they were so strong, and I feared the panic and shame would soon follow. I could see Eddie wringing his hands as he looked down at me, and I blinked to see Dalton kneeling next to me, worry etched across his handsome face.

I squeezed my eyes shut, fighting the tears that were pooling as I pushed up from the couch into a sitting position. Dalton sat next to me, and I scooted away from him as I looked up at Eddie and the tears began to flow.

"I'm sorry," I tried to say, only to have my voice betray me and the words squeak out.

"No, Grace. You don't apologize to me. Not now. Not ever," Eddie countered and reached his hand down to me.

I took his hand and felt the familiar comfort from him. He was the father I lost, the friends I left, and the family I never had, all rolled into one. He was the witness to my years of darkness, and he was the light that brought me back from the edge.

Dalton sat silently next to me as I gripped Eddie's hand, needing the connection to bring me back to the present. When I felt the last of the panic ebbing from me, I released Eddie's hand. He asked, "Do you need me to stay?"

His eyes cut to Dalton before coming back to mine, and I glanced at the handsome man who saved me from injury. I always trusted my gut, and there was nothing about him that gave me fear or panic. I sensed no bad intentions. "He saved me. I doubt he wants to hurt me. Right?"

I looked at Dalton, and he reached for my hand. "I'd never do anything to hurt you or any other woman. She's safe with me. I promise."

"I need to close up, so I'm going to trust you to keep an eye on her until I get back. Don't make me regret it."

"Yes, sir," he replied and turned his full attention back to me.

I was embarrassed that he or anyone else had to see me losing it, but he didn't seem fazed by it. In fact, he seemed protective of me, and I didn't know what to make of that. No one, besides Eddie, had given a crap about me in more years than I cared to think about. The false love I once received made me leery of people's words and it eroded my trust in others. I learned the hardest lesson of them all.

People will say what you want to hear to achieve their goal. No matter how twisted and sick their goals truly were.

Chapter 4

Skid

I watched Grace carefully as the sounds of the bar grew to silence. Her gaze was locked on the far wall of the small office, her mind lost somewhere that was causing her pain. Not wanting her to dwell on whatever it was that was pushing her to the brink, I cleared my throat to draw her attention. She slowly turned her head to me, and that's when I saw it in her eyes.

Shame. Regret. Pain. Loneliness. Anger.

All the things I witnessed my sister deal with alone and the same emotions that echoed from Aubrey. Remembering what Eddie said about her personal space, I asked, "Are you okay?"

Sliding my hand across the couch, I brushed my fingertips across the back of her hand, and she lowered her eyes to where I was touching her. She didn't object or even appear fazed the connection, so I placed my hand flat down on the couch, extending my fingers up, offering her a hand to hold onto. I wasn't expecting her to reach for it, but when her palm connected with mine, she exhaled softly and curled her fingers around mine.

"Why do I trust you?" she asked quietly, almost to herself.

"Because you know I'll never hurt you. I understand you, Grace," I answered, and she lifted her eyes to meet mine.

"You don't know me. How could you understand me? I hardly understand myself," she muttered, and I stroked the back of her hand, hoping to reassure her.

"I see something in your eyes that tells me you're looking for the same thing I am." Her forehead drew into confusion, so I explained. "A friend. I don't have many in my life, and from what you said, it's just you and Eddie. I'd like to get to know you, as a friend. Maybe we'll get a laugh or two out of it." I shrugged and waited with shallow breaths for her to respond.

She tilted her head to the side an insignificant amount, but after watching her for three weeks, I'd learned that's what Grace did when she was making up her mind about something. One cheek lifted in a smile. "I'd like that." I gently squeezed her hand as the hallway lights turned off outside the office.

Eddie walked in a moment later and stumbled when he found Grace and I holding hands across the center cushion of the couch. His eyes grew wide, and he glanced quickly at me before recovering and offering Grace a smile.

"You ready to head home?" he asked, and she stood from the couch, dropping my hand in the process. "I'm going to drive you, and you can get your car in the morning."

"I can take her home," I offered, knowing she lived twenty minutes away in an even smaller community.

Eddie's house was next to the bar, and I may have followed her home the last week or so. He wrinkled his forehead and went to speak when Grace interjected. "That would be great. Thank you, Dalton. Can you pick me up tomorrow?" she asked him, and he nodded before responding.

"Grace, are you sure?" They had a silent conversation as I stood there, watching.

After a minute, he turned fully to me and rose to his full height, almost looking me in the eyes.

"Straight home, and if anything happens to her, I'll hunt you down," Eddie threatened.

"You have my word that I'll make sure she gets home and inside without a scratch on her."

Reaching my hand out to her, I waited for her to decide, and when she linked her hand with mine, Eddie shook his head with a small smile. We followed him out of the darkened bar and waited for him to lock up before watching him walk across the parking lot and open the fence to his yard.

"Are you ready?" I asked her, and she looked up at me, her gaze still distant.

"Sure."

Walking over to my new bike, I pulled an extra helmet from the saddlebag and placed it over her head before securing the strap under her chin. I could feel Eddie watching us as I climbed on the bike and offered her my hand to sit behind me. Grace slid her small body against my back and wrapped her arms around my waist, linking her fingers together. I put my helmet on and cranked the bike, the loud pipes on my 2021 Harley CVO Street Glide. She was painted bright red with enough chrome to make her unique.

There was a tremble in her hands, and I reached up and placed my hands over hers, gently rubbing the backs until she relaxed. "Hang on," I instructed, pulled the kickstand up with my foot, and put the bike into gear. Pulling away from the Backwater Bar, I drove slow on the dirt road until we hit asphalt.

When I ensured we were clear, I squealed tires on the blacktop and skid through the turn, laying rubber down before shooting down the road lightning fast. Grace gripped me harder, and I slowed down to the speed limit, not wanting to scare her. When we got to the end of that road a minute later, I yelled over my shoulder, "Which way?"

I knew exactly how to get to her front door, but I didn't want to scare her off, thinking I'd been stalking her. Even if I had been. Having spent so many years with Callahan, I learned that a little surveillance was a good thing when it came to protecting someone you cared about. It only took two visits to the bar until I was busy installing cameras in and around her small house while she worked. She lived secluded near a large expanse of thick pine trees, and I didn't trust anyone—especially where Grace was concerned.

My brain told me she was meant to be mine, but I knew she wasn't going to be easy to convince. She needed to learn to trust me, so I would take it at a snail's pace until she made the first move. Grace would yell where to turn, and soon, we were pulling into her yard. Motion-activated security lights flooded the yard in bright light as I parked my bike and killed the grumbling motor.

She removed her helmet as I stood from the bike and extended my hand to her. She placed her soft hand into mine and carefully climbed down. I pulled my helmet off and set it on the seat as she wrung her hands in front of her, unsure of herself. This wasn't the same Grace I witnessed earlier this evening knocking an asshole unconscious, and to see her vulnerable was killing a piece of me. All I wanted to do was pull the beautiful woman into my arms and shield her from any harm.

She tucked a lock of brown hair behind her ear and looked up at me. "Thanks for the ride. I guess I'll see you later."

She went to turn toward her house when I spoke her name. "Grace."

She looked back at me, and I stepped closer to her. She maintained her stance, and when I was inches from her with her bright eyes looking up at me,

I grazed my thumb across her cheek and whispered, "Sweet dreams, beautiful. I'll see you soon."

A genuine smile pushed at her lips, and she blushed slightly before responding. "Good night."

I watched from the yard as she unlocked the front door, and when she looked back at me, I stood taller. Her beautiful face slowly disappeared behind the closing door, and I listened to hear two locks and one chain slide into place. Knowing she was safe for the night, I cranked my motorcycle and drove the three minutes down the road to the trailer I rented. Climbing the rusty stairs, I unlocked the door and secured it behind me.

My laptop was open, and I immediately sat down, watching Grace's house but not allowing myself to see into her bedroom. That was her privacy, and I wouldn't invade it. Yet. One of the cameras covered the entrance to the bedroom. She left the door open as she changed out of her shorts and T-shirt from work and into a pair of pajamas that showed more skin than I was ready to handle.

I watched as she rolled another joint from a small metal jar on the kitchen counter and switched cameras when she stepped onto the covered porch spanning the entire front of the small house. She kicked her feet up on a table as she settled into an oversized chair and smoked the joint in peace.

Her shoulders relaxed as she opened a book under the light from the porch and began to read. For an hour, she sat outside in the cooler evening air and turned page after page until I saw her eyes blinking heavily. Closing the book, she walked inside, and I witnessed her secure both locks, slide a chain into place, and with a glance at a small table next to the door, she turned and walked into her bedroom.

The door was open, and I could see the pillows on her bed as she laid her beautiful head down and closed her eyes. For an hour, I watched her sleep peacefully before carrying my laptop into the bedroom and placing it on the other pillow facing me. After kicking off my boots, I slid my pants down and kicked them against the wall of the room, followed by my T-shirt. I hung my cut up the moment I walked into the trailer, and I glanced at it, missing my family, my brothers, and knowing I'd need to get home sooner rather than later.

I rolled onto my side in the bed and turned the fan on, cooling off the warm bedroom as I watched Grace sleep. Closing my eyes, I left the monitor in front of me, allowing me to check on her throughout the night. It was my own way of sharing a bed with Grace without actually being next to her. It would have to do until I could have her in my arms every night, where she belonged forever.

Chapter 5

Grace

"Are you ready for your trip this weekend?" my friend, Kelly, asked, and I shrugged.

I'd lived with the Ringmans for so long, my former life felt like a distant memory. Every so often, my mom would pop into my life, but she never kept herself clean long enough to gain custody of me back. She liked her drugs more than me, and since my father was gone, I got tossed into the system. Kevin and Connie weren't terrible, I guess, but they had so many strict rules that frustrated me. I was supposed to go camping with them this weekend and I was not looking forward to dealing with Connie.

She loved to pick apart everything I did wrong, reminding me that bad children who don't listen to their elders go to hell. By her thinking, everyone was going to hell for everything, except her. She saw herself as perfect, and I didn't want the camping trip to be all about my mistakes.

"I guess. Connie's been difficult lately, and I don't want to hear her griping all weekend," I reasoned, and Kelly nodded in understanding.

She was in the system for three years, but her foster parents adopted her and made a real family. The Ringmans didn't seem interested in adopting anyone, so I kept trying my best to make them happy. Kevin wasn't so bad. He'd roll his eyes at me when she would leave the room, and it made me feel like we had a special bond.

"I don't know why you don't tell your caseworker about how she talks to you. It's bullshit," Kelly said, and I looked over both shoulders to make sure there wasn't someone nearby.

"Shh. Keep it down," I told her and lowered my voice. "What good would it do to tell my caseworker? If anything, she'd move me to a new placement, and they could be a hundred times worse. Connie is crazy, but Kevin's all right."

"If you say so," she replied and stood from her swing. "I've got to get home, but call me when you get back. Maybe Connie will let you spend the night since it's the summer."

She gave me a quick hug and held up her pinky to me. I wrapped mine around hers before she turned and walked down the block to her house. We met on the first day of my new fifth grade class. She offered me a seat next to her, and we've been close ever since. Connie didn't like her, saying her adoptive parents didn't spend enough time in church and were leading Kelly into damnation.

I didn't know about all that. It seemed like some angry man in the sky, punishing people for honest mistakes without remorse. I sang their songs and repeated the words they taught me, but deep down, I didn't know if I believed like they did. I would never tell anyone that, but I knew it in my heart to be true.

I walked the three blocks from the park to my house and let myself in the side door, careful to wipe all the dirt off my shoes before stepping inside. The house was quiet, so I slipped my shoes off and placed them on the rack in the kitchen before tiptoeing into the living room.

"Grace?" Connie's voice sounded from the back of the house, and I sighed before walking toward her voice.

"Yes, ma'am?" I replied, standing outside her closed bedroom door.

"Come in," she instructed, and I turned the knob before slowly pushing the door open.

The room was dark and she was laying across the bed with a rag over her eyes. Just perfect. She had another migraine, and I usually caught the worst of her condemnation when she was sick.

She lifted the rag from her eyes and motioned for me to come closer. I stepped silently across the floor until I was standing next to the bed. "My migraines are starting again, so I'm not going camping with y'all this weekend. Can you handle packing the items in the kitchen notebook before Kevin gets home?"

I wanted to jump up and down and cheer for a weekend away from her, but I whispered, so as not to make her headache worse, "Yes, ma'am. Do you want me to get your medicine?"

"That would be nice, Grace. And a glass of ginger ale, please."

"I'll be right back." I walked out of the room, closing the door to stop the light from filtering into the room.

When I was in the kitchen and knew she couldn't see me, I danced around the kitchen, pumping my arms into the air and twisting my hips. A noise from behind me had me turning as I dropped my arms, and I saw Kevin walk into the kitchen from outside.

He smiled at me and walked up, whispering, "I guess it's just you and me this weekend, kiddo."

I smiled, and he nudged me with his shoulder as he walked into the living room and down the hallway to their bedroom. I quickly made her a glass of ginger ale and pulled her migraine medicine from the cabinet. After placing them on the nightstand, I returned to the kitchen and began packing the items she put on the list, adding a few extra sweet snacks to enjoy.

Within an hour, Kevin and I were pulling away from the house with the radio blaring top forty music louder than Connie would ever allow. The three-hour drive to the cabin he rented for the weekend was nice, and before long, my eyelids grew heavy, and I fell asleep. I felt him shake me awake, and I stretched my back and blinked away the sleep as I took in our getaway for the weekend.

"Grab some things from the back and let's get settled inside. We can go swimming before it gets dark," he remarked, grabbing our gear from the trunk.

Two trips and everything was inside the two-room cabin. We changed into our bathing suits and raced to see who could jump in the lake first. He won and hollered into the air as I broke the surface of the water, feeling its cooling effects on my heated skin.

I hadn't been that happy since my father was alive, even if the memories of him were faint. My mom always had addictions, and when I lost him, I lost the only person who ever loved me, so to have Kevin on my side was reassuring.

"Let's get dried off and start the grill. I don't know about you, but I'm starving," he said, and we swam to the stairs on the small dock and pulled ourselves out of the water.

We camped here on and off for as long as I'd been placed with them, so it was like a second home. The chilly air caught me off guard, and I crossed my arms over my chest, not wanting to be indecent, as Connie would say. Kevin looked at me and offered his elbow as we walked away from the lake and onto the large back deck overlooking the water. As we entered the cabin, I asked, "What can I do to help with dinner?"

"Why don't you get showered and changed, and then you can make the salad."

Before long, we were eating steaks, grilled bread, and salad on the back porch of the isolated cabin. When we finished, he took my plate, even though it was my job to wash dishes, and placed them in the sink.

When he returned, he handed me a glass of soda and sat down next to me with one in his hand. I sipped the beverage, and within a few minutes, my body felt a warm tingling sensation, making me smile into the darkening sky.

I felt a hand brush against my cheek, and my head lulled to the side as my eyes tried to focus on Kevin. "You're so beautiful. My Grace."

I felt myself smile, and I let my head turn away from him as I took another swallow of my drink. Setting the empty glass onto the table, my hand missed, but Kevin caught it before I dropped it to the wooden deck. I couldn't focus and I was sleepy, fighting to keep my eyes open as I fell back into the chair.

"Let me take you to bed, Grace. It's been a long day, and you need to rest," Kevin said as he scooped me up into his arms and carried me into the house.

No one had been this nice to me since my father was alive, and through my confusion, I whispered, "Thank you, Daddy."

Kevin inhaled deeply, and he whispered, "My Grace. My beautiful saving Grace."

He carried me into the bedroom and pulled the covers back before placing me on the soft mattress. I could feel him sit on the edge of the bed, his hand caressing my cheek. Turning into it, I heard him ask, "Do you want me to be your daddy, Grace?"

I wanted nothing more than to have a dad who would protect and love me, and I blinked hard against my heavy lids until Kevin came into focus. He had a look in his eyes that I'd never seen, and through the haze I was swimming in, I replied, "Please be my daddy."

He leaned over and whispered softly into my ear as sleep dragged me under, "I'll be your daddy, and you can be my sweet baby girl. I'll teach you everything you need to know, my saving Grace."

I snapped out of the nightmare and gasped, trying to catch my breath. My heart raced in my chest, and I felt the tears falling down my cheeks as the memories bombarded me from every direction. Squeezing my eyes shut, I tried to force the pain back into the box I kept it locked in, but there was no escape from it.

Realizing sleep was over for the night, I got out of bed and made quick work of my morning routine before walking into the small kitchen. After starting the coffee maker, I opened the windows, allowing the cool morning air to filter into the warm house. Crickets and the occasional dog were the only sounds in the stillness of the early morning, the silence allowing his words to ring louder in my mind.

I stared into the darkness outside and wished I would have been stronger, but knowing deep down, I wasn't given the chance to be strong. When the coffee was done perking, I poured myself a cup and moved to the front porch to watch the sunrise.

As much as I wanted to stop the voices repeating in my head, I couldn't, and the shame it filled me with lashed another piece of my self-esteem. I never expected a fairytale life, but I never asked for the four years of pain and betrayal I endured. All I wanted was someone to love me. Not someone who took an innocent moment of vulnerability of a young girl and twisted it into something so sick that it haunted my dreams. I didn't know what followed was wrong until Kelly saw something that I thought was innocent, but it was deeply wrong on many levels. I just wasn't aware

When she made me understand what was going on and how twisted it truly was, I remember throwing up for hours as the tears fell unchecked. No matter how much I scrubbed my skin, I could feel the touch that obliterated my trust in people. Kelly made a report to my caseworker, and when they came to inspect the home, they found two other foster kids happy and thriving, and me, labeled as a troublemaker. That's when the anger started, and through the years, it's grown into a hardened shell around me.

No one believed me.

I took the small amount of money I'd earned from odd jobs and, with the help of Kelly, made my escape a few days later. She was the only person who knew where I was going, and she kept me informed of what was happening back home for the first few months.

I was listed as a runaway and feared the authorities would drag me back to the Ringmans, forcing me back into a silent nightmare. When Kelly told me the two younger kids with the Ringmans were returned to their parents shortly after I left, I exhaled a sigh of relief. They were the last fosters Kevin and Connie took in.

Kelly helped connect me with people who understood what I lived through, and I was able to directly deal with the mental torment of running away from what I thought would be my future. I spent four months learning how I was manipulated and they, for lack of a better word, deprogrammed me.

I met Eddie a short time later, and he helped me find my way, learning to distance myself from my past and giving me a future to look forward to. He was the closest person in my life, and I feared where I would be without him.

The sun pushed through the trees, turning the darkness into shades of gray until the first patches of orange rose from the ashes of the night. The rays fell across the porch, warming my feet and legs and the sounds of the country came alive. Trucks carrying the early morning workers filtered past my long driveway as I stood from the porch and walked inside to make another cup of coffee. My phone sat on the kitchen counter, and I picked it up to find a missed call from Eddie.

I called him back and smiled when he answered, "Good morning, sunshine."

"Good morning yourself. Are you ready for breakfast?" I asked and walked into my bedroom to pick out some clothes.

"I was waiting to head over until I knew you were awake. Are you ready now?"

"I'll meet you at the end of the driveway," I answered, and he grunted his reply before the line went dead.

After pulling on a pair of jeans and a T-shirt, I slid my feet into my comfy tennis shoes and grabbed a hoodie from the coat rack. Locking the door behind me, I walked down the dirt driveway and waited for Eddie. The entire time, Kevin's whispered words played on a loop in my mind.

Be a good girl for Daddy.

Chapter 6

Skid

The sounds of Grace whining and thrashing on her bed woke me a few hours after I fell asleep with my laptop open on the pillow next to me. Sitting up, I grabbed it and ran my fingertips over the screen as I watched her fight an invisible enemy in her dreams. She whimpered and moaned as she twisted under the covers, and I wanted nothing more than to drive to her house and save her from whatever was haunting her dreams.

If I showed up in the darkness of the night, she would think I was a stalker. I was, just not the bad kind. I watched her as she moved around her house, and when she sat down on the front porch of her house, I saw the faraway look in her eyes and closed my eyes, feeling her pain.

When Eddie called and invited her to breakfast, I decided that was my opening. I needed to see her with my own eyes to know she was okay, so I quickly dressed and cranked my motorcycle before pulling out of my road. When Eddie's truck passed by a few minutes later, I followed behind him and waited down the road as he picked Grace up from her driveway. They drove west, and twenty minutes later, they pulled into a mom-and-pop diner tucked along the interstate.

When I saw they were seated, I pulled my bike in and made my way inside. I walked in, and Eddie looked up from his menu, seeing me take a seat behind them. Grace had her back to me, and I could see a smile pushing against Eddie's cheeks as I ordered a coffee and looked at the menu.

"Why don't you join us, Dalton?" he spoke. Grace snapped her head backward, finding me sitting behind her.

"Is that okay, Grace?" I asked, and she nodded with a look of confusion.

I grabbed my cup of coffee and moved to their table, taking the seat on Grace's side of the table, across from Eddie.

"What has you out so early?" he asked as the waitress stopped at the end of the table and took our orders.

"I couldn't sleep, so I decided to go for a ride," I explained. Grace lifted her coffee, taking a deep swallow and placing the mug back on the table.

"Since it seems you're going to be around for a while . . ." He paused for my reaction, and when I looked at Grace and nodded, he continued. "Why don't you join us for dinner at my house? On Sundays, I put on a full spread, and we eat until we can't move, then usually pass out on the couch watching some silly romance Grace insists we watch."

I could see her eyes grow wide as she waited for my answer. Turning to face her, I asked, "Is it okay if I join you, Grace?"

She tucked a lock of brown hair behind her ear, seeming unsure as she replied, "I think that would be nice."

"Then it's settled. You can drive Grace to her car while I pick up the provisions for dinner. You're welcome to hang out, or you can come back at five. Your choice," he offered as the waitress set our food in front of us and turned silently to check on another customer.

I smiled at him and shifted my foot under the table to touch Grace's. It was a small gesture, but I wanted, no, I needed to touch her after what I witnessed this morning. She was hurting, and I didn't know what the cause was, which made my mind race. I didn't want to be right, but the one word I heard her mutter during her distressful sleep made my stomach churn.

Daddy.

We made small talk while we ate, with Eddie asking most of the questions. I explained about the Death Hounds without going into any club business. He inquired about my family, and I told him how we all were immersed in the club life. Grace smiled when I told them about Jacob and his desire to patch in, and my sister's insistence that he have an education also.

"Your sister sounds like she only wants what's best for him," Grace remarked, and I agreed with her.

"Sadie was a mother to both of us, but Jacob more so. She worries about us all and only wants him to have a way to make a living outside the club."

"Have you ever been arrested, Dalton? Or do you prefer Skid?" Eddie asked, and I leaned back, wrapping my arm around the back of Grace's chair as she looked at me.

"No, I've never been arrested, and either is fine, but I prefer Skid."

"I prefer Dalton," Grace replied, and I winked at her.

The waitress brought the check, and I glanced at it before tossing two twenties to cover the food and tip. We finished our coffee, and I followed Eddie and Grace into the parking lot. She handed him a list, and he promised to be back to the house within an hour, so I helped Grace get settled on the back of my bike and pulled away from the diner into traffic.

We were stopped at a light, and I yelled over my shoulder, "Can I take the long way back to Eddie's?"

"Please," she yelled back and gripped her arms tighter across my stomach as we pulled away from the light.

I got the bike up to speed and turned onto a backroad, feeling her settle against my back. Grace was the first woman I ever had on the back of my bike, and I suddenly understood what Gunner meant when he said carrying Sadie was like carrying precious cargo. I loved the feel of the wind pushing against me as I rocketed down the road but with Grace behind me, I was extra cautious.

The rays of sunlight filtered across the road through the tall trees as we wove through the country, over small bridges, and past farmhouses. There was barely anyone on the road so early on a Sunday morning, and when I glanced into the rearview side mirror, I could see the huge smile on Grace's face as she hugged herself closer to me.

Approaching a four-way stop sign, I brought my hand down over Grace's and gave her a slight squeeze. She gripped my hands into my abs, and I felt her touch deep into my soul. Willing my cock to behave, we drove down the road, each mile bringing us closer to Eddie's Backwater Bar. I pulled the bike into the dirt parking lot and killed the motor before kicking the stand down.

Grace pulled her helmet off, and I helped her from the bike. She was still smiling, and when I stepped off the bike, she tugged me to her and kissed me on the cheek. I brought my hand up to the spot where her soft lips touched, and she blushed as she smiled up at me.

"Not that I'm complaining, but what was that for?" I asked as we began walking across the parking lot to Eddie's house.

"I wanted to say thank you for the ride," she reasoned and shrugged her shoulders.

I opened the gate for her and followed her through before closing it behind us. Slowly, I took her hand into mine, and she stopped walking to look at the connection. I didn't grip her tight, allowing her to remove her hand if she wanted. When she linked her fingers with mine, my chest inflated, and I stood taller. Somehow, I was going to claim this woman and I pray she didn't fight the inevitable.

We sat on the back porch to Eddie's house, watching the water of the river flow past. She kept her eyes on the water, and I worried she was inside her head instead of with me. I stroked the back of her hand and said, "Penny for your thoughts."

She looked at me, and I saw a haunted look in her eyes before she wiped it away with a fake smile. "I was just thinking about my friend Kelly."

"Does she live around here?"

"Arizona with her husband and daughter. It's been years since I've seen her."

"You should take a trip to visit," I urged, and she shook her head.

"Eddie needs me here, and that's a long way for a visit," she explained, and the sound of the back screen door closing had her looking over her shoulder.

"Eddie doesn't need you here, and anytime you want to take some time off, all you have to do is say so." He grunted and plopped into a chair on the edge of the porch.

She flipped her hand at him, rolling her eyes and scoffing. "Please. You can't make it one day without me and you know it."

He laughed at her silliness, and I could feel her anxiety lessen the longer we sat on the porch. Eddie was able to pull her from the darkness that overtook her, and I was going to have to talk to him if I wanted to learn how to pull her back into the light. He may tell me to go to hell, but I hoped he saw that I only wanted to help her.

Grace stood from her chair and looked at us. "I'm going to start dinner. You two need anything?"

We both shook our heads, and she smiled before walking inside. A radio turned on from the kitchen, and I could see her through the doorway as she began to prep the meal. I looked at Eddie and spoke quietly, not wanting her to hear me.

"Can I stop by tomorrow and talk to you about something private?"

He eyes me up and down before leaning in. "I've never seen her take to anyone as quickly as she's taken to you, so I'm going to say this once. If you're just trying to get into her pants, leave now and don't bother that sweet girl ever again. If your motives are less than pure where she's concerned, she will cut you off and never give anyone else the chance to get to know her. Do not damage her. She deserves more than that."

"I meant what I said last night. I won't hurt her or any woman. I'm not looking for something quick. I'm looking for forever."

"Then I'll see you at noon tomorrow," he replied and stood from the chair to stretch his back.

Eddie walked inside, and a minute later, Grace walked out with a puzzled look on her face. "He said to take the boat out while he's cooking and not to bother him while he works his magic."

"Do you feel like going on a boat ride?" I asked, and she looked over her shoulder before turning back to me.

"I guess so."

Extending my hand toward the water, I instructed, "Lead the way."

We walked an overgrown path to the water and tucked to the side was a small dock with a pontoon boat tied up. She climbed on board, and I followed, helping her untie the mooring lines and pushing the floating party barge away from the shore. She took the wheel and started the motor before turning the boat and motoring into the river.

The sun was warm, and I removed my cut, gently placing it over a chair near the wheel. She looked at me, and for the first time, I could see desire staring back at me as she took in my toned arms covered in ink. Needles did the work on my sleeves, and from her gaze, she appreciated my ink.

"There's extra swim trunks under the seat if you want to change. Don't worry, I won't look."

Swim trunks sounded nice, so I stepped behind her and whispered, "You can look all you want."

She blushed and tucked her chin down as I lifted the bench seat and pulled out a pair of shorts. Looking around the river, there was one other boat on the water, but they were far enough away not to be able to see me, so I kicked off my boots and pushed my jeans down my legs. The trunks were a little tight in the front, so I left my shirt on, hoping to hide the embarrassing hard-on I'd been fighting since the first moment I laid eyes on Grace.

When I was redressed, I approached her. "I can take the wheel if you want to get changed."

She looked over her shoulder at me and her blue eyes twinkled in the early afternoon sun. "Thanks."

I fought to keep my eyes straight as I heard her open and close the seat. I wanted to see her beautiful perfection but wasn't going to ogle her, so I slowed the boat and waited for her to signal she was dressed. Her small body stepped up beside me and she was wearing a black one-piece suit and a pair of shorts. Her pert breasts pushed against the top and her hard nipples poked through the material.

I slid to the side, and she took the wheel as I settled in next to her. She maneuvered the boat down the river and into the lake before parking us under some shade trees and tossing the anchor. She reached into a cooler and pulled out two bottles of water before handing me one. We moved into the sun, and she stretched her legs out across the bench as we sipped on our drinks.

The sun shining on her hair gave her an angelic glow, and I wanted nothing more than to kiss her, to feel her lips pressed to mine. She was beautiful without a stitch of makeup on, and I could only imagine how sexy she would look in a pair of leather pants and a Death Hounds tank top, professing her commitment to me.

I was putting the cart well before the horse, so I placed my drink down and looked at her. "You're beautiful, Grace."

"Thank you," she muttered and bit into her lip. "You said you were in town for business?" she asked, and I nodded. "What kind of business are you in, or is that something I'm not allowed to ask?"

"I work for Callahan Cyber Security as a code writer and do odd jobs for the club when needed." My answer was vague but honest.

"I've heard of Callahan Cyber. That's an impressive job," she commented , and I shrugged, not used to anyone being impressed with me.

We sunbathed, and when it got too hot, we jumped into the lake, cooling off and splashing water on each other. We laughed and smiled so much, I feared my cheeks would hurt the next day. When it was time to return to Eddie's for dinner, she let me drive while she kicked back in the captain's seat and instructed me on which way to take the boat.

Eddie was sitting on the back porch when we returned and walked down to the dock to help secure the boat. He kissed Grace on the cheek before she walked to the house to change, leaving him and me alone.

"She looks happier than I've ever seen her."

"I hope so. I want to keep that smile on her beautiful face."

As I went to walk up the hill, he grasped me by the elbow, and I turned to face him as he spoke quickly and quietly. "She needs someone like you, Dalton. I just hope you're strong enough to fight her demons when they rear their heads."

I replied with the same menacing tone I had when anyone mistreated a woman. "I'll send every one of her demons to hell, and if someone tries to hurt her, I'll bleed them dry."

He nodded with a satisfied smile, and we returned to his house for dinner. Grace and I were on the couch with overfull stomachs watching a football game when I felt her lean against my shoulder. Looking down, she had closed her eyes and was softly sleeping against me. Eddie chuckled from his seat as I wrapped my arm around her, and she settled further onto the couch, her beautiful face resting against my heart.

The game was over, and the sun had set over an hour ago when Grace stirred from her nap. Gently, I lifted my arm as she sat up, blinking into the room.

"Did you have a good nap?" Eddie asked, and she looked at me with confusion before a blush crept up her face.

"Sorry. I didn't mean to fall asleep," she explained, and I winked at her with a smile.

"You looked too peaceful to wake up, so Eddie and I've been enjoying the game while you rested."

Grace stretched, revealing a sliver of skin at her waist, and I shifted, not wanting to show my growing erection. She looked beautiful this afternoon on the lake, but I noticed she kept her shorts on over her one-piece suit. Most women her age would have been more revealing, from my experience, and it was refreshing and unexpectedly arousing to see her modesty.

"Would you like some dessert? I think there's some apple and cherry pie left."

"I'd love some. Can I help? I'm handy in the kitchen, or so Sadie says." I shrugged, and she looked at Eddie.

"Apple and ice cream, please." His smile was deep, and she stood from the couch.

"Follow me," she said, and I jumped from the couch and walked behind her, noticing a small sway in her hips.

She was tiny compared to my six foot three, and I gave her some room as we walked into the large kitchen. It was an older-style kitchen and, from the looks of the island in the middle, well used. There were pies, cookies, half a cake, and candy filling the counter, and my sweet tooth kicked in as I looked at all the homemade creations.

"Can you get us some plates?" she asked and pointed to a cabinet next to the stove.

I pulled three mismatched plates from the counter and handed them to her as she opened the pie safes and lifted the delicious-looking desserts on-to the counter. Since I'd been in Alabama, I've missed Sadie's homemade desserts. To see Grace had the same talents was ironic and gave me an idea. I tucked it away for now as she handed me a slice of cherry pie and waited with nervous excitement as I took a bite.

I loved my sister's desserts, but this was the best cherry pie I'd ever tasted. Moaning around the bite, I swallowed the sweet and tart pie before explaining.

"That is hands down the best pie I've ever tasted. And my sister owns a bakery," I explained and took another bite.

"I'm glad you like it," she replied and smiled brightly. "I tried a new crust and I think it's my best one yet."

Finishing the pie in one last bite, I closed my eyes in euphoria and savored her creation. When I opened my eyes, I batted my eyelashes at her and gave my best sad eyes. "My pie's all gone."

She cut me another piece, twice the size of the first one. Taking another huge bite, I spoke around the sweet treat, "Lead the way." She laughed and her smile brightened her already beautiful face as she grabbed the other plates, and we returned to the living room.

Chapter 7

Skid

I followed Grace home and parked my motorcycle at the rear of her car as she turned off the ignition, casting the yard into a peaceful quiet. She exited the car and smiled as she walked up to my bike. I could see she was unsure, and I didn't make a move to get off the bike. I expected nothing from her and didn't want her to feel like I was pushing for anything.

"Thanks for letting me crash your day today," I spoke softly, and she took one step closer to me.

The floodlights turn off, and the mostly full moon illuminated the yard, giving the area an almost ethereal glow. Grace bit her plump lip and replied.

"I'm glad you joined us. It was a nice day."

"And there was pie." I smiled, wiggling my eyebrows.

She chuckled and asked, "What's your favorite? I'll make one for you."

"Can you make a Kentucky Derby Pie?"

"I'm sure I can. Why don't you stop by tomorrow afternoon, and I'll have it ready."

She twisted her foot in the dirt and glanced down before bringing her blue eyes to mine. Her mouth opened, then closed before she exhaled and gently shook her head.

Slowly, I reached out and brought my hand to her cheek, brushing my thumb across her soft skin before I asked, "What's on your mind, Grace?"

"Would you ... I mean ... I want ..."

"What do you need, Grace. Tell me," I urged, and she leaned into my touch before she spoke.

"Would ... would it be okay if I kissed you?" Her words were filled with vulnerability, and I slowly stood from my bike and swung my leg over the side.

Sitting back down on the seat sideways, I placed my legs in front of the pipes so she wouldn't hurt herself and leaned over, bringing my face closer to hers. The light from the moon filtered across her face, and I watched as she closed her eyes, just before my lips pressed against hers. I purposely kept the kiss soft, allowing her to push it further.

Electricity jumped across our connection as she stepped against my legs and slid her hands up my arms, resting them on my shoulders. When I felt her lick tentatively against my closed lips, I opened and felt the first brushes of her tongue against mine, causing my cock to lurch in my pants. Willing him to behave, I followed her lead and lost myself in her lips.

She moaned and her hands moved to the back of my neck as I brought my hands to her hips. I needed to slow this down for both our sakes, so I tapered off the kiss, gently pecking her across her lips until she opened her eyes and smiled at me.

"That was . . ." she whispered, bringing one hand to her swollen lips and gazing deeply into my eyes.

Pecking her softly, I whispered against her lips, "That was fucking perfect." I should temper my words, but she needed to know there was a rough man inside the softer version of myself she was getting to know. "You're so goddamn beautiful, Grace."

"You're not so bad yourself," she returned, and I smirked at her.

"Let me walk you to the door," I knew if I touched her for much longer, I wasn't going to be satisfied with a kiss on the lips.

She linked her hand with mine, and the floodlights turned on as our movements brought us closer to her house. Unlocking the door, she turned to me and seemed reluctant. I leaned over and kissed her on the cheek before stepping off the porch.

"I'll see you tomorrow," I promised and walked back to my bike. Speaking over my shoulder, I said, "Sweet dreams."

"Good night." I heard her say and waited until I heard the locks engage before cranking my loud bike and grudgingly leaving.

As soon as I pulled into the yard of my trailer down the road, I ran inside and turned on my laptop, impatiently waiting for the secure feed to connect. Pacing the old, well-maintained trailer, I listened for the ping to alert me I was secure before pulling up the feed to the cameras I had in and around Grace's house.

She was sitting at the counter in her kitchen with a huge smile on her face and a laptop open in front of her. Making a list on a notepad, she closed the computer and walked into the bedroom, closing the door behind her. Even after the amazing day I had with her, I wasn't going to invade her bedroom, so I focused the camera on the paper she left behind, trying to read it.

When I saw what she wrote, I smiled to myself. It was the ingredients for the pie I requested, and my name with a heart around it. It might not be a declaration of love, but it was progress on winning my woman over.

**

The next morning, I drove to Eddie's after checking that Grace was still sleeping peacefully. I slept with the laptop opened to her bedroom door every night, needing to make sure she was okay. A few times, she'd had nightmares and it killed me to not have her in my arms, to soothe her pain. Seeing she slept soundly through the night, I drove quickly, wanting to glean as much information from Eddie as I could.

After seeing the two of them together at the bar, as close as they were, I started digging into Eddie, and I still couldn't find a connection between the two. How did a sixteen-year-old runaway from Missouri end up closer than family with a Gulf War Veteran from Alabama? It made no sense, and I hoped I could ferret the information from him, or at least a direction to refine the search.

He was waiting on the front porch when my headlights rolled across it, and he stood from his seat as I turned the bike off and placed my helmet on the seat. He walked inside, and I caught the door before it closed, following him into the kitchen.

Seeing the delicious desserts on the counter, I heard my stomach grumble. Eddie glanced over his shoulder as he poured me a cup of coffee, and when he turned around, he had two forks in his hand. I took my coffee from him, picked up the chocolate cake that tempted me last night, and carried it to the table.

"Good choice," he remarked and sat down across from me.

We both took a bite from the cake, knowing it would be gone soon as we began to talk. I glanced at his weathered face and could see in his stuttered eyes that he had painful secrets he kept buried as well. Most people did, but there was those few who, when they made eye contact, you knew they'd seen more than most.

"I checked you out," Eddie remarked, and I looked up quickly, fearful he knew the real reason I came looking for Grace. He held his hand up to stop me before I started making excuses, and I leaned back, pursing my lips, and waiting. "I needed to know what kind of man was pursuing Grace, so I called a friend over at the Army base."

I didn't show any outward sign of distress, but knew if he dug too deeply, he could cause problems for not only me but the Death Hounds and Callahan Cyber. I was back dooring my way through too many lettered government agencies to need that kind of attention.

"Before you freak out, I didn't ask him to dig through your entire life, just skim the surface." I exhaled and ran my hands through my hair.

"There are aspects of my life that don't need to see the sunlight, and other areas that have to remain hidden in the darkness. Nothing about my life would ever touch Grace, but I need you to stop digging."

"Funny, that's what he said too. Off the record, of course. What he did tell me is you're a man of your word, you're honorable, and most importantly, you would kill anyone who tried to hurt Grace. Am I right?"

"Without a doubt, I would kill anyone who thought they could cause her pain. And they would never find the body. I promise you that, and if I can't protect her, my club, my family, and my closest business associates would ensure her safety."

He stared deeply into my eyes, and I never faltered, letting him look into my soul. Grace was mine, and it was time for Eddie to fill in some of the blanks. When he got whatever answer he was looking for, he sat back and lifted his fork to take another bite of cake.

"Ask your questions but realize I won't tell you if Grace promised me to secrecy. My loyalty is to that sweet girl who got a raw fucking deal in life."

He chewed on a bite of cake and washed it down with coffee while I formulated where I wanted to begin. Deciding the beginning was the best place, I took a swallow of coffee then asked, "How long have you known Grace?"

"I met her five months after her sixteenth birthday."

"How did you meet?"

"Mutual friend who I won't bring into this," he explained and stood from the table to retrieve the coffee pot.

Pouring us both another cup, he placed it on the table and lifted his eyebrows.

"How did she come to live here?"

"She needed a place, and I gave her a room until she was able to afford her own place."

He was better at this than I expected, so I changed tactics, "When did she come to work for you?"

He smiled and sat forward. "She's been working with me for close to eight years. Started out stocking coolers and sweeping the floor, but eventually, she wanted to pour, so I kept her behind the bar with me."

"How would you handle it if I took Grace away from here?"

"If you were giving her a loving, supportive, safe home and not going to drag her to your club to turn her into a trophy, I'd be supportive. If you just want her to hang off your bike and follow you around like some kind of love-struck fool, then leave her alone."

"Do you know the bond between an old lady and her man?" He shook his head, so I explained, feeling a little insulted by his accusations. "She is coveted by her man to the point of worship, she is respected by every member of the club, she gains a network of support, family, friends, and an unbreakable bond that will follow her until the final days of her life."

"And that's what you want from her?"

"I want whatever will make her happy. I don't know what it is, but something happened to her that dimmed the light in her eyes. I saw the same thing in my sister's eyes after . . . let's just say, she survived and is stronger because of it, but it broke a part of her that never healed the same," I looked down at the table, shaking my head slightly at my memories of Sadie after her attack.

I knew in my heart that something had happened to Grace. The same man who spent *six visits* with Aubrey all those years ago in the shed was the man tasked with taking care of Grace for close to *twelve years*. I know deep in my soul something happened to her, and I only hate I can't kill him myself. Not that I could tell Eddie any of this. Hell, he might not even be aware of that part of her life.

"Are you in love with Grace?" I blurted out, and he leaned his head back, laughing from deep in his belly.

He wiped an errant tear leaking from his eye as he clarified, "I was in the military when 'don't ask, don't tell' was the standard. I love Grace like a daughter, but she's not my type. In my day, you were closer to what I was into, just without the beard."

I rubbed my chin and smiled. "I'm flattered, but I only have eyes for Grace."

He shrugged. "Pity."

"I do have a friend back home that has a thing for older men who keep themselves in shape. I think you'd like him."

I pulled out my phone and showed him a picture of Mathias, Aubrey's best friend, and he whistled low. "Damn. That's more my speed."

"If you're ever in Portstill, I'll set you up," I mentioned, and he looked at me with a serious expression.

"Do you promise to give her a good life free of expectations and love her when the demons who haunt her rear their heads?"

This was my opening, so I took it. "What kind of demons am I dealing with? Ones that I can slay or ones that have already met their demise?"

"Both," he cryptically responded, and I felt my stomach drop.

I needed to call James and have him start digging deeper into Grace's life. Somehow, I missed something if there was someone who still needed to be dealt with. Who could it be? Kevin Ringman died four years ago, so who was still haunting her?

Chapter 8

Grace

I woke up still feeling his soft lips pressed against mine. I couldn't believe I asked Dalton to kiss me last night. It was out of my character to be so forward, but spending the day with him, seeing his beautiful smile aimed directly at me, his hypnotic blue eyes looking deep into my soul, made me bold. I had some painful things I deal with when it comes to intimacy, but desire was something that I experienced like everyone else. Through the years, I had random hook-ups, needing to have a connection, but I never allowed anyone to take it past a night or two of fun.

With Dalton, I could see forever, and I needed to get my head out of the clouds. He was just passing through, and soon, he would be gone. Deciding to have fun while he was here and to keep my heart from becoming involved, I vowed to let our connection go wherever fate took us, for as long as we had together. I already knew I'd miss him when he was gone, so I would make the most of our time now.

After drinking a cup of coffee and doing my morning yoga in the living room, I took a quick shower and grabbed the list for the dessert he requested. I was excited to try a new recipe and I drove to the nicer store in town, choosing to use all fresh ingredients for his pie. After gathering all the ingredients except the liquor, I headed back toward my house, deciding to use my key to grab some liquor from the bar.

Eddie was already inside when I pulled up, and I announced my presence as I opened the door and yelled, "Eddie, it's me. I wanted to grab some whiskey for a new dessert."

He stuck his head out of the office behind the bar and motioned for me to join him. Stepping around the newly delivered boxes of beer and liquor, I walked into the small office and sat down in my chair in the corner as he plopped into his creaky desk chair.

"What's the new dessert?" he asked, and I smiled.

"Kentucky Derby Pie," I answered, and he chuckled.

"I haven't had that in years. Let me guess, Skid wants some pie?"

I blushed and glanced down at my folded hands before meeting his gaze. "I asked him what his favorite was."

"He's a good guy, Grace," Eddie stated , and I nodded in agreement.

"He seems like it, but he'll be gone before we know it, I'm sure," I explained, and he shook his head, leaning back into the old chair.

"I know what you're afraid of, but I can tell from the look in his eyes, he's an honest man who would treat you right."

"How can you know something like that?" My lip trembled and I closed my eyes briefly, fear pushing through the lovesick haze I allowed his kiss to wrap me in. "He could be worse than . . ."

Eddie stood from his chair and kneeled in front of me as the tears welled up in my eyes, "Grace, honey, I know trusting people doesn't come easy to you, and I fully understand why. But you have to take a chance on someone or you're going to be miserable. Real love exists, you just have to open your heart and let someone in."

"I let you in," I replied, hearing the sadness in my voice.

He took my hands into his. "It's not the same thing, Grace, and you know it. I love you with everything in my soul and I want you to be happy, but I can't be the only person you show love to. You deserve someone who can give you the family you want, and no matter what, I'm not going anywhere. I'll always be right here to tell you when you're screwing up."

"Are you saying Dalton is that one? I just met him and hardly know anything about him."

"What does your gut tell you about him?" Eddie asked, moving back to his seat and stretching out his legs to alleviate the pain in his joints.

For years, my ability to trust my own judgment had been completely fucked up. What I thought was right and normal was anything but, so I questioned my decisions, resulting in anxiety. Eddie taught me to trust my gut. Evaluate, look for deception, and let my gut decide.

I exhaled deeply. "My gut says he's a good guy."

"Mine does too, so trust your instincts and give him a chance, for however long he's here. Maybe, when he goes home, you'll be ready to take the next step. Maybe not. Whatever happens, give your heart a chance to experience all the joys a new relationship can bring you, and don't look for the bad things that could happen."

A knock on the outer door of the bar drew our attention, and Eddie checked the security camera to see another delivery driver waiting to offload more provisions for the bar. I followed him to the door and went to grab a box when Eddie stopped me.

"I've got the new barback coming to help get set up. You're off tonight so you can spend some time with Skid." His brown eyes twinkled, and he gave me a sly smile.

"Are you sure?" I asked as the driver pushed a hand truck full of boxes into the bar, and Eddie walked me to my parked car.

"I'm positive, and if you don't feel like working tomorrow, you don't have to." He wiggled his eyebrows, and I shook my head, rolling my eyes at him.

"I'll call you later."

I climbed into the car, and he stuck his head through the open door. "Shave your legs, girl. No man wants furry calves wrapped around their waist."

I gasped, mocking outrage, before joining him in laughter. "For your information, I shaved this morning."

"Brat." He pecked me on the cheek before closing my door and reentering the bar.

I drove home and pulled into the yard, parking my car close to the walkway. After carrying the groceries into the kitchen, I started some music playing over my sound system and got to work on Dalton's dessert.

Dancing around the kitchen, I smiled, thinking about his lips pressed to mine. I had just put the pie into the oven when my phone dinged with a text message.

Unknown: I may have begged Eddie for your phone number, so don't be mad. It's Dalton, by the way.

I smiled at the phone and checked I had a timer set for the oven before walking onto the front porch and settling into my overstuffed chair. Debating on how to respond, I decided to follow Eddie's advice to trust my gut. After saving his number into my phone, I responded.

Me: I just put your pie into the oven.

The three little dots popped up, and I smiled, thinking about him. He was so damn handsome, and when he kissed me last night, I felt myself falling for him. After talking to Eddie, I chose to live instead of hiding.

Dalton: I can't wait to taste it. What time are you working tonight?

Me: I'm off tonight. Would you like to have dinner? It won't be fancy, but I promise dessert will be delicious.

Dalton: That sounds great. Can I bring anything?

Me: Just your appetite. Dinner is at six.

Dalton: I'll be counting the minutes until I see you again, beautiful.

Me: Until then . . .

It was just after lunch, and my stomach grumbled, reminding me to eat. Walking into the house, I pulled some cold cuts and cheese from the fridge when I heard a motorcycle getting closer. Butterflies took flight in my stomach, and I walked to the open front door to see Dalton pulling into my yard. He turned the bike off, and I stepped onto the porch, shielding my eyes from the sun.

He removed his helmet and climbed off the bike before he approached the house. His faded jeans and tight-fitting shirt gave him an edgy vibe but knowing the leather jacket he wore was from an actual motorcycle club took him to a whole different level of hotness. He had a swagger to his hips as he walked up the stairs, stopping a foot from me and leaning down, placing a soft kiss on my cheek.

I smiled as he stood up and pushed his sunglasses to the top of his head. His blue eyes twinkled as he looked down at me, and I fought the urge to throw myself at him. He was hotter than should be legal, and I felt heat creeping up my face.

Clearing my voice, I asked, "Not that I'm not happy to see you, but what are you doing here?"

"I just wanted to see you and to give you a kiss before dinner tonight," he rationalized , and I inched closer to him.

"And now that I have my kiss?"

"That was just a hello, darlin'," he replied, his voice filled with need.

I licked my lips and met his gaze with mine, seeing his desire for me burning brightly in his eyes. Stepping closer until the smell of leather, smoke, and something distinctly Dalton filled my senses, I touched my hands to his toned chest and whispered, "Then where's my kiss?"

He brought his hands to my hips and tugged me closer to him before he slammed his mouth to mine. I groaned as his soft beard rubbed against my lips and opened my mouth, feeling him sweep his tongue against mine. His thickness was growing against my stomach as I brought my hands to his shoulders and linked them behind his neck.

His strong arms wrapped around me, dragging me impossibly close to him as our kiss grew in intensity. I felt myself moving backward until I collided with the wall of my house. He began to kiss across my jaw, and I angled my neck toward him until his lips pressed against the column. Shivers broke out along my body, and I moaned into the air. With a slight drag of his teeth across my pulse point as he pressed his hard length against me, he reluctantly slowed the kiss, placing soft nips on my lips until we were panting for air.

I fluttered my eyelids open and saw him looking down at me with such fire that I was ready to jump into the flames. Nothing about him made me scared, even though I'm sure there are parts of his life with his club that I might not agree with, I couldn't resist the pull to him.

I've seen the motorcycle TV show with the sexy actor and know that most clubs are less than legal, but his claim of working for a company that made the news for the technological innovations was reassuring. Until he showed me the bad, I would only see the good.

I just hoped I wasn't being manipulated again. I wouldn't survive any more betrayal.

The buzzer in the kitchen sounded, and he lifted his nose into the air and smiled. "Something smells delicious."

"It's your dessert," I smiled and went to slide out of his embrace when he tugged me closer to him.

He whispered, "It's not the dessert."

He placed a soft kiss on my neck and released me. My legs were wobbly, and my panties were damp from his amazing kiss, but I needed to get his pie out of the oven before it burned. Opening the door, I walked inside and looked over my shoulder, expecting him to be behind me. He stood with his arms crossed, but not moving.

"You're welcome to come inside," I remarked and walked to the small kitchen.

The door closed in the living room, and I saw Dalton step into my house. He looked around quickly before he walked into the kitchen to find me placing the pie on the counter. I was pleased with how it turned out and hoped he liked it.

"Damn, Grace. That looks amazing, and I have no doubt it will taste even better."

He looked at the cold cuts and cheese on the counter and gave me a quizzical look. "Have you eaten lunch yet?"

"I was just making me something. Would you like to join me?"

"Can I take you to lunch?"

I looked down at my shorts and T-shirt before shrugging. "Sure. Let me freshen up really quick."

I went to move around him in the kitchen doorway when he placed a hand on my side and whispered, "You look beautiful, now."

"Thank you," I replied and brushed a piece of hair off my forehead.

His compliments were hard to take when you weren't used to believing people's words, but hearing them fall from his lips, somehow made them feel real. I left him in the kitchen while I went to my bedroom and closed the door. Quickly, I changed shirts and pulled my hair into a clip, not wanting to take the time to fix it. He'd seen me free of makeup after we swam yesterday, and my hair was a curly nightmare by last night. If he was okay with that, then the need to make myself into someone else to impress him was absent.

Somehow, I liked being my real self with him. If my gut was truthful, he might be the person who can accept me for the painful things I endured and my inability to trust. Being near him pushed the memories deeper, and I prayed they stayed buried. No good came from kicking that hornet's nest.

I slipped my feet into a pair of tennis shoes and opened the door to find him sitting on my old couch, looking at his phone. He lifted his head, and a brilliant smile filled his handsome face as he stood.

"Are you ready?" he asked, and I nodded.

After locking the house, he helped me onto the bike and secured my helmet before climbing in front of me. After his helmet was in place, I wrapped my arms around his toned waist, and he cranked the loud bike, vibrating me as he pulled away from the house. It was freeing being on the back of his motorcycle, and I had the urge to spread my arms out, imagining it would feel like flying.

When he got to the end of my road, he stopped and yelled over his shoulder, "Hold on."

I wasn't scared when I was on his bike, knowing deep down, he wasn't going to hurt me. The only person I ever felt that way toward was Eddie, and I trusted his opinion on Dalton. I gripped tighter onto him as he revved the engine and squealed tires, laying down rubber as he peeled away from the stop sign and shot down the road like a bullet.

And after it happened twice now, I knew how he got the name Skid.

Chapter 9

Skid

Spending the last two days with Grace was more than I could have asked for. She seemed more relaxed the longer we spent time together, and I didn't want to do anything to cause her any more pain than what I knew she already experienced. I may be guessing on her past, for the most part, but the haunted look in her eyes, even through laughter, was a tell-tale sign I was on the right track.

I was texting with Devlin and James about digging deeper into her past when she walked into her living room, looking like a dream. Her curly hair was piled onto her head, she was makeup free, and her ability to make shorts and a T-shirt look sexy had my needy cock begging for relief.

During lunch, she kept her hand in mine when we were eating, and I stood taller with her by my side. I'd never taken the time to really talk to a woman, and hearing her tell me crazy stories from the bar made me miss home. Between the Dog House and Falcon's Tavern, I'd spent years seeing some of the craziness that goes on when people are drinking.

"Do you think you'll stay working at the bar long-term?" I asked when we were done eating, and she shrugged as she stacked our plates to help the waitress clear the table.

"I've been there for so long that it's home, but I don't see myself pulling drinks forever."

"What would you do if you could choose your career?"

"Eddie always told me I needed to start a bakery or a catering service, but that takes a lot of overhead, and banks don't loan money to people like me."

I leaned closer to her and asked with curiosity, "What kind of person are you?" Lowering my voice, I continued, "Are you secretly on the run from the law?"

I made my eyes wide and looked around, only to look back and see her giggling. I knew what kind of self-deprecation someone can go through when questioning themselves, and I didn't want her to think she was somehow less worthy than anyone else.

Besides, if she wanted a bakery, I could build her one. Not that I'd brag about it.

"Nothing as exciting as that. I . . . I only have a GED, so no bank is going to give me money to start a business." Her eyes cast down before she shook her head and looked up at me. "I'm happy where I am, and Eddie needs me."

Making the remark in passing, I wanted to plant a seed that would hopefully grow into more. "You could always come to Portstill with me. My sister would hire you on the spot with the level of excellence you put into your pies. She's always on the lookout for talented bakers."

As we walked out of the restaurant, she absently said, "I guess that's something to think about."

After securing her on the bike, I pulled into traffic and turned toward her house. When we were a few miles from her house, she yelled over my shoulder, "Can you take the next left?"

I nodded and made the turn, waiting for her instructions. Wherever Grace wanted to go, I'd be happy to take her. Every second we were together, I learned a little more about her, so I was eager to see what she wanted to show me. She pointed where to turn, and after another few minutes, she yelled, "When we get to the bridge, can you stop on this side?"

Giving her a thumbs up, I slowed down as the bridge came into view. It was a low-walled bridge crossing the river that flowed past Eddie's bar a few miles away. I looked over my shoulder at Grace as I stopped the bike, and she confused me when she asked, "Can you drive slow across the bridge?"

Just as I went to put the bike into first gear, she stood with her feet on the pegs and leaned her legs against my back. Smiling to myself, I kept the bike under twenty as we rolled across the bridge. Her hands rested on my shoulders for a few feet, and when I saw her throw her arms out and tilt her face to the sky, I knew the feeling she was going for.

Wrapping one of my arms around the back of her leg and steering with the other, I yelled, "Hold on, darlin.'"

She leaned into me, so I increased the speed, and I could practically feel her joy as she laughed into the air. When we approached the other side of the bridge, I slowed down, and she grasped my shoulders before sitting back on the bike and wrapping her arms around me.

"That was amazing," she yelled, and I patted her hand in agreement.

Being on a bike was freeing, and if my Grace was anything like me, she just wanted to fly. I took the roads a little faster than normal but made sure to keep her safe as I returned her to her house. Turning off the bike, she hopped off and took her helmet off as her laughter rang into the air.

"That was fucking amazing. I know why you like your motorcycle so much."

I pulled her into me and kissed her until we were breathless. "Best fucking feeling in the world."

I left it open as if I was either speaking of my bike or kissing her. They were tied as my favorite things to do, but I could see Grace quickly taking first place.

She asked with a blush on her face, "Would you like to come inside?"

Placing the helmets on the seat, I followed her into the small house, wanting to feast on her.

"Do you want some of your dessert now?" she asked, and I slowly approached her.

Her blue eyes ran up and down my body as I grew closer, and when she licked her lips, I decided to push my luck.

"I'd like dessert, but not the pie," I stated, and her eyes met mine.

She could tell me to go, and I would leave, but if she gave me one chance, I'd show her my devotion. Leaving no room for error, I explained, "I want you, Grace, with a hunger I've never felt before, but I won't push you for something you're not ready for." Stepping closer, I leaned over and felt her shiver as I whispered into her ear, "But if you say you want me as much as I want you, I'll take you to paradise and make you mine."

I saw her clench her knees together as he chest rose and fell and her pupils dilated. Something inside her gaze shifted and she stepped up to me, pressing onto her tiptoes to bring her face closer to mine. Thinking I may need to duck like Eddie reminded me, I held my breath in anticipation as she made her decision.

Her soft lips drew closer to mine, and I clenched my fists, not wanting to touch her until she said yes. She kept her eyes locked on me as her mouth brushed against mine, her whispered words an answered prayer.

"I want you so badly."

Closing the short distance between us, I wrapped my arms around her waist and lifted her into the air as I slammed my lips to hers, tasting her want on my tongue. She moaned into the embrace as her arms snaked around my neck, and I encouraged her to wrap her legs around my waist. She felt right draped around me, and I knew, from that moment forward, she was mine.

Walking across the small living room, I sat on the couch with her straddling my lap as I grasped the back of her neck and brought her closer to me. Any space between us was too much, and when she began to make small twists of her hips over my hard length, I groaned, breaking the kiss.

Placing my forehead against hers, we panted into the air as her unfocused gaze met mine. I could see some hesitation in her, and I asked, "Are you sure, Grace? We can stop."

She looked down at her lap and bit into her swollen lip. I gripped her hips with a squeeze, urging her to look at me. Her worried eyes met mine, and she admitted, "I don't want you to think I'm easy. I know we just met, but—"

"I would never judge a woman for her sexual choices, Grace. If you want me and I want you, who gets to put a timeframe on what *we* feel is right?" She looked directly into my eyes, and I asked, "Do you want me?"

"So much," she replied.

"Do you want me to stop?"

She shook her head, and I gave her one final chance to end everything. "Do you think I'll hurt you or make you do something you don't want to do?"

"Of course not."

I gripped into her hair and brought her mouth back to mine. "Then take your pleasure, baby. I'll never judge you. I only want to worship you."

Her small hands fell to my chest, and she ran her fingers under my cut as she licked her lips. I loved to watch a woman's inner vixen come to the surface, when she lets herself have the freedom to explore without fear of judgment. It was okay for men to sleep around, but if a woman did it, she was somehow less.

Well, fuck that, and fuck the judgmental assholes who believed it.

Her hands pushed at the sleeves of my cut, and I leaned forward to remove it, feeling my cock press into her core as the leather came off. Taking the jacket and folding it in half, I handed it to her and asked, "Can you put that on the back of the chair, please?"

She stood from my lap and took my cut to the chair next to the door, gently placing it on the back before turning to me. Her eyes were running up and down my inked arms as she swayed her hips and returned. When she climbed back onto my lap, her legs straddling mine, I reached out and pulled her fully over my erection.

She gasped, and I took the opening to kiss her, invading her mouth. She gripped my shirt and met my kiss with equal energy. Kissing across her jaw, I licked and nipped at the tender flesh of her neck, feeling her shiver in my arms. Smiling against her neck, I kissed the sensitive spot below her ear as she rocked on my lap.

I kissed down her neck and across her collarbone, pulling her shirt to the side as I tasted her skin. She reached to her waist and pulled her shirt off over her head, forcing me to break our connection. I looked down to see her pert breasts heaving under her pink bra.

"Fuck, you're beautiful," I groaned as I leaned her back and kissed her chest over her bra.

Sucking a nipple through the lacy material, she grasped my head and moaned my name.

"Dalton."

No one had called me that during sex. Ever. And it made this first time with Grace somehow more important. Not to sound overly emotional, but it made everything special.

Hearing her desire, feeling her hot pussy pressed against me through layers of denim, was testing my patience. I needed to let her lead when all I wanted to do was fuck her until we passed out from exhaustion.

She stood from the couch and offered me her hand. "Let's go to the bedroom where we can be more comfortable."

I stood and adjusted my cock, seeking any relief as I was led to her bedroom. I glanced up to the corner outside her room as we walked in and saw the pinpoint camera I'd installed weeks ago to monitor her. I should've turned them off, but I couldn't be bothered to stop as she turned to me.

Grace released my hand and stepped in front of me, looking up at me with desire and need. She fisted my shirt in her hands and tugged the material from my jeans. I pulled it off over my head and tossed it to the floor as she took in all my ink.

My Death Hounds tattoo took up my right chest, and there were countless skulls, daggers, and whatever I felt was cool at the time permanently inked into my skin. Her fingertips brushed along the designs, and I watched her with fascination as she examined me like a piece of art.

"Beautiful," she commented after inspecting my chest and back.

"I don't think that's something anyone's ever said about me," I replied with a chuckle as she came back in front of me.

"It's the truth. You're a walking masterpiece."

I brought my hand up, caressing her cheek as I explained, "I'm glad you like them."

She leaned into me, and I brought my lips to hers. Her bra-covered breasts pushed against my chest as she pulled me to her bed. Our mouths clashed, fighting for a connection as she fell backward and I followed, covering her small body with mine. She was so delicate under me, but she felt right.

Pulling back from the embrace, I sat up and raised an eyebrow at her, silently asking to proceed. She kicked her shoes off and reached down to unbutton her pants when I whispered, "Please, let me."

She nodded, and I kissed her again until we were fighting for breath. Working my way down her body, I nipped and kissed at her breasts until she squirmed under me, rubbing against my leg, seeking relief. I methodically worked down her body until I came to her blue jeans. Lifting my eyes to hers, I popped the button and urged her to lift her ass into the air.

When she complied, I tugged her jeans and panties down in one motion before discarding them onto the floor. She reached behind her, freeing her breasts from her lacy bra, and I groaned as I took in the sight of her beautiful nakedness. I'd seen countless women naked, but she was by far the most beautiful creature I'd ever laid eyes on.

Settling onto the floor on my knees, I pulled her ass to the edge of the bed and kissed her toned stomach, feeling her tremble under me. Slowly, I worked my way to her core and found my own personal heaven. Her pretty pussy was on full display, and she allowed her legs to fall open as I brought my nose to her curls and inhaled deeply.

"Fuck, you smell so good," I told her, and she brought a small hand to the back of my hair, running her fingers through my black locks. "I bet you taste even better."

Kissing down, I licked her clit fully and held a hand to her stomach as she tried to lift her ass off the bed.

"Oh, god," she moaned as I licked her up and down before swirling her engorged clit in tight circles.

Her legs clamped my head as I worked her higher and higher, the taste of her an elixir for my soul. Grace rocked her hips, chasing her release, and I pushed a finger into her tight pussy, feeling her walls squeeze against me. Knowing I would be a tight fit for her with my endowment, I pumped one then two fingers into her as I felt the first shakes in her legs.

"Dalton," she stuttered, and I felt her pussy contracting as her orgasm broke free. I pushed a third finger into her, pumping my hand as her release overtook her.

She was almost angelic when she came, and I licked her through her tremors until she pushed against my head, asking me to stop. Withdrawing my fingers from her, I kissed her clit and rested my head on her hip, watching her as she basked in her afterglow. I purposely kept my pants on in case she wanted to put the brakes on it now, because even though not being inside her might kill me, I would honor her request.

She looked down her naked body at me. "Fuck, that was amazing."

"Have you had enough, darlin'?"

I prayed she'd say no, and when she sat up, I mirrored her. She brought one hand to my cheek and leaned in, kissing me deeply and groaning as we shared her taste. When she pulled me back onto the bed with her, settling me between her spread legs, I knew she was okay with continuing.

"Please, Dalton."

Leaning over, I whispered, "Don't worry. I've got you, baby."

Reaching into my pocket, I pulled out a condom from the box I'd bought that morning as she turned and put her head on the pillows. She watched as I unbuttoned my pants and pushed them down my legs, exposing more tattoos along my lower half. Her eyes grew wide as my cock came into view.

Rolling the latex over my shaft, I positioned myself between her legs and asked, "Are you ready?"

She nodded and pressed her head into the pillow, so I followed her, kissing along her neck and plucking at her hard nipples until she was rubbing her wet center along my cock. When she got to the point she couldn't take any more, her small hand grasped my thickness and ran it along her pussy.

Locking my gaze with hers, I removed her hand and guided myself into her center, watching the expression on her face as I gathered her release on the tip and slowly pressed into her. Her mouth fell open as her eyes closed, and she moaned under me. With small thrusts, I worked more and more of my cock into her tight core until we were fused together at the pelvis.

At that moment, my soul connected with hers. It sounded lame, but I now understood what the married brothers said about finding the one and how perfect it was.

Slowly, I retracted my hips before pushing back into her perfection. Her hands gripped onto my back as I began to thrust with more force, long stroking her as she met every thrust with her own. Our panted moans filled the room as each push of my hips brought me closer to orgasm. I'd never finished that fast, but I wouldn't tip over the edge until she was with me.

Gripping her leg behind the knee, I pressed it against her chest with one hand and brought my other hand to her center. Rubbing her clit, I felt her walls clenching my shaft, and my vision grew spotty as the pleasure became too much to bear.

"Dalton . . . more," she begged, and I increased my speed, giving an extra shove of my hips into her as I felt her orgasm break free. "Yes, oh . . . yes!"

"Grace," I moaned as her release pulled mine from me, filling the condom.

I collapsed to her side, not wanting to crush her as our stilted breathing filled the room. She giggled, and I looked down at her with a smile as she stared up at me.

"That was . . ." she started, and I kissed her nose before finishing her sentence.

"Perfect. Amazing. Breathtaking."

Her beautiful eyes met mine, and for a moment, I could see our forever.

Only I had no idea at that time just how much blood there would be on our path to happiness.

Chapter 10

Grace

I'd never experienced anything like what Dalton and I shared. He was a perfect lover, and as we got redressed, I couldn't keep the smile off my face. Something clicked when he was inside me, and I felt a connection to him, unlike anything I'd ever experienced. He took me by the hand and dipped me backward, kissing me softly before placing me back on my feet.

The way he treated me was unexpected. From outward appearances, he looked to be a tough, sexy, tattooed biker who would rather hit you than talk to you. I'm glad he was persistent in his pursuit of me, or I would have never got to see this side of him. I had no doubt his tough side was something I hoped never to experience, but in his arms, I felt safe.

"Ready for dessert?" I asked, and he chuckled.

"I'll need a few minutes to recover."

I slapped his shoulder with a smile. "Not that dessert. Your pie."

He tugged me closer, pushing his growing length against me. His blue eyes were filled with heat as he gazed into mine. "Is that what we're going to call it?"

I laughed deep from my belly as we got dressed before I pulled him into the kitchen. His smile was contagious as I guided him to the counter and pulled down two plates. He came up behind me, leaning his hard body against my back as he took the plates from my hand and set them on the counter.

I turned, and his eyes met mine again. He was always bringing his gaze to mine, and normally, I glance into someone's eyes, but never peer into them. With him, I got lost in his stare. He was looking deep into my soul, and I tried to remain as open as I could with him, hoping I hid the shame and humiliation I carried with me. He lifted one side of his mouth and pecked me on the cheek before taking the plates to the other counter.

Cutting into my newest creation, I plated the two servings, and Dalton took the plates from me, carrying them into the living room. I sat next to him with one leg tucked under the other and my body facing him so I could watch him enjoy his treat.

He took a forkful and when he tasted it, his eyes closed, and he groaned as loudly as he did when he was inside me for the first time. I felt my tender core clench and fought not to shift in my seat.

"Fuck, baby, this is delicious," he praised before kissing me with chocolate on his lips. "Thank you."

"You're welcome," I returned and took a bite, enjoying the pecans and chocolate on my newest crust.

The sun was setting in the sky, the living room filled with long dark shadows, so I stood and turned on a few lights, casting us in a warm glow. I was full from lunch and dessert, not to mention the two amazing orgasms he gave me. So, when I sat down next to him, and he wrapped his arm around me, I fought to hide my yawn.

"If you're tired, sleep. I'll be okay while you rest," he said, and I looked up at him with my cheek on his muscled chest.

"I feel bad that I keep falling asleep on you," I admitted, not wanting to tell him he was the only person in my entire life, including *those years*, that I felt comfortable enough to sleep around.

"Why? You're tired, and I'm the lucky bastard that gets to hold you while you sleep. I say I'm getting the better end of the deal," he rationalized with a smile and a wink.

He took a pillow off the end of the couch and placed it over his lap as he lifted his sexy bare feet onto the coffee table and settled in with the TV remote in his hand. Patting the pillow, he urged, "Rest now, baby, cause when you wake up, I'm going to fuck you until we both pass out from exhaustion."

My breathing accelerated, realizing he was easy on me the first time. If he was going to ravage me, I would need some rest to keep up. A man like Dalton probably had his pick of the ladies, and I didn't want to leave him wanting.

I pressed up and brushed my hand across his cheek. His beard was soft under my fingertips as I kissed him softly. He kept the kiss chaste and patted the pillow on his lap again. I laid down, and he rested his hand on my side, his thumb rubbing slow circles against my skin until I felt the heaviness of my lids drag me into sleep.

"Are you sure this is right, Daddy?" I asked him as we walked up the driveway to the house.

I was only allowed to call him Daddy when Connie wasn't around. It was part of the rules he explained to me when we went camping two months ago, and I tried hard to follow them. When he was my daddy, he was nicer to me, telling me how pretty and special I was. It made me feel good to know he cared about me, and he told me that he wanted me to be his daughter, but it wasn't possible. He explained they got a check for me every month, and they couldn't afford to help other kids if my check was gone.

I didn't want another kid to have to stay somewhere unsafe like my old house was when I was little, so I smiled and told him I understood.

He squeezed my hand and looked down at me, his eyes soft and kind as he brought his hand to my shoulder.

"This is what is expected of us. I promise, it will be okay. Don't you want to be Daddy's special girl?" I nodded quickly, scared he changed his mind. "Then we have to go inside."

He released my shoulder and tugged my hand, urging me closer to the house. I could see a few men walk inside, and I turned my eyes, trying to see anyone my age. I'd been to gatherings with Connie and Kevin through the years where I was the only young person, and I hated being alone all night. Without Connie, I had Daddy to spend time with, and I was excited but also a little scared.

I didn't want to do anything to make him mad, and he told me if anyone found out, they would move me to a new house. I didn't want to be placed somewhere else, so I agreed to secretly call him Daddy when no one was around, and tonight was the first time I could say it in front of other people.

What made tonight so different confused me, and as we walked up the stairs to the brick house, I smoothed my hands down my dress like I was taught by Connie. 'First impressions matter,' she had said over the years, and I wanted to look my best in front of Daddy's friends. The door opened, and a lady smiled as she invited us inside.

Daddy reached over and kissed her on the cheek as he dropped my hand and placed it on her side. "Stella, it's good to see you. How are you?"

"I'm well, Kevin." She turned her eyes to me and asked, "And who's this beautiful young lady?"

Daddy turned his attention to me and smiled deeply before placing his arm around my shoulder and pulling me to his side. "This is my daughter, Grace. Grace, honey, this is Stella. This is her house."

"You have a beautiful home," I replied like I was taught, and she nodded.

"Thank you, Grace. Would you like to come with me while your daddy gets settled in with the gentlemen?" I looked up at Daddy, and he closed his eyes briefly before meeting my curious gaze.

He nodded before leaning down and kissing my cheek softly, whispering into my ear. "Be Daddy's good girl, and I'll see you soon."

"Yes, Daddy," I responded with a smile.

That was the first time he kissed me on the cheek, and I smiled, knowing this was how fathers treated their daughters. With kindness, respect, and love. He stood tall and stepped away from me as I turned to Stella.

"Come on, sweetheart. I'll get you something to drink," she explained, and I walked behind her, watching her hips sway as she moved down a hallway and into the kitchen in the back of the house.

"How old are you, Grace?" she inquired as she sat down at the small table near a large window and patted the chair next to her.

Sitting down, I replied, "I'm twelve."

"That's a wonderful age. You're growing up and able to accept more responsibility." She stood from the chair. I watched as she pulled two glasses down and began to make us some drinks. "Tell me. How do you like Kevin being your daddy? It's okay to be honest. It's just us girls."

She turned her back to me as she poured some soda into the glasses and returned, setting one in front of me as she sipped on hers. I lifted the glass and took a swallow before answering.

"I love it. Kevin is a good daddy but . . ." I let the words fade as my eyes fell to the table.

She lifted my head and turned my face to hers as she asked, "But?"

"I wish he could be my daddy all the time and not just when we're away from Ms. Connie," I whispered, and she smiled at me.

"If there was a way to make sure that no matter what, he was your daddy all the time, even if you couldn't call him that, would you do it?"

I placed my glass down on the table and turned my body to hers. She was so sophisticated, and if she could tell me how to make Kevin my daddy for real, I would do it.

Bobbing my head up and down dramatically, I quickly answered with urgency, "Yes. I'd do anything."

She pushed my glass closer to me, and I lifted it, taking a deep drink before placing it back down on the table. She smiled at me and explained. "There is a ceremony that we can do. That's why he brought you here, but you must agree to it. It's your choice, Grace. It might be unpleasant at first, but you'll be fine, and by the time it's over, Kevin will be your daddy for real. No matter what you call him or what some piece of paper says."

I was almost jumping in my seat as she spoke. "Yes, please. I want to do it," I rushed out.

"If you do the ceremony, any time your daddy wants to show you how much he loves you, he will reenact it with you, and it will bring you closer." She leaned in and lowered her voice. "You can never tell anyone about what you and your daddy do, though. Not everyone wants to have the kind of connection your daddy wants with you, and they won't understand."

"I won't tell anyone. I promise," I whispered and took another swallow of my soda. My throat was dry, and I was a little dizzy with excitement at the thought of making Kevin my daddy. I've craved the love my birth father gave me, and Kevin had been so invested in me since our camping trip, that I was eager to get started. "What kind of ceremony?"

"Well, it's a ritual of sorts. It's a binding of you and your daddy in the eyes of our community," she explained, and I looked at her, confused.

"Our church?" I asked, and she shook her head with a smile.

"The church only guides part of our lives. Our community guides the rest, and the ceremony is what makes you a member of the community. I did what you said you wanted to do when I was your age. My daddy helped me find a husband when it was time and made sure I knew what was expected of me. He taught me everything I needed to know to become a good wife, mother, and member of the community. I owe everything to my daddy, and I want to help you have the same thing." Her eyes were filled with a promise. "What's your decision, Grace?"

I swallowed thickly, a little scared and a lot excited as I replied, "I want to. Please help me."

She pulled me into a hug and whispered, "You may be scared, but your daddy will make everything all better. I promise. Trust your daddy and remember your promise."

She stood and urged, "Drink up. We don't want to keep your daddy waiting, do we?"

I finished the small glass in a couple of big swallows and wiped my mouth. "Let's go."

I was eager to get whatever this was over so I would know for certain, my daddy loved me. I wanted to be sophisticated like Ms. Stella, and if it meant Connie couldn't break my connection with Kevin, all the better.

I stood from the table and my head felt fuzzy as Ms. Stella took me by the hand and led me out of the kitchen. We walked down another hallway, and at the end were two closed doors. She knocked once, and someone said, "Come in," from the other side. She released my hand and looked down at me with a smile.

"Are you ready?"

I nodded and wobbled a little on my feet as she opened the doors. Taking me by the hand, she led me into a large den with heavy red curtains hanging over what appeared to be floor-to-ceiling windows. The room had bookshelves lining one wall with a long wooden table in front of it, and the other side had an ornate screen blocking a large section of the room. There were five men sitting at the table, all facing toward the screens, and when I stepped into the room, they all turned their gazes to me.

Stella released my hand and whispered, "Congratulations, Grace."

I smiled up at her, hoping my nervousness wasn't showing. Standing tall, I wanted to make Daddy proud, so I waited for someone to tell me what to do.

"Welcome, Grace," one of the men said.

"Thank you for having me," I replied.

A noise from over my shoulder made me glance in that direction, and I saw Daddy standing near the screen with a huge smile on his face. I smiled at him and turned my attention back to the men at the table. They all wore suits and had a drink in front of them. They looked important, and I was getting a little scared. Remembering Stella telling me it may be unpleasant, I suspected this is what she meant.

Were they looking at me to make sure I was a good daughter?

Did they know my mother threw me away?

Would they change their minds, and I lose Kevin?

Daddy approached me and placed his warm hand on my shoulder, encouraging me to turn toward him. "Did you talk with Stella?"

"Yes, Daddy."

"And you want this? For me to be your daddy? To teach you everything that will be expected of you later in life?" I nodded, and my head spun briefly before I focused again. "And you promise never to tell our secret?"

"I promise, Daddy."

"You may proceed," another man said, and Daddy led me across the room to the ornate screens.

Pulling one to the side, I looked behind them, unable to see what they were hiding. He moved another one, and I was unsure why there was a bed in the den. Confused, I looked up at Daddy, and he smiled down at me.

"Follow me, Grace. If this is what you truly want." He reached his hand out to me, and I willingly placed my palm into his.

He smiled, and the men stood from the chairs, moving closer to us as Kevin walked me to the bed and urged me to sit down. The mattress was soft, and he scooted me back until my knees hugged the side and my feet were dangling above the floor. He kneeled in front of me and took my hand, "With these actions, I choose you, Grace, to be my little girl. I vow to guide and teach you all the lessons that you need in life. I promise to be a good daddy to you. I pledge my love to you, Grace."

"I love you too, Daddy," I explained, and he smiled before leaning over and kissing my cheek.

The longer I was in the room, the heavier my head became until I was so tired, I couldn't keep it up anymore. Kevin helped lower me to the bed, and I smiled up at him as he turned me on the covers and laid down next to me. My eyelids were heavy, and I blinked as he rubbed his hand on my knee.

I jumped up from the couch and spun around, not knowing where I was for a moment. Dalton was in front of me, speaking calmly to me as I tried to focus on something, anything, to get my brain out of the memory.

"Grace, darlin', it's okay. You're safe. I'm here with you, and we're alone. No one can hurt you," he said, and I met his worried eyes, feeling the tears well up in mine. I never wanted him to see me like this. Shame filled me, and I turned away from him, hiding my face as the tears fell.

"Can you leave, please?" I stuttered through broken tears and prayed he would leave before he saw how much of a mess I really was.

He wouldn't be back after seeing me like this, and I couldn't bear to watch him leave.

"I'm not leaving until I know you're okay," he replied, and I turned to him with tears falling down my face.

Defensive, I yelled, "Is this what you want to see? How much of a disaster I am? Well, now you've seen it, so you can go."

"You're not a disaster, and I'm still not leaving until you've calmed down."

He reached over, grabbed the box of tissues from the end table, and handed me one as he stood with his tattooed arms crossed and worry filling his handsome face. I wiped the tears and blew my nose, not caring if I was unladylike.

"Can I get you some water?" he asked, and I nodded as I sat down on the couch.

The memory was receding, and my heart rate was slowing down as I watched him grab us bottles of water from the fridge. He entered the living room and handed me one before asking, "Can I sit down?"

I took a swallow and glanced up at him before nodding and moving my gaze to the far wall of the room. He sat with a cushion between us, giving me space as he watched me. His concern was admirable, but I knew he wanted to bail.

"I'm okay now. You don't have to stay if you don't want to." I gave him a way out, and he slowly reached over and took my hand into his. I loved the connection to him, grounding me in the present, and I looked at him with a tremble in my chin. "I'm sorry."

"Never apologize for a nightmare. Ever. You can't stop the demons that chase you in your dreams, and I won't ever judge you for it." I wanted to smile but couldn't as he continued, "My sister, Sadie, had nightmares for years after she survived something pretty bed. Something no woman should have to experience. I won't give the details, but I understand how monsters can be real when they find us asleep."

"Does . . . does she still have nightmares?" I asked, curious if it's possible to slay your demons or if I was going to be haunted by my naivety and stupidity forever.

"Not anymore. She finally found a way to put them to rest, and she's thriving now."

I scooted closer to him, and he cut the distance, gently wrapping his arm around my shoulder. I rested my head against his chest before I asked, "How did she put them to rest?"

His voice grew dark, and I felt the words vibrate in his chest as he replied, "I killed them and sent them to hell where they belong."

Looking up, I could see the hardened truth in his eyes, and I asked myself, could Dalton be the one who could finally help me put my shameful past to rest once and for all? Would he be willing to kill for me the way he did his sister?

Not wanting to ask anything more, I explained, "Thank you for not running. I know it would have been easier than seeing my crazy join the party."

He kissed the top of my head and replied, "You're not crazy, Grace. But if you are, you're my kind of crazy."

If I ever trusted him enough to tell him everything, I hoped he meant what he said. Not many people could fathom the whole truth.

Chapter 11

Skid

Leaving Grace that night was the hardest thing I'd ever done. I wanted to hold her, praying to keep the nightmares at bay, so I quickly rode to my trailer, and I watched her most of the night to ensure she slept. The next day I showed up before breakfast, and when it was time for her to go to work, I patted the back of my bike, encouraging her to climb on.

She shook her head and explained, "I can drive myself to work. I'm sure you have better things to do than sit at the bar all night."

Handing her the helmet, I waited for her to get seated on the back before I explained, "What's better than getting to spend the evening with my woman?"

She hesitated as she asked, "Is that what I am? Your woman?"

I leaned over her and brought my lips to hers, whispering against them, "Hell, yes. Unless you want me to be your man. Either is fine with me."

She smiled, and I winked before climbing in front of her and cranking the motor. She secured her helmet and wrapped her arms around me, squeezing my middle as I pulled away from her house. Skidding away from the stop sign at the end of her road, she hooted into the air as I shot down the road, gaining speed as we traversed the miles to Eddie's bar. I slowed down to pull into the parking lot and parked next to the fence securing the employees' area on the side of the building.

Helping Grace from the bike, I linked my hand with hers and watched her face illuminate with happiness as we entered the bar. It was still early, and the band was setting up on the small stage as Eddie and the barback filled the coolers. The waitress that kept hitting on me was wiping down the tables and placing the chairs onto the floor when we walked in, turning her head toward the light shining into the darkened bar.

"I'm glad you finally came to your senses, Grace," she joked and offered me a wink as I led Grace to the bar.

Eddie smirked at Grace as she walked behind the bar and pulled on her apron. He caught my eye and lifted one eyebrow in question as I sat on a stool at the opposite end of the bar. Not a man to kiss and tell, even to her best friend, I shrugged and settled in. He cracked a smile at me as he pulled a bottle from the top shelf and poured me two fingers of whiskey.

For the next five days, it was a repeat cycle. I'd meet Grace for breakfast and spend all our time talking, getting to know each other. I would take her to and from work, spending some time with her in my arms before I left for the night, and return the next morning to start over again. We hadn't had sex again since that first time, and I was dying to be buried balls deep inside her but felt her reluctance. When she was ready for me, I'd take her to paradise, but until then, my blue balls and I would have to deal with my hand and her beautiful face on my computer monitor.

Saturday night was swinging at the bar. The college in the next town won their football game and everyone was celebrating. There wasn't a seat to be found, and dozens of people stood around, enjoying the live music as Grace and Eddie filled order after order. He told me to keep my table in the corner and no one bothered me during the evening.

Maybe it was my 'drop-dead asshole' stare, or my Death Hounds cut, but everyone gave me space. I watched everything, ready to jump in when needed and when Grace caught my eye, she would offer me a sly smile as she made another drink. I wanted to ravage her, and she seemed more relaxed tonight. I know her nightmare freaked her out, and she was embarrassed, so I needed to show her that the darkness she lived in didn't scare me, and I would patiently wait for her to break her silence.

Devlin and James were diving deep into Kevin Ringman's life, and we were all growing frustrated at the lack of direction we were finding. There was no indication that there were real dangers still existing for Grace, but they vowed to turn over every rock until they found something. My phone vibrated in my pocket, and I pulled it out, seeing Sadie's face on the screen.

Placing the reserved placard Eddie gave me as a joke onto the table, I waved at Grace and wiggled my phone before nodding to the outside. She acknowledged me and waved before turning back to a group in front of the bar. Eddie lifted his chin, and I stepped outside, the loud music and noise filtering to muffles as I answered the phone.

"Hey. How's things going back home?" I asked her as I stepped away from the building to get some quiet.

"Hey, yourself. I thought you were going to call me at least once a week while you're gone."

Sadie still wanted to mother Jacob and me, and it was tough not to remind her I wasn't a child anymore. Not only would it upset her, thinking she wasn't needed or wanted, which she was, but Gunner would kick my ass for upsetting his old lady. I used to joke with Sadie about his possessiveness, but after having Grace in my arms, I realized I would beat anyone who made her cry.

"I'm sorry. I've been busy," I replied and ran my hands through my growing hair.

"What's her name? Or do you even know her name?" she joked, and I snapped at her without thinking.

"Don't talk about her like that." My tone was harsh, and I immediately felt like shit for being defensive.

Sadie chuckled and asked again, "Who is she, Dalton?"

Sighing, I moved to the edge of the lot and leaned against Eddie's fence as I explained. "Her name is Grace, and you're going to love her. She makes the best pie I've ever tasted."

"Better than mine?" She scoffed, and I laughed.

"Yes, dear sister. This one is better than yours, and if I can get her to agree to come home with me, I'll let her prove it."

"You seem happy, little brother." Her voice softened, and I smiled at her words.

"I am happy. Sadie, she's perfect. Smart, funny, kind, giving, and sexy as hell." There was a pause, and I looked to make sure the call was still connected before I asked, "Are you still there?"

"Can I ask you something without you getting mad?" I could hear the worry in her voice.

"You can ask me anything, but I may not answer." There was club business and Callahan business that Sadie wasn't privy to, so I needed to be cautious. "Go ahead," I instructed and waited for her to speak.

"Is this the girl you told Kade about?"

My vision grew red and I clenched my fists, angry that my President, my brother, my friend had betrayed his promise to not discuss Grace's situation with Sadie. "That motherfucker," I grumbled, and she quickly interjected.

"I don't know what kind of business you're dealing with, and he only told me that you wanted to make sure a girl was safe. After what happened with Elise a few years ago, I was worried. I promise, he didn't tell me anything more than that. Only that she was lost, and you were trying to find her." Her voice grew worried, and she asked, "Is she okay?"

Sighing deeply, I looked up at the dark sky filled with stars, and the sound of the band filtered into the air. "Yeah, she's okay."

"I'm glad. Whenever you bring her home to visit, tell her I want to try this best pie ever created."

Laughing, I replied, "Don't get butt hurt, Sadie. You make amazing desserts."

She laughed with me and said, "I'm glad you're happy, Dalton. Promise to call me soon."

"I will. Tell Jacob I'll call him in a few days."

"Love you, brother."

"Love you too, Sadie," I replied and hung up the phone.

Shaking my head, I walked across the parking lot and nodded to the doorman as I went inside. Sliding through the crowd of people, I tried to see Grace behind the bar, but there were too many people lined up in front. Moving to the bar, I stepped to the side, seeing Eddie but not Grace. I pushed through the people, and the few that gave me lip shut up when I looked down at them.

Eddie saw me and walked straight to the end of the bar, leaning over as I yelled over the music. "Where's Grace?"

"I told her to take a break before the band stops, and we get swamped with orders. She's out back," he explained and smacked the bar as he turned and began to pull beers from the cooler of ice.

Walking around the bar, I dodged drunks and a few groping hands as I made my way to the break area Eddie built for the staff. At first glance, a breakroom outside made no sense, until the noise got too much to think. By having the secluded area, you could give your eardrums a rest while you got some fresh air. It was a nice oasis away from the smokey bar.

As I approached, I saw there were two douche bags standing near the door, their eyes moving through the crowd as everyone around them drank and enjoyed the football win from today. When I got closer, I saw them step together, trying to block the exit.

Standing in front of them, I crossed my arms over my chest and rose to my full height, my gut telling me something was very wrong. "Move."

The pimple-faced douche shook his head with fear in his eyes and glasses douche started to step to the side, only to be tugged back in front of the door.

"I said fucking move, asshole." My voice grew louder but was still lower than the excessive volume of the speakers from the band.

They both swallowed deeply, and I was done with their stupid shit. Gripping into both their shirts, I fisted them and pulled them away from the door before shoving them to the ground. I went to open the door, and it wouldn't open from the inside.

Something was definitely wrong, and I stepped back, kicking the wooden door with my heavy boot, splintering it from the frame as it swung open. I ran through the door as Eddie yelled at me, and when I got outside, blinding rage overtook me.

Grace was pinned over the table with a man pushing her down, trying to shove his body between her legs. She was punching and kicking at him, but his size was so much greater, that he had her at a disadvantage. Her cries for help gripped the monster deep inside and dragged him to the surface, ready to kill for my woman. I ran toward the table and grasped him by the shoulder, spinning him toward me.

Grace scrambled from the table and fell to the ground as I punched him in the face, blood spraying from his nose as he yelled into the night air.

"What part of no don't you understand, you stupid motherfucker?" I screamed as he tried to push me away from him.

The music was coming through the door as I hit him over and over, bone crunching under my fist as his face became a bloody mess. Reaching into my waistband, I grabbed my knife in its sheath and was ready to sink it into his chest when I heard her voice, breaking the monster's hold on my anger. Hearing Grace yell was the only thing that snapped me out of the murderous rage I was locked in.

"Dalton, please. You'll kill him." Her small hands tugged at my shirt, and I turned to see tears flowing down her cheeks and her shirt torn at the collar.

Jumping up from my position over him, I pulled her into my chest as she wrapped her arms around me and sobbed into my chest. "Grace, baby, are you okay?"

She nodded into my chest as the tears continued. A noise over my shoulder had me turning to see Eddie entering the area, and his eyes grew wide as he took in the scene in front of him.

The asshole on the ground was moaning and wailing, "I'm going to have you arrested. You don't know who you're messing with."

Eddie ran to Grace and pulled her away from me as he inspected her for injuries. She had bruises coming up on her arms and inner thighs, and there was a drop of blood on her lip, enraging me again. I kicked the asshole on the ground in his gut as his two friends stumbled outside, threatening to call the police.

"I've already called the police," Eddie yelled as the band's music came to a stop, and some of the regular customers stuck their heads outside to see what the ruckus was about.

Grace was wrapped around Eddie, and he made eye contact with me before I stepped up and swept her into my arms. Carrying her to the other side of the fenced-off area, I sat down with her on my lap, her legs dangling to the side, as her tears subsided and the shaking started. Her adrenaline was wearing off, but her fear was palpable.

I sat there with her, stroking her back and whispering, "You're safe, Grace. I promise no one will ever hurt you again. I'm sorry I wasn't there to stop him, baby. I'm so sorry." She looked up at me, and I gently brushed her hair away from her damp face as she focused on me. "Are you okay?"

"I am. Thanks to you. You saved me." Her bottom lip trembled, and I kissed her on the forehead.

"I'll always save you, Grace. You're mine."

"Do . . . do you really mean that?" she asked, and I offered her my most reassuring smile.

"Forever won't be long enough." I don't know where the sappy shit was coming from, but she needed soft and nurturing right now. Whatever Grace needed, I would provide, and if it meant being soft for her, I would be a marshmallow.

Eddie kept the three douches away from us with security standing guard over them as he watched me calming Grace. Security wasn't to protect us. It was to protect them. And when I get my hands on them, they won't ever be a problem for another woman.

The sirens were getting closer, and I kissed Grace on the head, asking her, "Will you be okay for a minute? I need to make a phone call."

She nodded so I stood with her in my arms and placed her gently on the seat. Taking her hands into mine, I waited for her blue eyes to meet mine before placing a kiss on the backs of each hand. Lifting my chin to Eddie, I stepped into the corner, keeping Grace fully in my line of sight as I dialed the one man who could guarantee I wasn't hauled off to jail tonight.

"Skid, what's wrong?" he asked instead of the usual greeting, and I got straight to it.

"Some asshole tried to attack Grace tonight, and I beat the fuck out of him. Cops are on the way."

"Is he dead?" he asked, and I could hear a door closing on his end.

"Negative, but he needs to be," I replied, hearing the sirens outside the fence.

"I hear the locals have pulled up. Answer their questions, and I'll make a few calls. As far as the asshole, he'll be handled promptly." Devlin's voice was deep and filled with rage.

"I can't go to jail and leave Grace alone, Devlin."

"Let me handle it," he replied and hung up.

I trusted Devlin with my life, as much as I trusted the Death Hounds, so I slid my phone into my cut and exhaled before walking back to Grace. She looked up at me, hurt and lost, as the police walked out into the area. Eddie pushed a few of the locals inside and returned to the assholes.

"Then he came out of nowhere and started hitting me. I didn't do anything wrong," the bloody asshole explained with a whine in his voice as he pressed a towel from the bar onto his bleeding nose.

The cops turned and appraised me with one look, making a snap decision on what happened before even talking to Grace or me. I was used to people judging me on my appearance. Tattoos and leather spell trouble for cops, but Grace didn't deserve that. They put their hands on their weapons and started to approach when Eddie spoke.

"This whole area is under surveillance. Let's watch the footage and get the real story since these assholes won't tell the truth, and you seem to believe them over my niece and her boyfriend."

One cop turned to Eddie and appraised him before responding, "I'll look while they keep everyone apart out here."

The younger cop stood with the three douches, and an older female came to stand with Grace and me. She looked at Grace, her shirt torn, her legs bruised, her hair matted, the blood clinging to her lower lip, and leaned in to ask, "Honey, do you need to go to the hospital?"

Grace brought her red-rimmed eyes to the officer and replied, "No, ma'am. I bit my lip when he pushed me onto the table."

"He didn't . . . ?"

She shook her head and explained, "Dalton saved me."

Her hand reached up and took mine, and I pulled up a chair next to her and wrapped my arm around her, wanting to get this over with so I could take her home. She was done for the night. Maybe forever. No way was I going to let her walk out here night after night, remembering how some fucker violated her peace and safety for his own selfish gains.

"Good man," the officer said and turned her attention to the three assholes who were trying to backpedal from what they tried to do.

A few minutes later, Eddie and the officer returned, and Eddie was livid as he looked at the guys. His eyes softened and he walked to Grace, kneeling in front of her and asking, "Will you let Skid take you home and stay the night with you, or do you want to stay at my house?"

She looked from him to me before deciding. "I'll let Dalton take me home, but he doesn't have to stay."

I knew she was embarrassed and probably afraid she would have another nightmare in front of me, but there was no way in fucking hell I was leaving her alone tonight. I kissed the back of her hand, and she met my gaze.

"I'll sleep on the couch if that would be better, but I really don't want you to be alone tonight. Please, Grace."

"Okay," she reasoned, and a commotion behind Eddie drew our attention.

"This is bullshit! Do you know who my father is?" the bloody asshole asked incredulously.

His two friends appeared unfazed, almost sure they would be let go. Little did they know, a madman was coming for all three of them, very soon. And his name was Devlin Callahan.

"Son, I don't give two shits who your father is. I have you on camera with attempted sexual assault, and your two friends will be charged as accessories. Now, put your hands behind your back, or this won't be pleasant for you," he spit at the three douches.

Grace was shaky next to me, and I stood, offering her my hand as the cops handcuffed the men and dragged them through the bar. Grace, Eddie, and I followed, and customers threw empty plastic cups at the three as they were led outside into the waiting squad cars. A few of the regulars stepped up to check on Grace, and I wrapped my arm around her and gave them a look that said. 'Don't get close to her.'

As angry as I was, no words were needed to tell everyone to stay away from Grace. I guided her to the bar and helped her grab her small purse before Eddie led the way to the front door. The crowd parted, most giving me a chin nod in acknowledgment of protecting Grace. I would kill for Grace, and now everyone knew she was mine.

Eddie walked us to my bike and pulled Grace into a deep hug, whispering into her ear as he looked at me over her shoulder. Murderous rage was in his eyes, and I drew my thumb over my throat, to let him know it would be handled. He released her and handed her off to me before wiping his eyes and returning to the bar.

"I'm going to help you with your helmet," I explained and secured it on her head, tightening the strap under her chin.

She held onto my hand as she climbed onto the back, and I quickly pulled my helmet on and moved in front of her. Cranking the bike, the sound of the band playing permeated around us as I squeezed her hands gripping into my stomach. She rested her head on my back, and I slowly pulled away from the bar.

The lights filtered away as we pulled onto the road and where I would usually lay down rubber, I refrained and drove cautiously back to her house. She had enough excitement for one night, and when I pulled into her driveway, I exhaled slightly. The anger was rolling through me, pulling my brain in too many directions. She needed me calm, so I dismounted the bike and removed her helmet before taking mine off. She sat on the bike looking lost and scared, so I scooped her up in my arms and carried her up the stairs to the front door.

She tried to wiggle out of my arms to unlock the door, and I leaned over, "Go ahead."

She smiled softly at me and replied, "I can walk."

"No need to when you fit so perfectly in my arms. Now unlock the door so I can get you comfortable and roll us a joint. I don't know about you, but I could use one right now."

I had yet to smoke with her and I had some premium smoke from the Death Hounds grow house stashed in my cut. I was hoping to relax her tonight, not to have sex, but to ease her worry. She looked at me, and I whispered with an eye wiggle, "It's DHMC primo."

She chuckled and pushed the key into the lock before turning the knob and opening the door. I carried her across the threshold, and thoughts of our wedding day played in my mind. Grace in a dress, her curly hair blowing in the breeze, and her *Property of Skid* cut on, declaring her love and loyalty to not only me, but the Death Hounds as well.

I took her into the bedroom and placed her on the bed. Kneeling in front of her, I met her gaze with mine as I explained, "You need to take a shower, and I'll be right here when you get done."

She twisted her hands in her lap and glanced down. I slowly lifted her chin, and her watery eyes stared at me as she admitted, "I'm scared to be alone."

That fucker had wrecked her independence in one selfish moment, and I would spend a lifetime rebuilding her. Making her stronger and teaching her how to protect herself if I'm not by her side. I rested my hands on hers and told her, "You're never going to be alone again. I promise on my life, Grace." I moved closer and cupped her cheek, needing to apologize again for leaving her vulnerable. "Grace, I'm so sor—" She placed her small hand over my lips and stopped me before I could finish the sentence.

"You saved me, Dalton. If you hadn't come when you did, he would have . . ." She inhaled and continued, "So, please. Don't apologize again. Okay?"

I softly kissed her lips and replied, "You're so strong, Grace. I stand in awe of you."

Chapter 12

Grace

I didn't feel strong, and it was killing me. I'd fought for years to take care of myself, not depending on anyone, and in one moment, my feelings of safety were stripped away. Eddie's bar was always a safe place for me, and I was careless when I took my break earlier. I heard the door open as I sat down to take a break and assumed it was Dalton.

When I turned around, I was shocked to see one of the customers stepping into the employee area and knew something bad was coming when he took the chair next to the door and wedged it under the handle. He was faster than I anticipated, and he had his hand slapped over my mouth, muffling my screams before I could make a sound.

From that moment, all I could do was fight him with everything I had in me, refusing to let him take from me and praying that Dalton came looking for me. I was filled with relief when he ripped the man off me, and the level of violence he showed to my attacker wasn't unexpected, but I had to stop him before he killed him.

Admitting to him or anyone about my vulnerability was difficult. I'd never seen myself as a victim, having something taken from me without my permission, and tonight was stirring all kinds of turmoil in my brain. Guilt, shame, and subsequent anger were common for me, but the fear of what might have happened was overwhelming me.

"Let me help you get showered, baby," Dalton whispered, and I stood from the bed, my legs weak and the pain of tonight settling in.

His blue eyes were filled with worry as he helped me into the bathroom. When I started to undress, he turned his back to me until I got into the shower. Just his presence was giving me reassurance as the spray of water loosened the knots in my back while I washed my hair. An audible groan broke free from me as I felt the tension seeping out of my muscles.

"Are you okay?" he asked, and I paused before speaking.

"I'm good if you need to head out." There was something in my brain screaming he was about to run, and no matter how hard I tried, I couldn't shake the feeling.

"I'm not going anywhere, but I need to grab a change of clothes from my bike if you'll be okay for a few minutes."

"I'll be okay. I'm almost finished," I admitted and ducked back under the water, letting a few tears fall.

"I'll be right back." I could hear the hesitation in his voice, and I stuck my head out of the curtain.

"Thank you."

He stepped up to the curtain and brought his hand to my wet cheek as he explained. "You don't ever have to thank me. I'm sorry for not being there sooner."

I glanced down and noticed the dried blood drops on his jeans. Bringing my eyes up to his, I suggested, "How about this? You don't say you're sorry, and I won't say thank you. Neither one of us should have guilt over tonight."

Gently kissing me, his gaze lingered before he whispered, "I'll be right back."

Nodding, I watched him leave the bathroom and I finished my shower quickly. Twisting my hair into a towel, I dried off then walked into my bedroom with a towel wrapped around my body. Dalton's cut was laying on the bed, and I picked it up, seeing small flecks of blood on the front. I removed my hair towel and wiped the blood, hoping to remove it without leaving a stain.

The sound of the front door opening and closing sounded into the bedroom, and I watched as Dalton walked back into the bedroom with a pair of shorts and a clean shirt tucked under his arm. His gaze ran up my body and grew soft as he saw me cleaning his cut. "I've got something that will clean it. You don't have to do that."

Turning the leather vest around, I brought it to my nose and inhaled deeply, smelling the rich leather, faint smoke, and the earthy smell of Dalton. Smiling over the leather, I admitted, "I didn't want any more of him touching us."

He smiled at me and took the cut from my hand, encouraging me to turn around. He stepped closer and inhaled against my wet hair as he slipped the cut over my shoulders. "I like the look of my cut on you."

Turning back to him, I gripped onto the towel and asked hesitantly, "Do you let many people wear your cut?"

My gaze met his, and he looked deeply into my eyes, the truth of his words reaching right into my soul. "No one has ever worn my cut, and if I have my way, no one but you ever will."

I bit into my bottom lip, trying to hide my smile as I said, "Maybe if you're lucky, you'll get your way."

He winked at me before pressing his lips to my cheek. "I'll be back in a minute."

Turning, he walked into the bathroom and closed the door as I heard the shower start. I hugged myself in his cut before carefully placing it on the bed and quickly dressing. I heard the water turn off a minute later and waited for him to return to me. Keeping my eyes on the door, I smiled when he walked out in a fitted T-shirt and basketball shorts, his black hair damp and clinging to his forehead.

He offered me his hand, and I stood from the bed, linking my fingers with his. Dalton reached into the inner pocket of his cut and wiggled his eyebrows before he led me into the living room and out the front door. Sitting down on the oversized chair, he patted his lap, and I settled in with my legs hanging off one side of his and placed my cheek against his chest, feeling his heart beating against my skin.

I'd never been this open with anyone, always fearful they would see past my fake smile and into the pit I shoved my past. With Dalton, I wasn't afraid, and from his comments about not only his sister, but a few of his friends, he wasn't a stranger to the dark and menacing parts of the world. That gave me hope that one day, hopefully, I could tell him a small part of what makes me, well, me. The whole story was too twisted and perverse.

"As much as I love you pressed against me, I think you need this more than me right this second." He chuckled and wiggled a strong-smelling joint in front of me.

I sat up and went to stand from his lap when he gently placed his hand on my hip and tugged me closer. Coughing our way through it, I felt my head floating and my body relaxing as we smoked. I rested my back against the side of the full chair and lifted my gaze to the sky. The black sky was littered with twinkling stars, and I wondered what I'd done to have someone as wonderful as Dalton take an interest in me.

"Can I ask you something?" I asked.

"I'll do my best to answer," he replied, and I brought my eyes to his.

"I know you have to go home soon, and I was wondering, um . . ." I glanced down at my lap, and he waited patiently for me to continue. "What's going to happen to us?"

"Grace, baby, please look at me," he urged, and I lifted my gaze to his.

I wasn't good at reading people, so I wasn't sure if he was going to brush me off, lie to me, or tell me the truth. I can handle anything but letting my heart get involved. It was already too late, and I realized I was head over heels in love with Dalton. I was before tonight, but him protecting me solidified my feelings.

"What do you want to happen?" he asked, and I shook my head.

"I don't need you to deflect back to me. I don't want to sound or act like a needy woman, so I need you to be honest with me. Where do you see us going? If this is just a vacation fling—"

He pulled me closer to him and his words were direct. "You are more than a fling. You're everything, Grace. You want to know where I see this . . . us . . . going?" I nodded, and he answered, "I see us going all the way. You as my old lady, a family, if we both decide we want one. Whatever we want in this world, we can have, as long as you're by my side."

"Why me?" I asked.

"Do you know what I saw the first time I laid eyes on you?" he inquired, and I shook my head. "I saw a warrior. A survivor. I saw unimaginable strength in your eyes, and I knew deep inside my soul that you and I were meant to be."

Tears filled my eyes, and he caressed my cheek with his tattooed hand. "Please tell me these are happy tears because I can't stand to know I'm the cause of your sadness."

Wrapping my arms around him, I hugged myself to his chest. He brought his arms around my back, and I spoke against his neck. "I promise, they're happy tears. I just don't know what I did to deserve someone as amazing as you."

"I'm just following what my heart tells me to do," he admitted, and I gazed into his clear blue eyes.

There were sad tears mixed in, realizing his home was eight hours away. How could we make it work with such a great distance? Not wanting to hash out all the details, I brought my lips to his and kissed him softly. It was chaste compared to every other kiss we'd shared, but after the night I had, this was as much affection as I could handle. He always seemed to know what I wanted or when I needed him.

A cool breeze blew across the porch, and I shivered. He put his arm under my knees and one behind my back before he stood and carried me into the house. After placing me on the couch, he locked the front door and grabbed us both a bottle of water. When he returned to the couch, he handed me two pain relievers and my water.

I took the pills as he settled in next to me. "Do you want to watch a movie?" I asked, and he shrugged.

"Whatever you want is fine."

Flipping through the guide, I settled onto some mindless medical drama and leaned into his chest. He wrapped his arm around my shoulder, and I snuggled closer. He was so warm, and soon, I felt a yawn building. Trying to stifle it, he looked down at me and asked, "Are you ready to go to sleep?"

"I think so. Your smoke is stronger than mine, and I'm sleepy," I said, and he smiled.

"Then let's get you to bed, baby. Sleep will do you good."

Dalton turned the TV off and helped me stand from the couch. The soreness from my struggle was setting in, and I knew tomorrow would be painful. As he followed me into the bedroom, the thought of being in the room alone started to fill me with apprehension. I'd never slept with anyone, except for the times that . . .

Pushing those thoughts deeper under the layer of concrete inside me, I turned to Dalton.

"Grace, what's wrong?" he asked as tears welled in my eyes.

I hated crying, but my emotions were all over the place, leaving me feeling vulnerable and alone. I briefly closed my eyes and returned my gaze to his as I whispered, "Would you stay with me? I . . . I don't want to sleep alone."

"There's no place I'd rather be than holding you all night in my arms, but I don't want to make you uncomfortable after what happened tonight," he replied with some residual anger in his voice, and a tear fell down my cheek.

"I . . . I don't think I'd feel safe without you here," I whispered, and he reached out, cupping my cheek with his tattooed hand.

He brushed the tear away with his thumb, and I leaned into his touch. Dalton took me by the hand, guided me to the bed, then pulled the covers back, encouraging me to climb in. After pulling the covers up, he turned off the light and walked around the bed before lifting the covers and crawling in next to me.

Opening his arm up, I lifted my head and placed it over his heart, then he wrapped his arm tight around me, tugging me closer. My leg shifted on top of his, and my arm fell across his chest as I wiggled into his side. We were both fully dressed, but I'd never felt more connected to someone.

"Sleep well, beautiful."

In a moment of sheer openness, I requested, "Please don't let me go."

"You and me, Grace, we're forever, and I swear on everything that I'll never let you go." He kissed the top of my head, and just as sleep began to pull me under, I heard him whisper, "You're mine, Grace, and I love you."

***

The sun shining through the blinds woke me. Dalton's warm body was wrapped around mine with his front to my back, and his arm and leg flung over me, pulling me closer to him. I was rested, and for the first time in years, there were no nightmares. I was terrified that I would have one after last night's incident, but having Dalton hold me close all night kept the demons at bay.

"Good morning." His voice was scratchy, and I rolled in his embrace to face him. "Did you sleep well?"

"Good morning. It was the best night's sleep I've had in years." I placed a soft kiss against his chest and felt his morning erection pressing against my stomach. "Thank you for staying."

He brought my gaze up to his as he explained, "I told you last night. You're mine."

I didn't know exactly what it meant, but it felt good to know someone wanted me for me. Not what I was expected to be.

"Would you like some breakfast?" I asked, realizing I didn't eat dinner last night after we got back here.

He pecked me on the nose and replied, "Why don't we get dressed, and you can call Eddie to see if he wants to join us. I have a craving for a waffle and some bacon."

"That sounds good." I went to leave the bed, and he gently pulled me closer.

"Where's my good morning kiss?"

I bit my lip and smiled before sliding up and pressing my lips to his, not wanting to make him suffer my morning breath. He deepened the kiss, brushing his tongue against my lips until I opened for him. Groaning, I placed my hand on his chest as our tongues battled, sweeping against each other until we pulled apart, panting for breath.

Brushing the back of his fingers down my cheek, he smiled and said, "That's more like it."

I slipped from the bed and took a moment to let the soreness in my body ease before I walked to my dresser. I could feel his eyes tracking me as I grabbed a change of clothes and ducked into the bathroom to take care of my morning routine. Drinking from the sink, I took another two pain relievers and stretched slightly, realizing my morning yoga may be on hold for a few days.

After running my hands through my messy hair, I settled on a hat and left the bathroom to find my bed empty and remade. Smiling at how thoughtful he was, I walked into the living room just as he walked back inside, carrying a clean pair of jeans and a black T-shirt.

"How much clothes do you have in your bike?" I asked with a smile on my face.

"One more shirt after this one, but usually, I keep one pair of jeans, three shirts, and fresh socks. I have a small bag back at my place with the rest."

"No underwear?" I chuckled, and he began to walk to the bedroom.

Glancing over his shoulder, he gave me smoldering eyes as he replied, "I don't like them. They suffocate me."

Quickly, I sent Eddie a text, and he confirmed immediately that we would meet us for breakfast. Lost in thought, I lifted my head when I heard him walk back into the room. Faded jeans, black fitted T-shirt, black boots, and his Death Hounds cut were just part of the picture as he returned fully dressed. He was covered in tattoos, and after seeing him naked last week, I knew there was very little clean skin left.

We stepped onto the front porch, and I heard the first tinkles of raindrops falling in the early morning hours. Looking at him, he explained, "If it was just me, I'd ride with my rain gear, but since it's both of us, I think we should take your car."

"Okay," I replied and locked the front door.

We walked to my car, and I was going to get behind the wheel when he took the keys from me. "I'll drive. You give me directions."

Nodding, I walked around the car and noticed he removed his cut and placed it in the back seat carefully. When we were secured and on the way down the road, I looked over and asked him, "Why did you take your cut off?"

"When we're in a cage, we turn it around or take it off."

"Cage?" I inquired, thinking of a jail cell.

He patted the steering wheel and explained, "Cage. Car. For me, it's like being stifled in a box. I can't feel the wind on my face or the road beneath me."

"There are so many rules to your club," I reasoned, a little worried.

"Don't worry, baby. It's easy once you're around it for a while." He took my hand into his and kissed the back with a smile as he drove down the road.

What if I didn't live up to what he expected in an old lady?

What if the club didn't accept me?

Would he leave me if they said no?

I couldn't put the cart before the horse. He hadn't even asked me to meet his club or his family yet. A few minutes later, we pulled into the restaurant, and I saw Eddie's truck already parked next to the front door. Walking inside with my hand in Dalton's, I looked for Eddie and found him in the back corner booth with three coffee cups already on the table.

Sliding into the seat across from him, he reached out and took my hand into his as he inspected me for damage. I was fine, sore and a little bruised, but I fared better than what could have happened. I could see his guilt, and after everything he did for me after I arrived here all those years ago, I never wanted him to blame himself for everything.

"It wasn't your fault, so stop beating yourself up. I'm fine," I reasoned, and Dalton observed with his arm behind my chair.

"Grace, I'm sorry. I should have been keeping a better eye on things." Eddie's voice was filled with remorse, and I leaned over the table, speaking softly.

"You can't always protect me from the world. Last night was a fluke, and I won't have him," I turned my head to Dalton before looking back at Eddie, "or you, blaming yourself for someone else's actions."

"I think you should take some time off from the bar," he uttered, and I sat back, shocked.

"Are you firing me?" I croaked out, feeling tears building.

"Hell no. I'm asking you to take some time off. You've been working for me for years and you need a break. Besides, I got a call from a nice gentleman last night, and he's going to be upgrading the security at the bar. Better cameras, additional security guards, and panic buttons for the staff. I need you to take some time and let me make the bar someplace where I know you'll be safe."

His eyes cut to Dalton, who sat up straight in his chair and asked, "Who called you?"

Chapter 13

Skid

Eddie offering to give Grace a few weeks off was almost an answer to a prayer. I hated the thought of her going back there, knowing I couldn't watch her every second. When Eddie met my gaze, I could tell he was on the same page as I was, but he was having to take a unique approach to get Grace to agree.

I also knew that Devlin and James would want to monitor the situation, and I was curious which one contacted Eddie last night. Offering an upgraded system is an expensive endeavor, and I wanted to make sure they let me pay for it.

"A man named James Callahan called me last night after you left and made the offer. I thought it was a scam until he mentioned your name, and I remembered Grace telling me about your job," Eddie explained, and Grace looked at me with curiosity.

"James is one of my bosses, for lack of a better term. I called them last night to make sure there wouldn't be any problems with the police," I reasoned, and Eddie nodded his understanding. "If he's making the offer, take it. He'll give you state-of-the-art security and the peace of mind that not only Grace, but everyone is safe at the bar."

"Why would they do something like that? I'm sure it's expensive, and we don't have a way to pay them back," Grace questioned.

"No one wants to be paid back, baby. This is the Callahan's way of protecting someone that I care about. They did the same thing at Sadie's bakery a few years ago."

"If you're sure," she said and turned her attention back to Eddie. "I don't have to take time off while the new system is being installed. I'll just be more careful."

The waitress delivered our breakfast, and Eddie pushed his plate to the side before he spoke. "You've been there every night for years, and the only time I can get you to take time off is when you're sick. I promise, I'll be okay for a few weeks."

Seeing the indecision in her eyes, I offered, "Why don't we visit my family, and I'll introduce you to my club. Sadie's been dying to meet you, and it's the perfect excuse to take a road trip. Whenever you're ready to come home, or when Eddie needs you, I'll bring you back."

"Are you sure? That's a lot to ask from you," she muttered.

Leaning in, I whispered, "You didn't ask, I offered. Besides, I've been dying to show my woman off to my brothers."

She blushed and looked deeply into my eyes, hopefully seeing the sincerity in my gaze. Taking Grace to Portstill, to my home, was the first step in making her my old lady. I just needed to convince her.

Eddie was digging into his breakfast, watching our interaction with a smile on his face. Grace turned to him and replied, "I guess I can take some time off, but just until the new security system is installed."

"That's my girl," he said and winked at her.

We ate breakfast, and when Grace finished, she pushed away from the table. "I'll be right back."

She stood and walked to the bathroom in the back corner, and as soon as she was out of earshot, he looked at me and spoke quickly. "If you can convince her to stay, do it. She's in love with you even if she can't admit it to herself. I've known that girl since she was a teenager and I've never seen her as happy as she is with you. She was barely living and part of that was my fault. I wanted her to be safe and comfortable, and somewhere along the way, I forgot to tell her to live."

"How will you handle her not being here? I know how close you are."

He shrugged before casting his eyes toward the bathroom and explaining. "I always knew I was only meant to be a safe place for Grace to land. You were meant to be her safe place forever. Or am I misreading the situation?"

"I love her, and I promise you, I'll devote the rest of my life to taking care of her and destroying the nightmares that plague her. She's mine, and I will kill any motherfucker who thinks he can touch her," I told him, leaving no room for error.

"Then give her the happy life she deserves, but don't ever push her past where she's comfortable. If you break her and I have to pick up her pieces, I swear I'll kill you, and no one will be able to find your body. Do we understand each other?" he asked, and I leaned back, crossing my arms over my chest.

I didn't like to be threatened, but because it was over Grace and it was Eddie, I would look past it. "If I break her, I'll willing let you." Grace exited the bathroom and caught my eye, and I whispered, "I promise she'll be treasured."

"Good," he remarked as Grace walked back to the table and sat down next to me.

"What did I miss?" she asked, and I kissed her on top of the head.

"I was just telling Eddie that I want to get on the road soon so we can be home by tonight. He said he'd watch your place until we got back."

"Are you sure you're going to be okay?" Her worried eyes met Eddie's, and he took her hands across the table.

"I'll be fine. The drunks may have to wait a few minutes longer for their drinks, but they'll live."

She chuckled as the waitress placed the bill on the table. Eddie snatched it from the edge and glanced at it before tossing a few twenties on the table. He stood, and we joined him, walking out of the diner and standing under the awning as a light rain fell from the sky. Turning to Grace, he said, "Promise to let me know when you get there."

"I promise," she answered, and he pulled her into a hug.

I could see him whispering to her, and she nodded before he released her. Smiling down, the older man kissed her forehead before reaching his hand out and shaking mine. Grace tucked herself under my arm as we watched him turn and get into his truck. With a wave out the window, he pulled the truck away, and I could feel Grace's sadness.

"Are you okay?" I asked after we got into the car.

"Yeah. I'm just going to miss Eddie," she admitted as I turned her car toward her house and began the drive back.

"How long have you known him?" I asked, wanting to gain her trust by asking small details, hoping to ferret out more information.

I knew some of her past, but when she disappeared, her background went dark, and there are years unaccounted for. I worried the real demons chasing her that Eddie hinted to were from the last ten years, and they posed no real threat to her. If it was from the years before she ran away from the Ringmans, I knew, whoever it was, would die at the end of my blade.

"I met him almost ten years ago. I'd . . . a mutual friend introduced us, and we became a family almost overnight," she replied, and I could hear the smile in her voice.

"He's a great guy. I'm glad you have someone like him in your life."

"Eddie's one of a kind, and I wouldn't have it any other way," she explained and turned her gaze out the window as the rain let up, allowing the sun to filter through the clouds.

We pulled into her driveway, and I pulled next to my bike before turning off the engine. Turning in my seat, I brushed a piece of hair off Grace's shoulder and rubbed her neck with my thumb as I observed her. She was tense but seemed happy, so I asked, "Would you like to go to Portstill with me and meet my family? I feel like we pushed you into this, and I'm never going to make you do something you don't want to."

She looked at me and smiled softly. "I want to meet your family, but . . . this is the first time I've left the area since I moved here, and I'm a little anxious."

"There's no reason to be anxious. Portstill is great, and my house is just outside the city limits on a beautiful lake. My sister is dying to try your amazing pies, and Jacob keeps emailing me, asking when we're coming to visit."

They were partial truths, but I knew once they met her, they would love her like I do. She twisted her hands in her lap, and I waited, knowing sometimes she needed a minute to work through her emotions. Finally, she spoke quietly, and I understood her apprehension. "What if your club doesn't like me?"

Leaning over, I brought her lips to mine, kissing her softly until she relaxed under my embrace. Pulling back, I stared into her eyes as I explained. "They are going to love you. The Death Hounds are a family. If you're important to me, you're important to them. Besides, I don't need their opinions when it comes to my old lady."

She smiled at me, and I winked, hoping that I dispelled some of her worries. She opened her door, and I followed, taking her hand into mine at the front of the car and walking back into her house. When the front door closed behind us, I tugged her, spinning her around until she crashed into my chest.

Looking up at me, her blue eyes twinkled in the morning light as I leaned her back and kissed her until we fought for breath. Standing her back up, I gently popped her on her ass and explained, "I have a sidecar that will hold a small duffel bag, so pack light. Anything that won't fit, I'll buy for you when we get to Portstill."

"What do I pack?" she asked, and I led her into the bedroom, encouraging her to sit on the edge of the bed.

Sliding the closet doors open, I pulled out a few pairs of jeans, a couple of T-shirts, and one thick hoodie. Tossing everything onto the bed, I explained, "You just need whatever undergarments and bathroom stuff that will fill out your bag."

She looked at the small pile and back to me, unsure as she asked, "That's all the clothes I'm taking?"

I leaned over, caging her against the bed as she fell onto her back. Following her down, I kissed her again, pushing my tongue into the wet recess of her mouth until she was wiggling under me. When she was sufficiently placated, I pulled away slightly and replied, "I plan to keep you naked most of the time."

Standing up, I adjusted my hard cock in my jeans and explained, "I need to run home and pack a few changes of clothes plus get the sidecar hooked up. I'll be back in less than an hour. Can you be finished packing by then?"

She nodded, her lips swollen, and her eyes glazed over with lust. "I'll be ready."

Walking to the door of her bedroom, I looked back at her propped up on her elbows against the bed, her eyes looking straight into my soul as I told her, "I'll be back, baby."

***

I packed up my laptop and the few articles of clothing I had with me before hooking up the small sidecar to my bike. With any luck, the only time we'd be back down here was to pack Grace's house to move her to Portstill. Sending a quick text to Sadie and Devlin, I let them know I was coming home with Grace. Devlin responded first, telling me we needed to meet soon, and, in my gut, I knew his digging into Grace's past was garnering information.

Sadie asked if she needed to stock the cabin with food, and I thanked her, sending some suggestions on things I knew Grace liked. My sister was going to make Grace feel welcome, and I know they will become good friends.

We had been on the road for two hours when we stopped for gas. I'd offered to let Grace ride in the sidecar so she would be more comfortable, but she said she wanted to ride with her arms wrapped around me, and I wasn't about to argue with her request. Feeling her pressed against me had my cock hard as steel in my pants, and all I wanted to do was bend her over the bike and fuck her until she couldn't stand.

One day, I'd take her every way I wanted to, but until then, until she was able to release the demons who plagued her mind, I'd give her the space she needed.

"Stretch your legs and make sure you use the bathroom while we're here," I explained to her as I stood from the bike and started pumping gas.

She climbed off the bike and pulled her legs up from the knee, stretching the muscles before she walked into the store. I finished pumping the gas and followed her inside. The store was clean, and I looked for Grace before seeing her exit the bathroom in the rear of the store.

"What would you like to drink?" I asked, and she grabbed a bottle of water from the cooler.

Mimicking her, I took the two bottles to the register and tried not to punch the young kid behind the counter who was checking Grace out while she browsed the display near the register. Clearing my throat, he met my gaze, and his eyes grew wide before falling to the floor.

The further north you went, the more prevalent the Death Hounds were, so I knew the little shit recognized my club or at least one of our chapters. We were known for violence, so checking out my woman could be grounds for an ass beating.

"Are you ready?" I asked Grace as I handed her a bottle of water.

"Yep," she replied, and I took her hand, leading her out of the store and letting the kid know she was mine.

For the next six hours, we would drive until we needed fuel before stopping. I thought Grace would complain about being sore from the drive, or her attack last night, but she kept a smile on her face and climbed back on the bike. She was too perfect for words, and when we pulled into Portstill shortly after midnight, I could feel her exhaustion in her grip.

"We're almost home, baby. Just a few more minutes," I yelled as I drove the backroad to my house.

She nodded against my back and gripped tighter into my waist as I traversed the familiar road. I inherited the house when Uncle Mick died a few years ago, and slowly, Claw, the club's VP, and I have been improving the cabin. What used to be a two-bedroom bachelor pad was now expanded to a five-bedroom, two-story house that I wanted to fill with kids.

I turned down the road leading to my house. Pulling down my tree-lined driveway, I felt the tension seeping from me, knowing Grace was here with me, safe and mine. I could feel her take a deep breath as the cabin came into view and the floodlights turned on, casting the parking pad and front of the house in lights. I glanced in the rearview side mirror for her reaction.

Her blue eyes grew wide, and her mouth fell open as I pushed a button on the bike and a garage door began to rise. The attached garage was added last year and housed my truck and three of my four bikes. Pulling my newest one into the open space, I felt relieved to finally be home.

Turning the bike off as the door closed behind us, I stepped off the bike and removed my helmet, placing it over the handlebars. Grace took hers off and looked around, unsure.

"You live here?" she asked as I helped her from the bike and walked to the door leading into the house.

I could see she was stiff, and I kicked myself for not making her ride in the sidecar. She was a ride or die throughout the day, but after last night, she must be in pain.

"It's been home for about ten years now," I explained as I disarmed the security system and unlocked the door.

Ushering her inside with my hand on her lower back, I watched as she took in my home, what I hoped would be her home too, and prayed she liked it. Turning back to me, she smiled. Her beautiful eyes showed her exhaustion, and I led her by the hand to my bedroom.

"Let's get you into bed, and I'll give you the tour in the morning," I urged, suddenly realizing Grace wasn't the type of person who complained.

It was something I noticed all those weeks openly watching her at the bar. Even if it was something she didn't really want to do, like serve drinks on the floor, she would still do it with a smile and never complain. I wanted to ask her so many questions but interrogating her was not something I planned to do. Now or in the future.

She yawned and I needed to get her into bed so she could rest. If I knew my sister, she would be here in the morning with a welcome basket of goodies for Grace.

"Let me get you a T-shirt to sleep in. The bathroom's through that door." I motioned to the left and handed her the shirt.

"Thank you," she replied through another yawn, and I watched as she walked into the bathroom and closed the door.

My phone chimed, and I glanced to see a message from Devlin.

Devlin: I'm glad that you're home. We really need to talk.

Me: Not tonight. I'll call you tomorrow once Grace is settled.

Devlin: Glad she agreed to come with you.

Me: Same.

Devlin: Now make her yours so you stop being an asshole to everyone.

Me: Fuck you.

I chuckled to myself as Grace walked back into the bedroom. Her face was washed, and my oversized T-shirt fell to her knees. She walked to me and wrapped her arms around my waist with her face pressed against my chest. I pulled her closer to me and kissed her on top of the head.

She propped her chin on my chest and asked, "Thank you."

I smiled at her and inquired, "For what, baby?"

Kissing my heart, she met my gaze and replied, "For being you."

I prayed she never found out how I ended up in Eddie's bar last month. She may never forgive me if she knew the truth.

Chapter 14

Grace

The ride was exhausting, but I held onto Dalton the whole way, knowing he would keep me safe. When we pulled into his house, I wasn't prepared for the giant wooden cabin tucked down a secluded driveway. He said he lived in a cabin next to a lake, but it was more luxurious than I was expecting.

As soon as we walked in, I felt the utter exhaustion overtaking me. After getting ready for bed, I felt the need to show him my gratitude. Not with sex, but I hoped that happened sooner rather than later. He helped me into bed and ducked into the bathroom quickly, returning with a pair of shorts on and his tattooed chest on display.

Smiling at him as he turned off the light and walked across the room with only a lamp illuminating the room, I felt at home. Like we'd been doing this for years instead of days. He crawled into bed next to me and urged me to roll on my side before he pulled my body against his and wrapped his arm around my waist.

"Sleep, Grace. I'll be right here if you need me."

His lips pressed against the back of my head before I snuggled into the soft mattress and felt the weight of the last day pushing me into a deep slumber. Sometime in the night, a noise woke me up, and I blinked through the fog of sleep, trying to remember where I was. Seeing Dalton's Death Hounds cut hanging on the door, I rolled over to ask him what the noise was, only to find myself alone in bed.

Sliding from the covers, I slowly walked out of the bedroom and down the hallway. It was still dark outside, and I tried to figure out where the sound was coming from. I saw the kitchen light on as I walked into the enormous living room. There was a light on what I assumed was the back of the house, and I walked to the glass door. Peering out into the night, I saw Dalton sitting on the back deck with a rubber ball in his hand.

He was hunched over his laptop, aimlessly tossing the ball onto the deck, only to catch it without looking. I knocked on the glass door, and he lifted his head with a smile. Placing his laptop onto the table, he motioned for me to walk outside. The cool air from the lake chilled my legs as I stepped onto the large, multi-level deck.

"What are you doing awake? I thought you'd be passed out until the morning," he said, and I walked to the table and took the seat next to him.

"I heard a noise and didn't know what it was," I replied and yawned behind my hand. "What time is it?"

He looked at the ball in his hand and ducked his head down slightly. "I'm sorry. It's a habit I picked up when I work. I didn't mean to wake you. And to answer your question, it's almost six."

"Don't worry about it. I'm on vacation, remember?" I joked, and he leaned over, kissing me softly.

"Do you want to go back to sleep, or would you like some coffee?" he asked, and I debated on more sleep.

Not wanting to miss a minute of time with him, I answered, "I'd love a cup of coffee."

He closed his laptop and stood from his seat. "I'll be right back," he kissed me again before walking inside.

The earliest rays of sunlight were pushing at the edges of the darkness, and I watched the sky illuminate, offering glimpses of his yard instead of the pitch black we drove home in. The door opened, and I looked over my shoulder to see Dalton with a blanket tossed over his now covered chest and two cups of coffee in his hands.

He placed them onto the table and laid the blanket over my legs, warming me from the morning air. Returning to his seat, he took my hand into his and sipped his coffee as the sky began to turn a warm peach color. The lake behind the house started to glow as the rays pushed into the sky, and I smiled at the beauty in front of me.

"Would you feel up to going to a cookout at the compound tonight? Sadie texted me an hour ago, and I managed to stop her from showing up first thing, but she insisted I bring you to meet her this afternoon."

"She's married to your President, Gunner?" Dalton nodded, and I admitted, "I think it would be fun."

"Fantastic. I'll let her know."

"Do we need to make anything?" I asked, and he smiled deviously.

"Not for the first visit, but I'd love for Sadie to try that amazing pie recipe you've created whenever you're up to it."

I nodded and smiled as I finished my coffee and placed the cup on the table. Looking at him, I asked, "What time do we need to be there?"

"The party usually starts at six and lasts until everyone's had their fill."

"I'm looking forward to it." The nerves of meeting not only his club but also his sister filled me.

A little while later, he offered me a tour of the house, and I gladly followed as he proudly showed me around. After explaining how he inherited the house from his uncle, he showed me what the original house looked like and detailed the expansion. He was proud of his home, and I wished I could say the same.

I rented the house from a lovely older couple and wished it was nicer, but it's all I could afford. My thoughts began to stray into the future he said he wanted and wondered if the house would become my home too. I didn't dream anymore, knowing all too painfully that dreams could turn into nightmares in the blink of an eye, but with Dalton, I let myself believe.

The four bedrooms on the newly added second floor were mostly empty. One was an office that he only let me pop my head into before ushering me quickly to his workout room. I finally understood how he got his physique with all the equipment he had in the room. When we returned to the living room, he sat on the couch and tugged me onto his lap.

I felt his hardness pressing against the back of my legs as he pulled me into a hug. Normally, I didn't like to be touched, but with Dalton, all I wanted him to do was touch me. His fingers pushed up the hem of my shirt, and when he brushed his hand over my outer thigh, I winced at the sudden discomfort. Sitting me up, he looked at me with concern as I pulled the shirt back down.

"I guess I'm a little sore from the ride," I said, wanting to deflect from the pain the bruises from the drunken asshole were causing.

His eyes hardened, and he asked gently, "Can I get you anything?"

I pressed my cheek back to his chest and felt his arms squeeze me tighter as I whispered, "This. You can give me this."

Exhaling, I felt the tension seeping from him as he held me. Not wanting to drag him into the darkness with me, I looked up at him and asked, "Can I make you breakfast?"

He smiled and replied, "You don't have to cook for me, but if you're hungry, then I need to feed you."

He stood from the couch and lifted me in his arms before strolling to the kitchen. Placing me on the cold granite counter, he grabbed his phone and made a quick phone call, keeping his eyes locked on mine.

"Gunner, I need a prospect to pick up an order from the diner and run it to the cabin." My eyes grew wide, and he winked before giving the man a few yeses to unheard questions then hanging up the phone.

"Breakfast will be here in less than thirty minutes. Do you want to shower before it gets here?"

Blinking, I was shocked as I inquired, "So, you can just make a phone call, and one of your club brothers drops everything and brings you what you need?"

He laughed and pecked me on the nose as he stepped between my spread legs and tugged me closer to the edge. "A brother would tell me to fuck off, but a prospect's job is to do what the club asks of him. It's a way for him to show loyalty to the club."

"He shows loyalty by bringing your breakfast?"

He laughed louder, and I smiled, joining in as he wiped an errant tear from his eyes. "If a prospect is eager to drop what he's doing to follow an order from the President, that shows dedication. If they are willing to do grunt work to earn their colors, that shows loyalty. Those are two important qualities in being a Death Hound."

"Wow. So, it's like the military, in a way?"

Shrugging, he answered, "In its own way, yes."

"Interesting." I smiled at him and reasoned we didn't have much time until our food would be here. "I think I would like to take a shower before they arrive."

He pulled my ass off the counter, and I shrieked as I wrapped my legs around his waist. He smirked as he carried me to the bedroom, and with each step, I could feel his hardness rubbing against my needy pussy. The ride yesterday was a giant tease of riding a huge vibrator for hours and not being able to come.

I knew I wanted to be with Dalton again, but so far, he seems to be letting me lead. His gentleness was a turn-on, but somehow, I needed to let him know I wasn't made of glass. I didn't feel like there was any lingering trauma, other than some bruises and residual anger over my incident, so I hoped to find a way to seduce him soon.

Walking into the attached bathroom in his bedroom, he sat me on the floor and turned the water on in the walk-in shower before adjusting the temperature. Stepping back to me, he brushed his hand down my cheek, and I leaned into his touch as he spoke, "I'm going to take care of a few emails while you're getting cleaned up. Make yourself at home."

I pressed up to my tiptoes and kissed him softly on the lips. Keeping the embrace chaste, I lowered to my shorter height and replied, "I'll be out soon."

"Take as long of a shower as you want. It's a tankless hot water system, so you literally have an unlimited supply of hot water," he said, wiggling his eyebrows before walking out of the bathroom.

This was the first time I'd been alone since the incident on Saturday night, and I exhaled, feeling the solitude wrap around me. Having spent years taking care of myself, it was a little overwhelming to have someone doting on me and my needs. It's what I always wanted, and somehow, I knew his promises were real and not some perverted version of the truth used to manipulate me.

Flexing my hands open and closed, I closed my eyes and counted to ten before the anger subsided. The more the thoughts of my time in foster care pushed to the surface, the madder I got, and I needed to remember that I was safe with Dalton. He couldn't hurt me the same way as what I had survived. That's all I needed to remind myself of.

After standing in the hot spray longer than expected, I quickly washed my hair and body before turning the water off and grabbing a towel from the cabinet next to the shower. Wringing the water from my hair, I dried off and secured the towel around my body before stepping into the bedroom. I could hear Dalton talking to someone with a deep voice, and not wanting to eavesdrop, I turned away and focused on getting dressed. After pulling on a pair of yoga pants and a T-shirt, I managed to fit into the bag, I ran my fingers through my unruly hair and clipped it into a curly pile on top of my head.

I stepped out of the bedroom as the sound of a door closing echoed down the hallway, and cautiously, I walked into the living room, hoping I wasn't interrupting. Dalton turned when I walked into the room and smiled at me, offering me his outstretched hand.

"You just missed my brother, Needles. He dropped off breakfast on his way out of town. He was hoping to meet you, but he had to get on the road."

I looked out the front window and saw a large man wearing the same cut Dalton had rolling down the driveway. "I'm sorry I took so long."

Dalton turned my face to him with a finger under my chin, and I looked at him as he explained, "No one expects anything of you here, Grace, other than to be yourself. If you want to shower for three hours, do it. If you want to take a nap, go for it. If you want to relax in the hot tub, just say the word. Whatever will make you happy makes me happy."

My stomach grumbled at that exact moment, and I giggled. "Breakfast would make me happy."

He offered me his elbow and escorted me the fifteen feet to the dining room table before pulling my chair out and helping me push to the table. Walking into the kitchen, he returned with four large to-go containers, two fresh cups of coffee, and a rolled-up shirt.

"Needles grabbed a shirt from the compound for you," he said, and I held it up in front of me.

Future Property of a Death Hound was imprinted on the front, and I looked at him with curiosity.

"That way, you don't have to worry about one of the club brothers hitting on you if I'm not by your side tonight," he explained as one by one, he opened the containers, showing an assortment of meats, omelets, fruit, pastries, and pancakes.

"It smells delicious," I said and started to fill my plate with the countless goodies. "And thank you for the shirt. I was wondering what I was going to wear since I have like three outfits."

"I'll have Devlin's wife call you to set up a day to go shopping," he reasoned with a smile as he sat down next to me at the table.

He'd mentioned Devlin Callahan and his wife, Elise, telling me how close he was with the Callahan brothers and their families. It would be nice to meet both parts of Dalton's life. I just hoped I didn't make a fool of myself at his club tonight.

We sat in peaceful silence as we ate our breakfast, and I couldn't help but sneak glances at him throughout the meal. All too soon, I was pushing my empty plate away and leaning back in the chair as I rubbed my full stomach.

"Would you like anything else?" he asked as he ate the last bite from his plate.

"I couldn't possibly eat another bite," I admitted, and he leaned over, kissing me with maple syrup on his lips.

I stood and gathered the dishes from the table, only to have him try and stop me. "I can get this."

"I'm not used to being so lazy. Please let me help."

"Okay," he begrudgingly agreed, "but I don't expect you to wait on me."

Most men would be happy with letting a woman take care of them. Cooking, cleaning, and waiting on a man were expectations from my youth that I vowed I'd never do as an adult. There was a difference between doing something because you wanted to and doing something because it's demanded of you.

Eddie and the two other people who knew what I'd lived through explained that I could choose whatever I wanted in my life, and no ingrained requirements could hold me hostage without my consent. I never understood what they meant until that very moment. I wanted to do for Dalton, and he was appreciative.

That's when I realized he was for real. Actions spoke louder than words.

After we threw away the empty containers and stored the leftovers in the fridge, Dalton refilled our coffees, then took my hand and led me onto the back porch. To the side was an oversized couch under a small roof and he sat down, patting the cushion next to him. Getting comfortable, I rested my head on his shoulder as he reached into the pocket of his shorts and pulled out a joint.

"A little dessert," he rationalized as he lit the tip and inhaled.

I chuckled before I took a draw and found myself coughing around the strong, acrid smoke. Handing it back to him, I took a swallow of coffee and felt the burn in my chest subside. Passing it back and forth, we smoked until it was gone, then he tossed the roach into an ashtray.

"Do you smoke often?" I asked him, and he shrugged.

"Define often. Do I stay stoned all day? Fuck no. Do I enjoy a little herb in my downtime to relax me? Hell yes. Do I mind others choosing differently than me? Not at all. I have a few friends who . . . survived some difficult things, and they use it instead of prescription medication. If you need more, let me know," he replied, and I leaned up, kissing him on the cheek.

Dalton wrapped his arm around my shoulder and pulled me closer to him as the sound of the lake filtered through the air. It was different from the river at Eddie's, but the sound was just as relaxing.

"Why does it seem like you know me better than anyone, and we just met? Like you understand what's going on in my mind without me having to say it?" I asked, feeling the heavy effects of the last few days, and the strong smoke.

"I'm not a mind reader, Grace, but I understand trauma and the lingering effects it can have on a person's life. I see that in you, and one day, I hope you can trust me enough to tell me who or what hurt you, so I can send them to hell where they belong." His voice was soft, but rage tinted his words.

Being with him felt so right, and I feared it was all going to blow up, leaving me more alone than before. Knowing what genuine affection and devotion looked like, or at least what I thought it looked like, I couldn't go back to my life of solitude. I needed to trust that if I ever told him, it wouldn't change how he felt about me.

At least, I hoped it didn't.

I never intended to fall asleep, but the big breakfast and strong weed pulled me into slumber as the sun shined down on the deck, warming the air, and blanketing me in comfort. Dalton's strong arms gave me the safety to let my guard down, and for the first time in longer than I cared to think about, I dreamed of my future.

Chapter 15

Skid

Hearing her breathing even out, I glanced down to see Grace snuggled into my chest with a peaceful expression on her beautiful face. I wanted her to have that same look all the time, and I hoped she heard my promise to avenge her. Without saying it, Grace confirmed my suspicions, and I was curious what Devlin needed to tell me.

Gunner hated that I still helped the Callahans from time to time, but I owed a lot to the men. They could have left me on the outside when the company sold the software I helped design, but they paid me more than my fair share, ensuring that my family, my club, and I would be taken care of for generations to come.

I also wasn't going to turn my back on his supreme hacking skills. Devlin and James spent too many years documenting people's lives and often saw invisible threads in people's actions that others would miss. Working with them to identify the man who hurt Aubrey led me to Grace, and I wouldn't change it for the world.

I wished I could change what happened, but I couldn't change the past. All I could do was give Grace a future and protect her from the nightmares when they plague her. My phone chimed from the table, and I reached over to pick it up, not wanting to wake Grace from her nap.

Devlin: We need to talk.

Me: Can you come to the house? Grace is asleep and I don't want to disturb her.

Devlin: James and I will be there in thirty.

I glanced down, staring at Grace's peaceful beauty. Not wanting Devlin and James to wake her, I shifted until she was lying down on the couch, and with slow movements, I picked her up and pulled her to my chest. She snuggled in and released a little snore. I smiled as I carried her into the bedroom and placed her on the bed.

Grabbing the remote, I closed the curtains, casting the room in dark shadows, before I pulled a soft blanket over her sleeping form. She snuggled into the covers, and I sat on the edge of the bed, gently stroking her hair as she slept. The sound of a car pulling into the driveway alerted me of the Callahans' arrival, and reluctantly, I leaned over and placed a kiss on her forehead. Grace sighed and smiled in her sleep.

I walked to the door and looked at her once more before pulling the door closed behind me. Moving through the living room, I open the front door and usher Devlin and James inside. I shook each man's hand and nodded toward the back deck, wanting to keep our conversation away from Grace.

Whatever they wanted to tell me had to be about her, and she didn't ever need to find out how I found her. Not only would it cause her pain, but it would bring additional pain to Aubrey, James's long-lost sister, and I would do anything to keep them away from the truth.

Sitting down at the table, I turned to two of my oldest friends and asked, "What did you find?"

James ran his hand through his hair and leaned back, shaking his head. I leaned forward and locked eyes with Devlin. From the look in his eyes, I wasn't going to like what they found. Running my hands down my face, I exhaled and demanded, "Fucking tell me already."

"What do you know about Grace's time after she ran away?" Devlin asked, and I gave him a quizzical look.

"She ran away ten years ago, and a few months later, she showed up with Eddie and lived there ever since. Why?" I inquired.

"We found what we think is a connection between the two of them," Devlin explained, and I rolled my hand, encouraging him to continue. "Eddie petitioned the state of Missouri for custody of a little girl about twenty years ago, a long-lost niece who had been in the system for two years and he'd just found out. Turns out Eddie is Grace's uncle." My eyes grew wide and my mouth fell open as he went on. "Well, half-uncle, to be exact. Grace's father had a half-brother who was raised by a different mother, and they barely knew each other growing up. Eddie was on his third deployment when he received word his half-brother was dead. Coming home, he discovered the state had taken his niece into foster care and he tried to adopt her. They refused on the grounds of his military obligations, and she remained in the system."

"Fucking assholes. She could have been out of the system when she was six or seven and spared the horrors of that fucking pervert. Aubrey may have been saved too, for all we know," James grumbled.

"After they turned him down, the military shipped him all over the world, and it took years for him to make contact with Grace," Devlin said, and I leaned back, needing to rethink what I'd learned. "How did they say they met?"

"Eddie said mutual friends, and Grace wouldn't expound when I asked," I said, and James shrugged. "From all indications, he never told her. I don't know why,"

"So, she doesn't know he's her uncle?" Devlin asked. I shook my head, and he wondered, "Why not tell her?"

"He's protecting her," I said, and they looked at me curiously. "Think about it. How did Amaya take it when she found out she really was wanted and not cast aside?"

James's wife lived through hell to save her sister and it was only after she passed that Amaya discovered a father who looked for her and a family that loved her. She'd spent years building a relationship with them, trying to come to terms with the knowledge that she was loved and not an afterthought. Like countless others.

James's eyes grew hard. "It was hard on her to find out that for years, someone wanted to save her from the horrors of her home but was unable to."

"I can imagine Eddie didn't want to confuse her. She hasn't said much, other than she was in foster care until she was sixteen, and even that was difficult to get her to admit," I said and picked up my phone to check on Grace.

I had cameras in every room of the house so I could check on her without disturbing her. Pulling up the app, I opened the live feed from my room and saw she was still cuddled into the covers, resting peacefully. I didn't want her to overhear this conversation, and I set the phone down once I knew she was sleeping.

"You're as bad as we are." Devlin chuckled, and I lifted my middle finger into the air.

I actually thought they were creepy for having cameras throughout their house but having Grace in my home, I wanted to take care of her every need and always have eyes on her. One day, I'd tell her about the cameras, but until then, I would let them stay my secret from her.

"So, what do we know about that fucker Ringman?" I muttered, feeling the rage building at the thought of him.

"There are some strange things I found from his archived bank statements that I want to look further into, but I have some initial ideas," James stated, and Devlin looked at his brother.

"You have guesses. I know you want justice for Aubrey and Grace deserves her justice, but I don't know if this idea of yours is fully developed enough to discuss." Devlin wasn't one to question his brother, and the interaction had me nervous. "Why don't we wait until you do some more digging before we plant that idea into Skid's head."

I leaned forward, flexing my hands on top of the table as I spoke, my tone deadly, leaving no room for error. "If you have information, I want it. Whatever it is may help me heal Grace. She's my priority right now, no offense to you or Aubrey."

James slammed his fist onto the table. "My sister doesn't get to be dismissed like her pain isn't valid."

"I never said her pain wasn't valid, but think of it this way. What she endured lasted for six visits. Six horrible, single incidents that destroyed her for years. My Grace lived with that man for twelve years. Twelve. Fucking. Years." I punctuated each word with anger. "I've seen her thrashing in her sleep, begging for it to stop. I've seen her slam a tray into someone's face for touching her without permission. I've witnessed firsthand what she's living with, and she hasn't been able to speak a word about it. So, while I'm not trying to minimalize Aubrey's experience, my focus is on Grace. I'm sorry if you don't understand that, but she's my woman and my priority."

Devlin, always willing to step in between James and me when we butted heads, held up his hand and stopped both of us before we continued. "I understand what you're saying, Skid, and I see where James is coming from too. For now, let's keep digging, and you have my word, by the end of the week, we will have something solid to move on." I nodded. "We need to know how the Ringmans and Aubrey are connected. We need to figure out where Grace went for those months she disappeared. We have to decide how to approach this whole situation without hurting those two precious women any further than they already have been." His deep voice took on an ominous tone as he said, "Ringman's filth touched my lamb, and I will kill any fucker connected with him, but until we can verify, we have to wait."

Exasperated, but knowing deep down they were right not to tell me, I leaned back into my chair and ran my hands down my beard. "Will you give me something to look into? I feel like I'm running in quicksand trying to figure out all the invisible strings connecting everything and coming up empty."

The two men made eye contact and had a brief but silent conversation. Devlin stood, and James and I mirrored him as he stepped closer to us. "Tell him your thoughts, James. But, Skid, I want your promise you will keep your cool until we know something definitive. Then, you can bring down the thunder of the Death Hounds on whoever needs killing."

James exhaled deeply before meeting my gaze with his green eyes. "Promise us, and I'll tell you."

I stepped closer and offered my hand to him. We shook, locking hands at each other's forearms as I replied, "I promise."

Releasing my grasp, he gave me the one sentence I never thought I'd hear. "Research the now-defunct cult called Servants of God, and you'll know which direction I'm looking."

My nostrils flared as I absorbed the information. Looking at the two men, two of my best friends, I told them in no uncertain terms. "I know who and what they are. You have until Saturday to give me the information I need. After that, I can't be held responsible for my actions."

James nodded and cut his eyes to Devlin before turning and walking down the outside stairs and disappearing around the corner of the house. Devlin explained, "Aubrey is having a tough time lately. James told her you were investigating what happened, and she's aware there may be another girl involved. He feels powerless to help her, and Hayden is helping her come to terms with the fact she may not be alone. It's not comforting, and I believe she thought it was just her."

"I don't want Grace to ever have to relive what she experienced. Even if she never tells me what happened, she doesn't need to bring that pain back to the surface. She struggles enough in her sleep with the demons, to bring them back to life."

Devlin turned to leave and looked over his shoulder at me. "Keep her safe and love her through the pain. One day, she'll trust you enough to share her past, and when she does, it's your job to absorb it. Never let her see the anger. She'll think it's because of her even though it's not. I've seen it with my lamb, and in time, you can chase her demons away. I'm happy for you, Dalton, and proud to call you my friend."

With those words, he walked down the stairs and turned the corner of the house. A moment later, I heard his car crank in the driveway and pull away from the house. Checking on Grace once more with the app, I saw she was kicked out of the covers with her flat stomach on display. I wanted to ravage her and take away every painful touch but would wait until she gave me the go-ahead.

I went inside and climbed the stairs, headed to my office. After closing the door and securing myself inside, I pushed a button to open the sliding panel on the wall, with nine monitors mounted. Sending the app image to one screen, I watched Grace sleep for a minute while my laptop logged on to the secure network for Callahan Cyber Security.

When the computer pinged that I was secured, I began to search for the cult James mentioned, and after reading two articles, I felt my stomach churning. I prayed to everything I didn't believe in that Grace wasn't touched by the depraved madness those religious zealots professed to be the word of God.

Closing my laptop, I walked downstairs and poked my head in to see Grace still resting, so I went to the garage and approached the punching bag hanging in the corner. Stripping off my shirt, I pulled my headphones on and played my workout mix while I punched my aggression away. After twenty minutes, my arms were wobbly and I turned the music off, sensing someone behind me.

I turned to find Grace sitting on the workbench in the garage with her eyes locked on me. Tossing the headphones to the side, I strolled up to her and kissed her softly on the lips. She brought her hands up to my shoulders and held on to me as I tried to pull away, pushing the kiss deeper. I fisted her hair with my gloved hand and held her in the position I wanted her as I kissed along her neck.

She moaned in my embrace, and I smiled against her skin as I placed another breath-stealing kiss on her swollen lips. Pulling back, I saw she was dazed with a smile on her face.

"Did you have a good nap?" I asked as I helped her from the bench, and we walked inside.

"I did. Thank you. How long until we need to leave?" she asked as we walked into the kitchen, and I grabbed a bottle of water from the fridge.

"We can get there whenever you like, darlin'. There is no official start time, more of a suggestion," I admitted and drained half the bottle. "But we have about three hours until we need to start over. Is there something you want to do in the meantime?"

I wiggled my eyebrows at her, and she ducked her head, smiling deeply before she looked back up at me. "You said something about a hot tub?"

I offered her my hand, and she linked her fingers with mine as I tugged her through the living room and down the hallway. My bedroom was on the right, allowing the morning light to filter into the windows. There was a door on the left that opened to a private, enclosed deck on the side of the house.

Opening the door, I ushered Grace outside, and she gasped when she saw my private oasis. The six-person hot tub was near the house with a roof over the top to keep it shaded from the sun. A table with overstuffed chairs sat close to the fence separating this area from the main deck, and all around the space were lush green plants and twinkling lights. The lights were off, but when they were illuminated, it turned the area into a private wonderland, free from prying eyes.

"It's beautiful," she remarked as she looked over the banister at the lake.

"I'm glad you like it. Let me get the tub turned on so you can take a soak."

Pushing a button on the side, I heard the tub turn on as I lifted the cover and steam rolled out. It looked inviting, and I glanced over my shoulder to see Grace leaning over the banister with her eyes closed as the sun shone down on her beautiful face.

I pulled my phone from my pocket and snapped a picture of her looking so serene before walking up to her. Gripping onto the banister on both sides of her, I stepped closer until I felt her lean against my chest. She inhaled deeply and released the pent-up breath as I placed a kiss on her neck.

"Thank you for bringing me here. I didn't know how much I needed a break until this very moment." Her words were soft, but I felt their hidden meaning.

"My home is your home, Grace. You stay as long as you want." There was weight to my statement, and I hoped she felt it.

She turned so her back was leaning against the railing as she looked up at me, her blue eyes shining like emeralds in the afternoon sun. "What if I didn't want to leave?" she asked, with playfulness and vulnerability in her voice.

I leaned over and whispered, "Then welcome home, baby."

Smiling, I kissed her before leading her to the hot tub. "Do you want to grab your swimsuit?"

"Nope," she replied before she spun her finger, and I turned away from her.

She removed her clothes and slipped into the water. Her groan made my cock lurch in my pants, and I turned to see her hidden under the turbulent waters with her head resting on the edge.

"This feels amazing," she groaned, and I smiled.

"Can I join you?" I asked, and she bit her lip with a nod.

I pulled my shirt off and tossed it onto the table before pulling my shorts off and turning back to her. My cock wasn't fully hard, but my desire for her was evident as I walked to the tub and slipped inside, sitting across from her. She had a blush on her face as I lifted her feet onto my legs and began massaging the bottoms. My hard length was bobbing against her toes, but she made no indication she wanted to move them.

Our skin was wrinkled when we climbed out an hour later, but Grace seemed to be moving better. I could see stiffness in her steps when she woke up this morning, and it pissed me off all over again. Those assholes were going to get what they deserved for hurting my woman, but for now, I would focus on Grace.

I made us a quick lunch, knowing the club was putting on a full spread for us. There was a worry that Grace would be overwhelmed with everything tonight, so when she got into the shower to get cleaned up, I sent Sadie a message.

Me: Can you make sure Grace feels welcome tonight? I don't want her to get overwhelmed.

Sadie: Don't be a dumbass. Of course, I'll make her feel welcome.

Me: Thanks. She's not fragile, but she is delicate.

Sadie: You really are a dumbass.

Me: Why?

Sadie: I'll explain later. Gunner's got the prospects setting the tables up in the wrong spot. I've got to go.

I shook my head, confused about what she meant, as I sat on the couch and surfed through the TV. Grace came out a little while later, and my mouth fell open as she entered the living room. She cut the shirt I gave her, showing slits along the back with no sleeves and a wide neck. It was tied at the waist, making it more fitted, and her jeans hugged her like a second skin. The boots she wore on the ride up finished off her outfit, and I swear I was looking at a wet dream.

"Do I look okay?" she asked with uncertainty in her voice.

I stood from the couch and walked to her, seeing her usually minimal makeup replaced with heavier eyeliner and bright lipstick. Not wanting to smear her makeup, I brushed my thumb across her cheek and replied, "You look fucking hot, baby."

She smiled, and I kissed her cheek softly. "I'll be out in a few minutes, and we can head over."

"Okay. I'm going to call Eddie and check in with him."

"Tell him I said hi," I remarked and walked into the bedroom.

Showering quickly, I pulled on a clean pair of jeans and a black T-shirt. Running my hands through my wet hair, I grabbed my cut from the closet door and slipped it on before walking back into the living room.

Grace was sitting on the couch, reading a book from my bookshelf, and when she heard me enter, she lifted her head. Her blue eyes ran up and down me, and all I wanted to do was bury my cock into her perfection. Placing the book on the coffee table, she stood and sauntered toward me with a sway in her hips.

"Are you ready?" I asked, and she fluttered her eyes up to mine.

"As ready as I'll ever be," she replied, and I took her hand into mine.

Helping her onto my bike, she went to grab her helmet when I stopped her. "Not necessary here, baby, unless you feel safer."

"I always feel safe with you," she replied, and I climbed onto the bike, feeling her arms wrap around me as we headed toward the clubhouse.

I was nervous that Grace would change her mind about me after she saw how rowdy the Death Hounds could be.

Chapter 16

Grace

Pulling up to the Death Hounds compound, I felt the nervous energy growing inside me. The tall fence surrounding the compound was menacing as we approached, and I squeezed my arms tighter around Dalton. He slowed the bike at a building outside the gate and patted my hand as a young guy with a cut declaring him a prospect stepped out to meet us.

"Skid, my man. It's good to have you back home. And this must be your old lady, Grace."

I went to correct him that I wasn't an old lady when Dalton swung his hand out and clasped forearms with the young man. "Thanks, Squid. It's good to be home."

He stepped back inside the building and pressed a button. The gate slowly rolled open, and the sound of music filtered out. Dalton put the bike into gear, and we drove into the compound. A large brick building came into view, and one side had doors rolled up, showing inside the building. To the left was a line of bikes, each backed in, and to the right was a covered picnic pavilion.

There were Death Hounds walking around, most with beers in their hands, and a few women moved around, shuffling food from inside to outside. Dalton backed the bike in and turned off the engine. He stood from the bike and helped me down as a few of his brothers approached.

"Hey, man. Welcome back," one man said, and I looked to see his patches said *Claw* and *Vice President*.

Dalton man hugged him as the man turned his attention to me. Offering me his hand, he spoke. "Grace?" I nodded and shook his hand as Dalton pulled me closer to his side. "It's nice to meet you. I'm Claw, VP of the Death Hounds. Welcome to the family."

"Thank you."

"Sadie told me to bring you to her as soon as you got here," Claw remarked, and Dalton shook his head with a smile.

"Let's go find her before she sends Gunner to track us down," Dalton said, and I took his hand in mine, needing the connection and reassurance.

A few other brothers tried to stop Dalton, but he kept remarking, "Sadie needs us," and they would nod and step aside. I could feel their eyes on me but not in a disrespectful way. I knew they were checking me out, sizing me up, and judging if I was good enough for Dalton. Knowing what we had was real, I stood taller and looked up at him to see him smirk as we grew closer to the building.

"That's my girl," he said and stroked the back of my hand as we walked into the building. "Never back down, Grace. Never let them see you second-guess yourself. Show them the strong woman who isn't afraid to hit someone with a tray."

He chuckled as I smiled. Knowing I needed to be strong, I channeled my inner badass and hoped I wasn't in over her head. A woman a few inches taller than me with Dalton's black hair and blue eyes pushed through the gathering and made a direct line for us. Her smile was contagious, and when she was in front of us, Dalton released my hand and pulled her into a hug.

"Grace, baby, this is Sadie." He introduced me and then turned to her. "Sadie, meet Grace."

She pulled me into a hug, whispering, "It's so good to meet you, Grace."

I wasn't used to being touched but swallowed down my discomfort as I returned the embrace. Pulling back, she remarked, "You are absolutely beautiful. What in the world are you doing with my little brother?"

"Hey," Dalton scoffed, and she chuckled.

A large man with reddish-brown hair and a full beard stepped to us and wrapped his arm around Sadie, pulling her close to him. She looked up at him the way I look at Dalton and turned back to me. "Grace, this is Kade, my husband and the President of the club. Kade, this is Dalton's girl, Grace."

"Nice to meet you, Grace. Welcome to the Death Hounds. I hope you'll make yourself at home while you're here," he offered, and I smiled up at him as Dalton tugged me into his side.

"Why don't we get to know each other better while these two catch up?" Sadie suggested, and I nodded with a smile.

Dalton kissed me on the cheek and whispered, "Come find me if it gets to be too much. Okay?"

"Okay," I replied and followed Sadie through the crowd.

Everyone gave her respect as we walked through and entered a large dining room with multiple long tables. She walked to one and pulled out a chair,
offering it to me while she sat down across from me. I sat down and clasped
my hands in my lap, unsure what to expect.

"So, how did you meet Dalton?" she asked, and I smiled.

"He came into the bar I work at and never left." I chuckled, and she
joined me in laughter.

"The Death Hounds usually know what they want when they see it, and
they don't stop until they get it," she reasoned and leaned closer. I mirrored
her movement, then she lowered her voice. "I'm glad you're here. It's nice to
see my brother happy."

I brushed a fallen curl behind my ear and responded. "I'm glad he was
persistent. He said you raised him and your younger brother?" She nodded,
and I continued. "Thank you for raising a gentleman."

She cackled into the room, and I was confused, feeling like I was missing
something when she explained, "I'm not laughing at you, but no one has ever
described my brother as a gentleman." She wiped her eyes and stated. "I'm
glad he's treating you right. Don't be afraid to stand up to him if he gets too
big for his britches."

"I won't," I joked.

"Do you have any family? Brothers or sisters?" Sadie inquired.

I swallowed the pain that shot through my chest and responded with my
fake smile. "I've got Eddie, my boss and best friend back home."

She reached across the table and gently gripped my hand. "You've got
Dalton and us now, and once you're family, you're family for life."

I desperately wanted a family and felt Dalton was meant to be my future.
But how do you explain to someone that the meaning of family was so dis-
torted in your mind that you didn't understand the concept? I had Eddie and
the occasional call to Kelly, but other than them, I was completely alone in
the world. Sometimes I liked it that way, but seeing the camaraderie of the
people around us, I realized I'd been missing out on the good parts of life.

Somehow sensing my discomfort, Sadie stood from the table with a
smile. "Follow me. I need to make sure everything's ready to eat."

Walking into the kitchen, I saw a few other women making side dishes
and plating food as brothers walked in and grabbed items, carrying the food

outside. After making sure there wasn't anything we needed to help with, Sadie took me to the bar inside the clubhouse and made us both whiskey and Cokes.

Clinking glasses with me, we sipped on the drinks as the music started up outside.

"Let's go see what's going on," Sadie said, and we walked out the side door closest to the picnic pavilion.

The fence was closing as we sat down on top of one of the concrete tables, and we watched as a group of ladies, scantily dressed and wearing wobbly high heels, exited a vehicle. Sadie rolled her eyes and huffed as the women dispersed throughout the gathering of leather vested men.

"Just wonderful," she muttered, and I glanced at her.

"What's wrong?"

She placed her drink down before turning to me to explain. "Those are the girls who work at the Dog House, a bar the club owns a few miles from here. They come to the parties and usually try to cause trouble."

"Trouble?" I asked, sipping the last of my drink and turning back to the party.

"Can I be honest?" she asked, to which I responded, "Please."

"A few years ago, when Gunner and I were dating, he did something stupid, something nearly unforgivable, and the club girls were the catalyst. I don't blame them, I blame him, but seeing them still pisses me off. I wish they didn't come around so often, but at least I got them to leave the committed brothers alone. Now they skulk around the single brothers, looking for an old man."

"Wow," I remarked, and she hummed around a swallow of her drink.

Sitting under the pavilion, I caught a glimpse of Skid across the parking lot and smiled as he threw his head back in laughter. Guys were slapping him on the back, and he joked around with them as I sat with Sadie, taking it all in. The grills were going with more meat than I'd ever seen cooked before.

"Let me get you another drink," Sadie remarked and took my glass. "I'll be right back."

Nodding, I turned back to people watch, feeling a little out of place. Dalton kept moving through the crowd, greeting different brothers. It was hard to keep track of him with all the different people, and I lost sight of him just before Sadie came back with my drink. Sitting next to me, she tapped her glass with mine and took a drink.

A minute later, she shook her head and looked at me. I could see the worry in her eyes, so I turned back to the crowd to see one of the women pressed against Dalton's side, rubbing her hands across his chest as he talked with someone. Confused, I watched as he said something to the woman, and she laughed, throwing her head back in delight.

"Can I give you some advice? From someone who's sat where you are?" I nodded, feeling sick to my stomach as she continued. "If I were you, I'd stake my claim before my stupid brother does something even stupider."

"Stake my claim?" I asked, and she turned to fully face me.

"Go out there and show that bitch who Skid belongs to," she explained.

"Won't that cause a problem? I don't want to embarrass him." She giggled, leaning closer.

"I guarantee my brother won't be able to keep his hands off you if you go and tell that bitch what's what. Look at your shirt. He asked Needles to come by and grab it this morning so everyone would know he was claiming you. Go out there and claim him. Show him you won't take that kind of shit. If you don't put your foot down now, they will keep coming back until they drive you away." She knocked her shoulder into mine and said, "Trust me."

Gunner walked up and sat next to Sadie, taking in the scene in front of us. He wrapped his arm around her shoulder as I watched Dalton step away from the half-naked blonde, only to have her push closer to him as he talked to someone next to him.

"I told her to go stake her claim, but I don't think she believes me," Sadie remarked to Gunner, and he leaned forward, catching my gaze.

"She's right, darlin'. Those women can be aggressive to the point of annoying. Skid made sure we told everyone you were with him, but I don't think he realizes how that looks to everyone." He pointed to the woman rubbing against Dalton's side, only for him to shift, putting space between them. "He's trying to be a nice guy and not shove her away, even though he should. You need to go set her straight. I promise, Skid won't be angry or embarrassed."

Inhaling deeply, I cracked my neck and finished my drink, needing the courage to do what I was about to do. I prayed Sadie was right and I wasn't about to make a fool of myself as I hopped down from the table.

"Go get him," Sadie urged as she and Gunner watched me walk through the crowd of Death Hounds. The large, leather vested men glanced at me and stepped to the side, somehow knowing where I was going.

Stepping closer to Dalton, I could hear the woman trying to be sexy with him as he talked to another man standing with them. Letting anger fuel me, which may have been a mistake, I walked closer to Dalton. Standing behind him with my arms crossed over my chest, I tilted my head and watched the desperate woman make her advances. She looked behind Dalton and smirked before rubbing her hand back up his chest, and that was it for me.

I could feel the presence of people behind me, but I focused on Dalton and the skanky woman rubbing her nastiness on him. Giving her a saccharine sweet smile, I spoke clearly, leaving no mistake in my warning. Until he said otherwise, Dalton belonged to me.

"Either take your hand off my man, or I swear I'll break it off and beat you with it," I menacingly stated, and Dalton turned around to see me standing behind him.

"Grace, baby. What's wrong?" he asked, his blue eyes filled with worry as he stepped up to me.

The woman whined, "But, Skid, you promised to take me for a ride again."

She reached out for him, and I slapped her hand away before stepping in front of him. Her eyes grew wide, and she moved to me, trying to use her height to intimidate me. Dalton was behind me, and he placed his hand on my lower back, giving me assurance as the skank squealed.

"Who do you think you are, bitch? I don't see his cut on you, so you have no claim." Her words pissed me off, and I tilted my head to the side, sizing her up.

I stepped closer to her as the noise around us quieted to a whisper. "I'm his. Cut or no cut, until he says otherwise, he's mine. So, keep your fucking hands off him, and we won't have a problem," I spat at her and heard a few 'fuck yeahs' coming from the gathering crowd.

Usually, I didn't want the kind of attention this situation drew, but the thought of her and him together pissed me off. I went to turn to Dalton when she gripped me by the shoulder to spin me around. I was prepared for her bitch move, and when she swung her hand toward my face to slap me, I blocked it with my left forearm.

Her eyes grew wide, and I cracked a smile as I explained, "Wrong move."

I could hear gasps from behind me as I came up with a right hook, popping her in the side of the face with as much rage as I could focus into the punch. She fell to the ground with a thud, and a few of the brothers whistled and hollered as I leaned over her prone form on the ground.

"That was your one warning. Do not touch my man. Are we crystal clear?"

She nodded in acknowledgment, with her hand across her face and tears streaming down, causing her makeup to smear down her cheeks. I stood and turned to Dalton, feeling a restless energy pulsing through me. I noticed the crowd had stepped back and I raised one eyebrow in question. Smoothing my hands down my *Future Property of a Death Hound* shirt, I waited for his response.

He'd seen me lose my temper once, but it used to be a regular occurrence. He seemed shocked and his eyes grew wide when I stepped closer to him. Fisting his shirt, I dragged him closer to me and kissed him forcefully. He groaned into my mouth, and the brothers cheered and clapped.

Pulling away, I spoke softly with a tremor in my voice. "Please don't ever make me do that again."

He grasped my hand and pulled me through the gathering crowd, with more than a few of the brothers patting him on the back. I struggled to keep up with his long strides, and I glanced to see Sadie clapping under the pavilion with a laughing Gunner standing next to her. Dalton kept moving faster away from the clubhouse until we got to the back of the building.

He hadn't said anything, and I was afraid I just screwed everything up with him. When we got to the rear of the building, away from prying eyes, he pushed me against the brick wall and stepped up to me, grasping my cheek and kissing me. His tongue was in a fight with mine, each of us wanting more as his stiff length pressed against my stomach.

"Fuck, Grace. That was hot as fuck." He moaned as he kissed down my neck, and I wrapped my arms over his shoulders.

"You're not mad?" I asked, and he looked me in the eyes.

I could see need staring back at me, and he replied, "Why would I be mad? You had every right to do what you did. She knew I was with someone, and she kept pushing." He kissed me again and brought his lips to my ear, whispering as he flexed his hips, rubbing his length against me. "And you just proved you belong here. You earned everyone's respect with your declaration. You claimed me, just like I claimed you."

Kissing me again, I pushed closer to him. I bit my lip and whispered, "I want you."

Feeling his desire, seeing his need made me want him with an urgency I'd never experienced. Something was shifting in me, making me bold. Dalton grasped me by the wrist and started fast-walking down a small path behind the building until a row of small cabins came into view. He reached into his pants and pulled out a set of keys as we walked up the two steps to the front door. Unlocking the door, he ushered me inside.

I looked around, confused. "My place," he remarked as he kicked the door closed behind us.

I turned to see him approaching, and at that moment, I surrendered myself to him. He picked me up, and I wrapped my legs around his waist as he walked across the small living room to a bedroom off the side. Tossing me onto the bed, He looked at me with rapid breaths as he explained, "One chance to say no before I fuck you into the mattress. I want to be gentle with you, but you have me so worked up, I don't know if I can."

His hard cock pressed against the front of his jeans, and I licked my lips at the memory of our only time together. He brought me to heights unlike any I'd ever reached, and to see him hanging on by a thread, made me want him even more.

I leaned back on my elbows and responded, "I'm not fragile, Skid."

He fell onto his knees at the end of the bed and husked, "Don't call me Skid. To you, I'm Dalton."

I whispered as he grew closer, "Please, Dalton, fuck me. Claim me."

I'd never been so forward, but my lack of fear or apprehension with Dalton gave me confidence. He crawled up my body, settling between my spread legs as he began to kiss me again, squeezing my breasts and rubbing his hard length against me. I was squirming under him when he pulled back and stood from the bed.

I sat up and watched, afraid he changed his mind when he removed his cut and reverently placed it over a chair before returning to me. Standing at the end of the bed, he pulled my boots off and tossed them to the floor, quickly followed by my socks.

The sound of music from the party filtered into the cabin as I sat up and pulled my shirt off, and dropped it to the floor. My bra quickly followed as he crawled up my body, unsnapping the button on my jeans and opening the zipper. He kissed my lower stomach, and I quivered as he worked his way up to my breasts. Pulling one hard nipple into his warm mouth, he pinched onto the other, and I arched upward, needing more.

Whimpering under him, he released my nipple with a pop and tracked his eyes to mine. I got lost in his blue eyes, and he sat up, pulling his shirt off and tossing it over his shoulder. His large, tattooed hand gripped into the waist of my jeans and pulled them, along with my panties, down and off my feet, leaving me exposed.

His gaze zeroed in on my wet pussy, and he licked his lips before moving between my legs and planting his bearded face into my center. "Oh, fuck," I moaned, and he pulled my clit into his mouth, battering the tip with his talented tongue.

Licking and sucking, he pushed me to orgasm as he worked me higher and higher. I felt pressure building in my core, and my hand grasped his black hair as I begged, "Don't stop. Please, don't stop."

He mumbled something against my wet lips as he pushed two thick fingers into me, the orgasm threatening to split me in half. Pumping his fingers into me, he flicked and licked me until I clenched my legs against his head and yelled into the cabin, "Oh . . . oh, fuck."

My orgasm was powerful, and he placed one hand on my stomach, keeping me on the bed as he licked me through countless tremors. My body was tingling as I brought my heavy eyes down to watch him strip naked and crawl between my legs.

Sitting up, I reached out and pulled him to me as I kissed him, tasting my release on his lips. He followed me down to the bed and propped up onto one elbow as he brushed a few damp curls from my face. "Grace, never question my devotion to you. You're mine now and forever. I love you."

My eyes filled with tears as the validity of his words pierced my heart. I never realized how much I wanted someone to say those words and mean it until he spoke them against my lips.

"I love you too, Dalton."

He kissed the tears tracking down my cheeks, and I felt his hard length brush against my pussy. My eyes rolled back as I shifted my hips, feeling the bulbous crown pressed between my wet lips. He went to pull back, and I gripped his hips, looking at him with uncertainty.

"Condom," he remarked, and I tugged him closer.

"IUD," I muttered, and he smiled down at me.

"Are you sure?"

"I trust you."

Those words shifted something in both of us as he reached between us and gripped his shaft, running the head against me until he pushed his hips, slipping into me. I gasped, feeling the stretch of his enormity as my eyes rolled back in my head, forcing my lids closed. He flexed his hips, slowly pushing his monster cock into me.

When his pelvis was pressed to mine, he groaned, "Fuck, baby. You feel amazing."

He withdrew his hips and pushed back into me, allowing me to feel every veiny inch of his shaft. Thrusting slowly, he stared into my eyes, and I clasped his cheek as he not only claimed my body, but my soul.

Faster he rocked his hips, and I lifted my ass, meeting his movements as we both grew closer to release. Leaning down, he drew a stiff nipple into his mouth and bit down on the tip, making me moan louder. The sound of slapping skin and grunting pleasures filled the room as my orgasm grew closer to the surface with every thrust of his hips.

Dalton licked his thumb and brought it down to my clit, applying pressure and rubbing circles until I dug my fingers into his back. My body shook and my legs pressed harder into his sides as the orgasm of a lifetime broke free, spotting my vision and making me tremble during his ministrations.

Dalton kept working his hips, drawing out my release, and when he felt my body relax, he pulled his wet cock from me.

"Roll over, Grace. Get on your hands and knees."

Feeling like every muscle is made of jelly, I rolled over and pushed myself up, presenting my ass to him as he pushed between my knees and gripped one hip. I could feel his head pressing against my pussy before he shoved his length into me. I came off my hands, and my back fell against his chest as he gripped into my hips and fucked me hard.

"Oh . . . oh . . . oh . . ." I chanted between hard thrusts and started lowering my chest back to the bed.

He grasped my hair and pushed between my shoulder blades, pressing my face into the mattress as he rode me. Maintaining the grip in my hair, he pounded into me, and I felt another powerful orgasm building. My walls constricted, and I heard him behind me, praising me.

"That's it, Grace. Come on my cock. Let that perfect pussy pop for your old man." he urged as my face rocked against the bedsheet with my ass in the air.

"Dalton," I moaned, and he released my hair, gripping into my hips and powering into me at a punishing pace.

The orgasm burst free, and a scream caught in my throat as everything exploded inside me. I could feel Dalton grow thicker in me before he slammed into me, filling me with his release. "Mine," he roared into the room as I blinked away the kaleidoscope of colors.

He leaned over, kissing me at the base of my neck on my back as he whispered, "I love you, Grace, and I'm never letting you go."

I smiled and replied, "I love you too, old man."

He chuckled, and when I joined him, he groaned, slowly pulling out of me and collapsing on the bed. I stretched my legs out and felt his release sliding out of me as I turned my head to face him, unable to roll over off my chest. We laid there, looking at each other with goofy smiles for a few minutes before my stomach grumbled. I covered my face in embarrassment, and he moved my hand to kiss the tip of my nose.

"Let me feed my old lady." He smiled and kissed me again.

I cleaned up in the bathroom, and we got dressed before returning to the party. When we walked around the edge of the building with Dalton's arm over my shoulder, a chorus of whistles sounded, and I ducked my head, feeling the blush across my cheeks.

Chapter 17

Skid

Eddie warned me about Grace's temper, so when she claimed me in front of the entire club, I couldn't help but smile. She worried she wouldn't fit it, but she proved to the whole club she was old lady material. We rejoined the cookout to cheers, and I smirked as I tugged Grace tighter to my chest. She blushed and cast her eyes down briefly before looking up at me with a sly smile.

"Don't be embarrassed, darlin'. You showed her who was boss, and I showed my gratitude." I leaned over and whispered as we approached the pavilion. "They aren't choir boys. We at least had the decency to do it in private."

Her eyes grew wide, and I chuckled as she leaned up and asked, "You mean . . . out in the open?"

"And then some." I laughed as we joined the line of people waiting to get food.

Sadie was saving us a place to sit with her and Gunner, and we squeezed in across from them. The music wasn't too loud yet, allowing for some conversation to take place.

"I told you so," Sadie joked, and Grace smiled at her.

"Sorry I caused a scene," Grace acknowledged to Gunner, and he leaned over with a smile.

"Grace, honey. I promise it was a pleasure to see you throw a punch. Where'd you learn to hit like that cause you may need to teach a few of the prospects the right way to knock someone on their ass," Gunner joked, and I shook my head with a smile, watching Grace fit into my family and my club seamlessly.

She scratched her neck and shrugged before replying. "I had a few months of self-defense training years ago and I guess some of it stuck."

"Whoever you worked with taught you well. Anytime you want to spar, we have a gym in town, and I know Sadie would like the company." He was watching her as he spoke, and to anyone else, you wouldn't know he was analyzing everything about her.

Gunner taking over was the right move a few years ago, and his leadership has been good for the club. He has the ability to somehow sense when someone wasn't giving all the information they could. Not lying but omitting parts of the truth, and he could ask the most benign questions to get the answers.

I didn't like he was doing it to Grace, but he was getting her to give information I hadn't been able to garner from her during countless hours of conversations of the last week. Giving him a subtle cue that not even Sadie knew, I let him know to push without being pushy.

"That sounds like fun. It's been years since I've been to a gym," Grace responded.

"What I want is to try this best pie in the world pie that Dalton raved about," Sadie interjected, and Grace covered her smile with her hand.

I leaned over and whispered against the shell of her ear, "Can I have some of your pie, Grace? I promise to lick the plate clean."

Grace cleared her throat and turned to Sadie. "I don't know about being the best pie in the world, but I'd love to make you one. Dalton said you own a bakery?"

"I do and for him to say it's the best in the world means I have to try it, then I'll be forced to hire you, so you don't become my competition," Sadie joked, and Gunner kissed her on the temple before draping his arm over her shoulder.

"I've always wanted to work in a bakery, creating new desserts and perfecting old classics," Grace reasoned, and Gunner subtly nodded to me.

"I'm going to get us another drink. Do you need anything?" I asked Grace, and she turned to me with a smile.

"I just need you," she replied, and I kissed her before standing up and joining Gunner.

We walked into the clubhouse, away from the music, and sat down at our usual table in the back of the room. I could see Grace sitting with Sadie, her head thrown back in carefree laughter through the rolled-up doors used to fortify the clubhouse. I was glad to see them getting along like old friends and to see Grace so relaxed was a relief.

A prospect quickly delivered two beers and scurried away before Gunner spoke. "I don't want to ask what you found out, but I kind of do. I can see it in her eyes, and Sadie does too. Is it as bad as you expected?"

I took a swallow of my beer and set the bottle down before I met his gaze and explained. "She's carrying around something darker than I could have ever imagined. Grace doesn't share information freely, and after this afternoon, I think I may understand why."

"What happened this afternoon?"

"James and Devlin stopped by while she was taking a nap," I explained and ran my hand through my hair. "They suspect something about her foster dad, and they wanted to compare notes."

"Don't make me keep asking questions. Tell me what you can so I don't step into something sensitive. The last thing I want to do is hurt your old lady. She is your old lady, isn't she?"

"Fuck, yes, she's my old lady, and as soon as Parrot gets back in town, I'm ordering her cut. And to answer your question, they think he was involved with the Servants of God somehow."

His eyes grew wide, and he leaned closer to me, looking around before he lowered his voice and spoke. "Isn't that the cult that used the Bible to justify sex with girls?"

I closed my eyes and exhaled. Looking at him, I spoke with a deadly tone. "If you repeat this, I swear I'll turn in my cut." His mouth opened, realizing the weight of that statement. I explained, "She has nightmares, whimpering one word as she struggles against an invisible enemy. If he was connected to them, it makes sense that she has trust issues and violent tendencies."

"Damn. Do you think he believed that sick shit?"

"I can't be sure, and I refuse to ask. They are digging into some of the defunct members and seeing if there is a connection. It's a long shot, and he may have just been a pervert, but after reading about their practices, I fear it's true."

I could see Grace and Sadie stand from the table, and I turned back to him, quietly speaking. "Sadie can't know, and I don't mind you asking Grace questions, but please be mindful she will sidestep on issues that connect to him. That's the only thing I've figured out. She glosses over foster care, and according to her, life began when she ran away."

Just as the ladies entered the far side of the large clubhouse, he asked in a whisper, "What's the word?"

Turning my back to Sadie and Grace, I mouthed, 'daddy' and his nostrils flared in disgust. They approached, and Sadie stepped under Gunner's arm as Grace linked her hand with mine. I looked down at her, and her blue eyes twinkled with happiness as she smiled up at me.

"I want to take Grace to the lake," Sadie remarked, and I shrugged.

"The path is clear. Just take some flashlights," Gunner urged, and Sadie giggled.

"Pierce Lake. Not the pond in the woods. I want to take her over to Pierce Bluff and grab some Papa Dough's. I'm off on Wednesday and would love to have some girl time."

I looked down at Grace. "Maybe you can grab some extra clothes while you're there. Since you couldn't pack much on the bike."

"Only if it's okay with you."

"Of course, it's okay with him," Sadie urged, and Grace raised her eyebrows, looking for an answer. "And since it's his fault you couldn't bring any clothes, he's paying for our shopping trip."

Grace shook her head to decline when I kissed her on the cheek and smiled. "I think that's a great idea." Leaning closer, I whispered, "Get some sexy lingerie while you're there."

The four of us walked back outside, joining the party. It was tame for a Death Hounds party, and I think it may have to do with Grace. They all seemed to be enamored with her, and I couldn't blame them. From the first moment I saw her, I was a goner.

The music blared from the speakers set around the front of the building, and I took Grace by the hand, pulling her to my chest as I swayed with the music. She wrapped her arms around my neck and pressed to her tiptoes as we danced along to the music. Her smile was genuine, and the love I felt for her was growing every second.

We drank, laughed, and talked until close to eleven, when Grace hid a yawn behind her hand. I looked over at her and could see the exhaustion on her face, so I stood from the table and scooped her into my arms. She shrieked as I walked away from the pavilion where everyone seemed to congregate.

"I'm taking my woman home. Later," I yelled, and Grace snuggled closer to my chest as I walked to my bike.

After making sure she was secure on the back, I climbed on the bike and cranked the loud motor. Grace wrapped her arms around my waist as I pulled away from the clubhouse. The prospect opened the gate as I approached, and when I got to the road, I urged, "Hang on, baby."

Her grip increased, and I hit the throttle and peeled out of the compound with a screech. The drive home was peaceful as I traversed the familiar roads. Having Grace on my bike, sharing my bed, and hopefully sharing my life gave me new hope, new energy.

I just prayed we could figure out what threats still existed and eliminate them before Grace realized what we discovered. I feared her ingrained shame would push her over the edge, and she would forever close herself off. If she took her heart back, I would go mad with loneliness.

***

Grace spent the next day reading on the couch while I 'worked' in my office. Digging through everything I could find on the now-defunct cult, I made a list of members who weren't arrested during the raid on their compound. The government had investigated them for three years, so there were extensive records on each member.

Devlin was able to use his connections, and we split the information, hoping to find a lead, and coming up empty at every turn. The frustration grew with each dead end. If Ringman wasn't dead, I would drive to his house and torture the information from him, making him admit what he did not only to Aubrey, which I could prove, but also to Grace, which I suspected but couldn't verify.

A knock sounded into my office, and I closed my laptop and turned off the monitor bank on the wall as I responded, "Come in."

Grace stuck her head through the door with a smile on her face. "I'm sorry to bother you, but I wanted to run to the store to pick up the items to make Sadie's pie. Would it be okay if I borrowed your truck?"

"I can drive you," I offered, and she shook her head softly.

"You're working, and if I go alone, we'll have more time together when you finish. I have GPS, so I'm fairly sure I won't get lost."

Standing from my chair, I walked to the door and stepped into the hallway with Grace. Brushing my hand down her cheek, I leaned over and kissed her, pouring love into the embrace. After reading how the cult treated and trained the young girls, I wanted her to know how much I cared and cherished her.

Without telling her, I was hoping to erase all the things she endured. Pulling back from the kiss, I looked down at her and winked.

"Wow," she remarked, and I wiggled my eyebrows at her.

Linking our hands, I escorted her down the stairs and into the living room. My wallet was on the small table in the kitchen, and I reached inside, pulling out a hundred dollars and handing it to Grace. "Take this for what you need." Then I handed her my credit card. "And use this for what you want."

She shook her head and handed the card back to me. "I'll take your money for the dessert, but I have no need for your credit card."

"I know you don't need it, but I want you to have it. Can you do that for me, Grace? Can you keep it, knowing it makes your old man feel better?" I wasn't playing fair, but I wanted to take care of everything she needed or wanted.

"I don't feel right taking your card, but if it makes you feel better, I'll keep it. Even though I won't need it."

I brushed my lips against hers before whispering, "Thank you, baby."

Walking into the garage, I took the keys to the truck off the hook by the door and helped her inside the vehicle. After making sure her seat and mirrors were set, I reminded her, "I'll be here waiting for you to return."

She bit her lip as the garage door opened from the remote in my hand. "Lucky me."

Watching her pull away from my house, I walked inside and ran up the stairs to my office. Turning the monitors back on, I opened my laptop and activated the monitoring system for my truck. I wasn't as bad as James by putting a mic in the truck, but I could see where it was on the map and had access to the cameras for the navigation system.

I could see every turn she made as she traversed the road into Portstill, and when I saw she was a few miles from town, I called Gunner.

"Hey, brother."

"I need a prospect to follow Grace. She's on the road leading to town going to the grocery, and I want to make sure she's okay," I remarked, and I heard him cover the phone.

"I've got Jackal already in town, so Claw sent him a message to keep an eye out for Grace," Gunner replied, and I exhaled deeply. "Have you found anything?"

"Not yet, and I want to be finished for the day when she gets back."

"Then I'll let you get back to it. I'm here when you need me. We all are." I could hear the worry in his voice, and I knew my brothers hoped this was the last job I took for Callahan.

They watched me slip further into the darkness the longer I worked for him but being connected to him has been beneficial to the club. Having Grace around, I no longer wanted to live in the craziness. Instead, I wanted to ride with my club and spend every free moment with Grace beside me.

Watching Devlin, James, and Hayden move on with their lives, even with the pain and trauma from the past, gave me hope that my future with Grace would be possible. I just wished I could keep her once the truth of our meeting came to light.

Chapter 18

Grace

It took four batches of dough for my new crust to set correctly. I was growing frustrated with my baking, and after three pies with over or under-done crusts, I cheered when the last one baked perfectly. I heard Dalton running down the stairs, and I turned to see what the emergency was. He ran into the kitchen and looked around with worry.

"Are you okay? I heard you yell."

Stepping up to him, I brought my hand to his chest and chuckled. "I'm sorry. I finally got the crust to set properly, and I got a little excited. I didn't mean to disturb you."

He's been in his office for long stretches of time the last few days, and I was quiet as he worked, trying to be respectful of his space. He kept encouraging me to interrupt, but I told him his work needed to come first. I had no idea what he was working on, but I knew it must be important from the stress he was carrying.

"You never disturb me." Dalton looked over my head to the counter and saw the four pies in various stages of cooling, and he smiled, licking his lips. "I can see you've been busy. I'm sorry I've been neglecting you the last two days."

"You're working, so you never need to apologize for that. I can find plenty to keep me occupied."

He pulled me closer to him, letting me feel his growing shaft as he whispered, "When can I have some pie?"

"Whenever you want," I replied and caught his gaze with mine.

He pulled my face to his chest and wrapped me in his strong arms, surrounding me with his love as he spoke. "I love you, Grace."

"I love you, Dalton."

Stepping back, I took his hand into mine and tugged him closer to the counter. "This one is for me to give to Sadie tomorrow, so hands-off." I pointed to the perfect pie cooling on the rack. "The rest you can have at," I explained, sweeping my hand over the three that didn't turn out as good as I hoped.

"We can take two of them to the clubhouse for the brothers, and I'll keep one for myself," he explained and grabbed a knife to cut into one of the sweet desserts. Picking it up with his hand, he took a bite off the end before turning and offering it to me.

The chocolate and pecans were slightly overcooked but still delicious as I swallowed my bite and watched Dalton licking his fingers with satisfaction. "So good."

"I'm glad you enjoyed it," I replied and sat down at the small table in the kitchen.

He joined me and took my hands into his as he asked, "Is there anything you want to do? I feel like I've abandoned you, and that wasn't my intention. I wasn't expecting Devlin to need me, but I hope I'll be finished in a day or two."

I could see worry hidden under his smile, and I refused to draw attention to it. I didn't know what he was working on, but it must be important. "You didn't abandon me. How many nights did you watch me pour drinks while I worked?" He shrugged, and I pushed on. "You have responsibilities, and I'm not going to make you feel guilty for not spending every waking second with me. I promise. I'm a big girl and can find something to keep me occupied."

He brushed his thumb across my cheek and asked, "How did I get so lucky?"

"You decided to stop for a drink," I reasoned, and he nodded.

"Why don't you get cleaned up, and I'll take you out to dinner."

"I can cook something for you," I said, and he smiled before leaning over and pecking me on the lips.

"I want to show my woman off. Dress comfortably, and I'll be ready in two hours," he instructed and stood from the chair. "I promise I'm close to finished."

He walked away, and I couldn't take my eyes off his tight ass. Seeing him so comfortable and relaxed, compared to the tough man who watched me for three weeks, was a dramatic change. I could see the real him where everyone else gets a diluted version of Dalton.

He cared deeply, loved fiercely, and was protective to a fault.

In short, he was the best thing that ever happened to me, and I prayed I could keep my secret from him. I couldn't stand to see the look in his eyes when he realizes what I said to him the first night he spoke to me was true.

I'm not worth the effort.

He took me to a taco truck for dinner then we walked through the bustling downtown area of Portstill. It was a nice town, and the people who walked by us nodded to Dalton with a smile. I was curious to know why the club was so highly respected, and he explained about the charity work and countless businesses owned by the club. To the town of Portstill, it appeared the Death Hounds were not to be feared.

Maybe I was wrong about the club, but something told me they had secrets that they would kill to protect.

When we returned to the house, I could see he was eager to get back to work but not trying to brush me off. Never wanting him to feel bad about his responsibilities, I offered, "Why don't you work for a while, and I'll settle in with my book."

"Are you sure? I don't want you to feel like I'm choosing it over you."

Taking his hand into mine, I led him to the couch in the living room and sat down, encouraging him to join me. Turning to him, I asked, "If you work now, will you be closer to being finished?"

"Yeah, but it can wait until the morning. I'd rather ravage you tonight." He leaned over and kissed my neck, causing chill bumps to erupt across my skin.

I needed him but would wait until he could focus all his attention on me. He was distracted and under stress, and if finishing whatever assignment Devlin gave him would give him peace of mind, I could wait.

"I'll be gone all day tomorrow with Sadie, so I need to get some rest. Why not put everything into it tonight and tomorrow while I'm gone. Then, when I get home, I can model some of the new lingerie for you."

"I think that sounds amazing and I think you're incredible."

"I'm just me," I reasoned, and he stood from the couch, keeping his hand in mine.

"I'll get you something to help you relax before I get back to it." His sexy wink was making me second guess my restraint as he went into the kitchen.

Battling the inner voice in my head, I tried to remain adaptable yet independent. Giving in seemed like I was falling into the trap that was laid shortly after my twelfth birthday, and no matter the depth of my feelings for Dalton, I feared I would slide into the mind games and resort to compliance to keep the peace.

My gaze was on the silent fireplace across the room when Dalton returned. Glancing at him, I saw him push a smile onto his face before reaching his closed hand out to me. Sitting up, I peeked into his hand as he opened it to reveal a beautifully rolled joint. Taking it from him, he leaned over and kissed me until I couldn't catch my breath.

"Enjoy your relaxation, beautiful, and if you decide to get into the hot tub, let me know. I don't want you to fall asleep out there," he joked.

Picking up my book from the coffee table, I stood and turned to face him. "I promise no naps in the hot tub. Now get to work so I can have my way with you tomorrow."

He wiggled his eyebrows and pecked me on the cheek before he walked upstairs. I could hear his office door close, and I smiled into the empty room before walking onto the back porch. I sat down on the overstuffed chair and lit the joint, inhaling deeply and leaning back to watch the sun set across the lake.

My phone chimed from my pocket, and I pulled it out to see Eddie had sent me a text.

Eddie: How's Tennessee?

Me: It's beautiful. You'd like it here.

Eddie: Do you like it there?

Me: I love it here.

It was hard for me to admit my feelings since they were twisted against me so cruelly, but Eddie was someone I could always be honest with. I don't know why he's been so wonderful to me through the years, but if it weren't for him and the two counselors I worked with after running away, I would be a basket case most days.

Eddie: Have you thought about staying for a while or are you planning to run back home?

Me: I want to stay, but I'm scared.

Eddie: Of Skid? Has he done something to hurt you?

Me: No. He's wonderful. That's what I'm scared of.

Just admitting that was cathartic. I took another draw off the joint before snubbing it out and letting my gaze move to the lake. The orange sky was casting a glow on the lake, and I couldn't think of anything more beautiful than the scene in front of me. Snapping a quick picture, I went to set my phone down to pick up my book when it rang.

Seeing it was Eddie, I answered, happy to talk to my closest friend.

"Hey. How's things at home?" I asked and could faintly hear music in the background.

"Things are good. We miss you here, but I'm happy you're having a good time," Eddie replied with a pause. "Now, tell me why you're scared, Grace."

Eddie always told me that one day, I would be able to tell the person I loved and who loved me in return, the truth of what happened. He said the person meant to be mine would never judge me for my past and would help me to navigate the uncertainty in my mind until *The Community* was a distant memory.

Just thinking those two words made me anxious, and I tried to focus on exactly what it was that had me scared.

"Everything, I think. What if I can never tell him about what happened? What if I'm creating something with him that's not real? What if he finds out and looks at me with disgust?"

"Grace, you can ask a thousand what-if questions and never be satisfied with the answers. What you have to ask yourself is this? Does Dalton show you love? Not with words, but actions? Does he think of your needs first, does he treat you like a partner and not a piece of property?"

"Yes," I whispered and wiped an errant tear that fell down my cheek. "He does all of that and more."

"Then you have to find a way to trust him. You have to talk to him and tell him something real about your past. However small, tell him and see his reaction. If he handles it without interrogating you or pushing you away, then you trust him with a little more. Eventually, you'll have told him everything and it won't seem so bad."

"How do you know that? How do you know he won't hear the truth and tell me to leave?"

"I don't know much in this world, Grace, but I know this. That man loves you. He told me so before you left, and I saw the sincerity in his eyes. He's a good man, Grace. Even if he is an outlaw, he's an honorable and decent man that is lucky to have such an amazingly strong and resilient woman by his side."

I was crying at Eddie's words, and I resigned myself that tomorrow night, I would share something with Dalton. A truth about me that will tell me if he's in it for the long haul like he professed, or if he was just looking for something perfect that I can't live up to.

"Thanks, Eddie," I spoke through tears, and he chuckled.

"Anytime, darlin'. No matter what, I'm always here for you. Love you, kiddo," he replied.

"Love you too."

I hung up the phone and turned my gaze back to the lake as the final minutes of daylight pushed into the horizon, blanketing the sky into darkness. As the light faded, the familiar feeling of regret filled me. The lights programmed to turn on flickered to life, illuminating the deck in a soft glow, and I wrapped my arms around myself, pushing away the memories that were spinning faster and faster in my brain.

"Happy birthday, Grace," Kelly cheered as she pulled me into a hug.

"Thank you. Come on in," I urged.

I was happy my best friend could spend the night for my birthday and couldn't wait to have girl talk. Technically, my birthday was last week, but it was special to have her here, just the same.

Kelly and I ended up at different high schools due to our desired career paths, and we only got to see each other on occasion now. We still talked and sent messages every day, but this was the first time in weeks I'd seen her. Connie was out of town, and Daddy agreed to let Kelly sleep over as long as I cleaned up any mess before Connie got home on Sunday.

"Where's the wicked witch?" Kelly whispered, and I chuckled as we walked to my bedroom.

The two younger kids who came into the house last month shared a room closer to Connie and Daddy's room. Connie was taking them to Memphis for their monthly visitation weekend with their parents. She got to stay in a hotel, and I got the weekend away from her judgment. I was surprised last year when they gave me the back bedroom, offering me some privacy and personal space.

"She's in Memphis with the two new fosters for monthly visitation. She'll be back with them on Sunday evening," I replied as we walked into my bedroom, and she tossed her overnight bag onto the bed.

Flopping down on our backs, we started catching up on school and the boys we liked, giggling about typical teenage crap. The sound of the front door opening let me know Daddy was home. He'd been a little distant with me over the last month or so, and last week, I heard him on the phone talking about a new girl he wanted to bring into The Community.

Aubrey.

I was hurt he was looking past me to another daughter, but I knew my time to marry was drawing closer. We went to a Community gathering last week, and I was shown a picture of the man Daddy picked for me to marry. He was the stepson to a member of The Community, and from first glance, I thought he was cute. I didn't want to marry someone I'd never met, but Daddy reminded me it was his choice, and he knew what was best.

"I ordered you girls some pizza for dinner, and I'm going to be in my room working on some things if you need me tonight," Daddy explained from the open door, and I rolled over to look at him.

"Thanks, Kevin," I replied, and he gave me a subtle nod. I stood from the bed and looked at Kelly. "I'll be back in a few minutes."

She knew how strict the Ringmans were, so she rolled her eyes and picked up her phone, getting lost in Candy Crush while I followed Daddy to his room. He pushed the door open as I walked inside and turned to face him.

"Have you been a good girl, Grace?" he asked, cupping my cheek with his hand.

"Yes, Daddy," I whispered, and he smiled down at me.

"That's good, Grace. I need for you to take care of something before dinner. Can you do that for your daddy?"

I glanced over his shoulder, knowing Kelly was on the other side of the house and engrossed in her phone. Worried she would see and make Daddy angry, I asked, "Can I take care of it in the morning before Kelly wakes up?"

"You'll wake me before you start?" he asked.

"Yes, Daddy. If that's what you want," I promised, wanting to get back to Kelly.

Lately, our connection had been frayed, and I knew what he wanted. I just didn't want to do it while Kelly was awake.

"First thing, Grace," he instructed and kissed my cheek before stepping aside.

I walked past him, and he rubbed my back, allowing his fingers to brush against my bottom as I left his room. All night, I tossed and turned, feeling like something was wrong, and when the sun started to peek through the window, I slowly crawled from bed, leaving Kelly sleeping. Walking out of my room, I closed the door and moved through the house to Daddy and Connie's room.

He was asleep, so I walked to the bed, gently nudging him. He blinked his eyes open and smiled at me. "Good morning, my saving grace. Are you ready to take care of what I need?"

"Yes, Daddy," I whispered and lifted the covers back.

He swung his feet to the floor and removed his sleep shorts. I slid onto the floor between his legs and did what he taught me to do when Daddy was stressed and needed relief. His hand was in my hair as he encouraged me. "That's Daddy's girl."

I had no idea the door wasn't closed. I was doing what I was taught a good wife would do for her husband when I heard a faint noise. Looking up, Daddy didn't seem worried, and I wished it was already over. A minute later, I felt his hand grip deeper into my hair as he whispered, "Yes, baby. Here it comes. Take Daddy."

When I was finished, I quickly brushed my teeth and slipped back into my room, finding Kelly on the bed, turned toward the wall. I slid in beside her and faced away from her, hoping she stayed asleep.

The front door opened and closed a little while later, and I heard Daddy's truck crank up. He had a meeting, so Kelly and I would have the house to ourselves until after lunch. Kelly rolled over to face me, and her face was covered in tears.

"What's wrong, Kelly?" I asked, and she sat up, pulling me into a hug.

"What he's making you do is wrong," she cried, and I pushed her back with confusion.

She told me what she saw, and I got scared, fearing Daddy's deal to find me a husband would be in jeopardy. "He's not making me do anything. He's teaching me, just like your dad teaches you."

"Grace, my dad doesn't teach me anything like that. That's abuse. That's wrong," she explained, but I shook my head.

"You're mistaken. That's how daddies show their love. That's how they teach you to be a good wife and mother," I rationalized, feeling like everything I knew was being threatened.

She took me by the hand, and for the next three hours, she told me about how wrong I was. She promised she would find someone to help, and when I couldn't take the feelings of disgust and shame anymore, she held my hair while I threw up, fully understanding what Daddy had been doing to me for years.

The following week, with no help from my caseworker and Daddy and Connie denying everything, I took the money I'd saved from small jobs and the occasional birthday present, packed everything I could fit into my duffle bag and backpack, and left without a note or goodbye.

Kelly had found a place for me to go to help fix some of the things the Ringmans had lied about, and after four months, the group helped me find my way to Eddie.

I'd carried the guilt and shame of his actions around for years, and if Eddie was right, Dalton might be the one to break my chains and set me free. Now to find a way to tell him without either of us hating me.

Chapter 19

Skid

After Grace left with Sadie for their day in Pierce Bluff, I dialed into a conference call with Devlin and James to go over the information we individually uncovered. I made sure my office door was locked, even though I was alone in the house, not wanting anyone to hear the conversation.

"What have you found?" I asked the two men who were sitting next to each other and waited for their response.

They owned and lived in the same condo building in Pierce Bluff, which meant they usually were together during these types of meetings. Over the years, we'd grown from a small house in the Flats to the state-of-the-art hub inside their building.

"I started digging through the government's files on those who were convicted and found no link to Kevin Ringman. No common school, family, jobs, or even gym memberships," Devlin explained, running his hand down his black beard with frustration. "What about you, Skid? What have you figured out?"

"I started looking into Ringman's life and found no relationship with the few members that didn't get convicted but were under indictment. There doesn't appear to be any connection to the Servants of God and Kevin Ringman," I explained, frustrated we couldn't connect anything to him other than he was a freak who took advantage of little girls and would never see justice.

"What about his wife?" James asked, and I sat back with confusion.

"What about her? I dug into her life, and she wasn't connected to anything. There were never any accusations against her when Grace spoke with the social worker, and it doesn't appear she was aware of what he was doing," I replied, and James shook his head.

"I disagree. Connie Ringman, formally Connie Philips, was part of a traveling family of preachers until her father died when she was thirteen. She was placed with a family in Texas who reported some strange incidents with her, resulting in her removal from the house," James clarified.

Devlin looked at his brother and asked, "What kind of strange incidents?"

"Hypersexuality for someone her age. Inappropriate touching of the foster father. After the third time it happened, she was taken from the house at his request and spent the rest of her time in a group home. The pieces fit, but I couldn't find where she had contact with the Servants. From everything I could uncover, her father was never affiliated with them in any way, so why would she act like that?" James inquired, and the three of us fell silent for a minute.

"When did she get diagnosed with cancer?" I asked.

James typed something into his computer. "Two years before Grace was placed with them. She had a hysterectomy six months after Grace moved in."

"What if Grace was meant to be a surrogate?" Devlin pondered, and my vision grew red.

"To bear them children?" I yelled, and Devlin held up his hand to the screen as I pushed my chair back and paced my office.

When I got my temper under control, I sat back down to see the two men watching me intently. Devlin spoke, offering some solace in the fucked-up mess my sweet Grace was dragged into. "Not for children. For his wife. Connie Ringman may have ignored his perversions or even connected Kevin with someone who put the idea into his head."

"Who? Because if there is someone still alive that's connected to the depraved shit Grace and Aubrey had to live through, I'm going to gut them and stuff their own intestines down their throat until they choke to death on them," I explained, and James looked at me with murderous rage in his eyes.

"The only way to find out is to ask Grace. She may have information or at least be able to put all the questions to rest," Devlin reasoned, and I shook my head.

"Fuck that. There's no way I'm going to ask her about him. She isn't aware I even know anything about anything, so I will not throw something painful and embarrassing in her face, just to satisfy our need for answers," I returned and crossed my arms over my chest, daring them to push back.

"What about my sister and maybe the countless other girls that were affected by him?" James threw back, and I leaned into the screen, happy we weren't in the same room, or I may have punched him in the face.

"How do you know there were others? What if I ask her, ripping open old scabs until she bleeds out, only to find it was just them? From everything

I can figure out, Ringman met Aubrey a month before Grace ran away. How do we know it wasn't just the two of them?"

They both sighed, and I knew we were at an impasse. Neither of us was willing to back down. James wanted justice for Aubrey, and I wanted Grace to forget the pain she endured. Bringing it up to them wouldn't fix anything. He was dead and couldn't hurt them or anyone else anymore.

"How about this? We ask her to undergo a background check since she's living with you now. It's standard for all Callahan Cyber employees, and it's a way to ask non-intrusive questions without digging. She can speak with Elise and Amaya, and maybe they can help garner some information," Devlin suggested, and I contemplated his solution.

"Look, Dalton, I know you don't want to hurt Grace. I can see how much you care for her, and I respect that. And you. But if there is someone out there hurting kids, we need to stop them. Let's see if she's willing to do the check, and I'll talk to Amaya. We can keep Elise out of it, for now, Devlin. I don't want to upset her, and Amaya is better equipped to discuss sensitive topics. We can decide our next move after that. Does that sound agreeable to everyone?" James inquired, and I reluctantly nodded.

Devlin glanced at his brother sitting next to him and then back to the screen. "I agree that may be the best way to go about this. Let's let it happen organically and decide what's best afterward."

"I appreciate it and I promise, if there is someone who needs to die, I'll be at the front of the line. But not if it means hurting Grace. I love her too much to see her in pain, and I refuse to be the cause of it," I returned, and it was decided.

I nodded at my two friends and disconnected the video call, casting my office into silence. How had I never thought of looking in Connie Ringman? Being focused on the man who physically hurt them, I never considered she could be a part of it. She could have been a victim as well, from her reported actions, and if so, I was sorry for her too. All too often, brainwashed or manipulated victims grow up, not knowing what they lived through was wrong. I don't know how many go on to become predators themselves, and I wished there was a way to rid the world of those sick perverts before they hurt anyone.

It was after one o'clock when I finished looking into Connie's family, trying to find anything James and Devlin missed. Not seeing anything promising, I stood from my chair and stretched my back. Sadie and Grace wouldn't
be home for another two hours, and I wanted to check on them.

Grabbing my laptop from the charging station, I walked downstairs to
the living room and logged onto the Callahan network to pull up the cameras in Pierce Bluff. It took a minute to load, and while I waited, I thought of
how I wanted Grace's claiming ceremony to go. I sent Parrot a message, asking him to get started on her cut as soon as he got back from Florida.

When the cameras came online, I scrolled through the ones around the
lake, looking for Grace and Sadie. They weren't parked in the lot, and I
scanned downtown, hoping to catch a glimpse of her. I needed to see with
my own eyes she was okay, and the longer it took me to find Sadie's car, the
more anxious I got. I wasn't worried about someone hurting them, I was just
worried.

Something was clawing at my gut, telling me everything was about to
blow up, and I couldn't shake the feeling. I finally located the car parked in
the side lot of Papa Dough's Pizza and exhaled the breath stuck in my throat.
We didn't have cameras inside the restaurant, but I could see the entrance
from the street camera.

I moved the laptop into the kitchen and rolled myself a joint while I
watched the screen, waiting for them to exit. Carrying the computer outside,
I sat down at the table and placed it in front of me before firing the joint up
and taking a deep inhale. A few nervous minutes later, I saw my sister walk
out, followed by Grace.

Through the screen, I could tell something wasn't right, even though she
had a smile on her face. It was the way she carried herself. She was withdrawn
and pulling in on herself as she carried two pizza boxes to the car. Sadie said
something to her, and I took another hit of the joint as Grace nodded in
agreement.

"Fuck it," I said aloud and grabbed my phone from the table.

I dialed Grace's number and waited for her to pick up. The car backed
out of the parking space, and I was going to lose sight of it soon. On the third
ring, she answered.

"Hello."

"Hey, darlin'. How's the shopping trip?" I wanted to keep it light and hoped to cheer her up from whatever had her upset.

"I got a headache when we were at the lake, so we decided to grab dinner and head home," she replied, and I hated she wasn't feeling well.

"I'm sorry, darlin'. I'll take you later this week when you're up to it and I can spoil you," I responded, and she chuckled slightly.

"You do that already."

"Drive safe, and I'll see you when Sadie drops you off. I love you."

"Love you too."

She hung up the phone, and I stared at the disconnected call, trying to figure out if there was something else going on. Knowing I wouldn't find out until she got home, I quickly showered and changed into a pair of shorts and a T-shirt. Waiting on the front porch, I watched the driveway for them to pull up.

When I saw Sadie's car turn into the driveway, I slipped a pair of shoes on and walked out to meet them. The car stopped in front of the stairs, and Grace opened the door, sticking her head out and inhaling deeply. Sadie got out and had a worried look on her face as she took two pizza boxes from the back seat.

I walked to the passenger's side and helped Grace from the car, seeing she was pale and sweaty. Feeling her forehead, she felt warm, and I was worried she was sick. Her blue eyes appeared dull in the afternoon sun as I wrapped my arm around her and helped her into the house. Sadie followed behind and closed the door when she entered. Taking the pizzas to the kitchen, she nodded to me as I got Grace settled onto the couch.

"I'll get you some ginger ale. You rest," I instructed, and she gave me a thumbs-up as she rolled to her side.

Sadie was standing at the counter when I walked in, and she motioned for me to join her.

"What happened?" I asked, and her eyes turned sad.

"We were walking around the lake, and she was having a good time when we bumped into James and his wife. We talked for a few minutes about the two of you getting together with them for dinner, and when we walked back to the car, she got sick. I told her I'd bring her home, but she insisted on getting dinner as we planned. On the drive home, she got nauseous, and I worried she was going to throw up. Is she okay?" my sister asked.

"I'm not sure, but I'll keep an eye on her. Thanks for taking care of her," I replied, and Sadie hugged me.

"She's a keeper, Dalton. Don't screw it up."

"I don't plan on it. Parrot's getting to work on her cut, and I planned to have my ring on her finger soon," I explained, and she pressed up to kiss my cheek.

"Smart man. I'll let myself out but text me later about how's she doing, and if she gets sick again, I'm sending Doc over to check on her."

Doc was the brother who took care of Sadie when she survived her attack. For years, he and Piper were the only two who knew what Sadie endured, and I trusted him with Grace.

"I'll let you know," I promised and walked her to the door.

Returning to the couch, I placed Grace's ginger ale on the table and sat down gently next to her. I brushed her hair away from her forehead, and she cracked her eyes open to look at me.

"Can I get you anything?" I asked, and she shook her head with small movements.

"If I could get my head to stop hurting, I'll be fine," she replied, and her voice was flat and dull.

"Do you want to stay here, or would you be more comfortable in the bed?" I asked, and she pushed herself up to sit on the couch.

"Bed, please."

I helped her stand and guided her to the bedroom before pulling back the covers. She kicked her shoes off and pulled her jeans down her legs as she sat on the edge of the bed. I could see she was struggling.

"Let me help you, baby." I kneeled in front of her and removed her pants, leaving her socks on. "Bra?"

"Off, please."

I reached under the back of her shirt and unhooked the clasp of her bra, trying to remember how I'd seen it done and getting confused. She took over and reached into the arm holes, pulling one strap down at a time before reaching under the front and pulling the bra out. I took it from her and helped her to lay down.

The sun was shining into the windows, and I pushed the button to close the drapes, casting the room into darkness. She closed her eyes, and I pulled the covers over her. A smile graced her beautiful face, and I kissed her head gently, whispering, "Get some sleep, and I'll check on you in a while. If you need anything, just call for me."

"Thank you," she whispered, and I walked to the doorway, watching her as she rolled onto her other side and nestled into the bed.

Once I was sure she was okay, I walked to the back deck and called James. The app was running in the background as I waited for James to pick up so I could watch Grace as she slept. If she made one move to need me, I wanted to be aware. On the fourth ring, James answered the phone.

"What's up, Skid?" he asked, and I clenched my hands together.

"Did you go looking for Grace today?" I asked, hearing the anger in my voice.

If he went behind my back to gather information, he and I would have a problem. "Hell no. Amaya was with her father, and I walked over to get her. We bumped into Sadie and Grace, and Amaya had no idea of our conversation. I wouldn't do that to you or Grace. Why? Did she say something?"

"She got sick shortly after she saw you, and I wanted to check," I responded, happy my gut was wrong about everything. Maybe, she was coming down with a bug, and I would nurse her back to health.

"Is she okay? Can we do anything?" he inquired.

"No man, I appreciate it, but I think she must have caught a bug. I'm going to let her rest and check on her later."

"Let me know how's she doing."

"Will do," I answered and disconnected the call.

Sitting on the back porch, I watched Grace sleep, praying she didn't have a nightmare as I continued to dig into the Ringmans. Two hours later, I was tired of looking into those assholes' lives and went to look in on Grace. She was sleeping peacefully, and I closed the door behind me. Not wanting to disturb her, I laid down on the couch in the living room and fell asleep, missing having Grace in my arms.

Chapter 20

Grace

Pierce Lake was beautiful, and Pierce Bluff seemed like the kind of town you wanted to raise a family in. Sadie and I were enjoying the peaceful view, talking, and getting to know each other when a man approached us. The woman with him was stunningly beautiful, and when he spoke to Sadie, I recognized who he was from Dalton's explanation.

James Callahan and his wife, Amaya, were nice people who seemed to be madly in love with each other. We visited for a few minutes, and before we separated, Amaya made an offer that, at face value, seemed nice.

"We'd love for you and Skid to join us for dinner sometime. We can invite Devlin and Elise, and maybe Hayden can take a night off so he and James's sister, Aubrey, can make it too." she said, and I smiled at her.

A couples dinner party sounded nice, and I replied, "That would be great. Just let Dalton know, and I'll make dessert."

"She makes amazing pies. I had one this morning, and I've been begging all day for the recipe," Sadie joked, and James looked at me with a smile.

"If Sadie says it's delicious, I need to try it. I'll make the arrangements with Skid," he remarked before he led Amaya down the path toward the front of the lake entrance.

Sadie and I were leaving the park a little while later, and as we walked up the path, I began to think about something Amaya said, something that kept scratching at my memories. The more we walked, the more it scratched until finally, it all clicked. The need to throw up hit me in the face, and I ran behind a tree, not wanting anyone to see me get sick.

Sadie checked on me, and I played it off as an impending migraine, when in reality, my past was crashing down around me, and I felt like I'd been set up. I couldn't figure out why or how, but something wasn't connecting. The closer we got to Dalton's house, the more my head pounded until I felt like it would explode.

I wanted to yell and scream. I wanted to find out what I was missing, but I couldn't do anything other than let the memories overwhelm me, pushing more and more pain into my heart and head. Feeling Dalton kiss me after he tucked me into bed almost broke me, but I rolled over, letting sleep drag me under.

I woke up in the middle of the night and rolled over to find I was alone in bed. Sitting up, I looked around and saw I was alone in the room, so I silently slipped from the bed and walked into the living room. Dalton was asleep on the couch with a blanket pulled up to his stomach, leaving his chest full of tattoos exposed.

Watching him sleep, I thought about what happened yesterday, looking to connect everything before I confronted him. I don't know if he lied or not, and until I had a better idea, I wouldn't go on the defensive. Eddie taught me through the years not to immediately fly off the handle, so I took a few deep cleansing breaths and turned away from the living room.

My eyes tracked upstairs, and with deliberate steps, I climbed to the second floor. The closer I got to the closed office door, the more my heart pounded against my chest. If I was wrong, I could potentially destroy the relationship I had with Dalton over my lack of trust, but if I was right, it was already over. If it was even real to begin with.

Reaching my hand out to the knob, I listened to see if he had woken up before testing the handle to see if it was locked. I closed my eyes and turned, finding the door unlocked and the office empty. Walking inside, I closed the door behind me and turned on the light on the desk. The room was mostly dark, and I didn't want to draw attention to my snooping.

I sat down at the large desk and looked at the bank of monitors, hanging silently on the wall. The computer on the desk was turned off, and I pressed the button, waiting for it to come alive. There was a security question that I didn't know the answer to, and I grew frustrated. He worked cyber security, and I barely knew how to use computers, so the chances of me cracking the code were slim.

I opened the desk drawer and reached around inside, hoping to find a password or hint. A noise from downstairs halted my movements, and I listened for footsteps approaching. After a few minutes of tense silence, I reached deeper, not knowing what I was looking for. My gut was saying there was more to this, to us, than I was led to believe.

Looking through scraps of paper, I went through each drawer and began to think I was going crazy. When my hand brushed against something small in the back, I grasped it and discovered an envelope containing an old thumb drive. It was outdated and out of place in the state-of-the-art office, and I held it up, wondering what could be on it. I couldn't find anything to help me unlock the computer, and I questioned if the thumb drive would even open without the password.

Worried I was about to blow up the best relationship that I would ever have, I pushed it into the side of the computer, waiting for it to load. The computer made some small noises as I stood from the chair. I rubbed my eyes as my feet moved me back and forth across the office with the silent monitors taunting me.

The memories of Kevin and the twisted games he played filled me with warring emotions, and I started looking for ways I was sabotaging my relationship with Dalton. Was I looking for something wrong so I could push him away before he hurt me? Were the mind games from my past ruining my chance at a future? Shame and anger filled me, and I couldn't process what was real and what wasn't.

A small ding from the computer sounded into the silent room, sounding much louder than it actually was. I peeked out the office door and heard no movement from Dalton, so I closed the door and walked back to the desk. Closing my eyes briefly, I debated on not looking at whatever was on the drive.

Not being able to push that nagging feeling away and letting the little voices in my head win, I opened my eyes and looked at the screen. The drive was open and had six files inside. Moving the cursor to the first file, I double clicked and waited for it to open.

My hands trembled the moment I saw what was on it, and when I heard his voice coming through the small speaker, I threw up in the trash can as tears rolled down my face.

"Is that how Tiffany taught you to say thank you?"

I didn't need to see what else was on the thumb drive, having lived through those exact words and knowing what came next. Yanking it from the computer, the images stopped playing, and I was once again alone in silence. I couldn't stop the pain and sheer betrayal that filled me when I realized how everything connected.

I was a fool for ever trusting Dalton, and now realized he never cared about me. He only cared about the secrets I held inside. Why would he make me fall in love with him when his intentions obviously weren't pure?

Taking the thumb drive, I placed it back in the envelope before tucking it back into the desk. Sitting in the empty office, the tears dried up as my eyes lifted to the closed door. I needed to get out of here and back to my real life of solitude. It will take years for me ever to trust anyone again, and I learned my lesson.

Women like me never find happiness. We were meant to be by ourselves.

I closed the computer and let myself out of the office, the anger inside building higher with every step I took. Seeing him sleeping so soundly, knowing he used me, killed a piece of me that no one would ever touch again. As quiet as I could, I descended the stairs and walked back into the bedroom. The unmade bed taunted me, and I turned away from the memories of him holding me, chasing the nightmares away. It was another ploy to somehow hurt me, and I refused to let his words deter me from leaving.

It was better to be alone, than to live without knowing if someone's love for you was real or another manipulation.

My duffle bag was on the floor of the closet, and I grabbed it, being as quiet as possible while I gathered the few items of clothes I had brought. I should have known I was meant to be temporary and was happy I didn't bring too much with me. I would have to walk out of here until I could get an Uber to take me to the nearest airport.

My clothes from yesterday would have to suffice for me to wear, so I picked them up and went into the bathroom to change. The woman looking back at me in the mirror had sadness in her eyes, and I felt my heart shattering into dust. Grasping my chest, I fought the physical pain of his betrayal and took one minute to mourn what could have been, but never was. When I met my gaze in the reflection a second time, the tears were gone and in their place was a rage unlike anything I'd ever felt.

I splashed some water on my face and pulled my hair up as I checked that I had all my stuff. After verifying I was all packed up, I pulled the small duffle onto my shoulder and walked to the bedroom door. A small part of me didn't want to leave, and I told that stupid bitch to shut up as I opened the door and quietly walked into the living room.

Dalton was still asleep on the couch, and I scooted around him, afraid he would try and stop me. I knew he would, just to cover his lies, and I couldn't hear his hurtful words of love and forever, knowing they weren't true. I should leave him a note to let him know I'm aware of his bullshit but decided that would burn time that I could use to get as far away from Port-still as possible.

The back door was my way out, and I slowly turned the knob and kept peeking into the living room as I scooted through the small opening and silently closed the door. Every step down the stairs was painful as I kept to the shadows. Walking in the tree line, I managed to avoid all the motion-activated lights, and as I got to the edge of the driveway, I gave the house one final glance.

Wiping a tear from my cheek, I turned and began walking down the road. It was almost sun-up when I got to the edge of Portstill, and I ordered a car to pick me up from the side of a gas station. Staying in the shadows of the building, I watched for my ride. The sound of a motorcycle pulling into the station filled me with panic, and I poked my head out to see a Death Hound filling his bike up at the pump. I didn't recognize him, but he was one of Dalton's brothers, which meant he could be a threat to me.

I didn't know if Dalton was even aware I was gone, but I couldn't take any chances, so I stayed pushed to the side of the building, listening for him to leave, and checking on my ride. The app said it was two minutes away, and I prayed the Death Hound left before they pulled in. My breathing was accelerating, and I was afraid I was going to pass out as I watched and waited.

The bike cranked up a moment later, and he pulled away as I watched my ride turn into the parking lot. Confirming he was gone, I ran to the car and quickly got into the backseat. The driver wanted to make small talk as he drove me the hour to Memphis, but I kept my words inside and my eyes out the side window, watching Tennessee pass by. Just after eight, my phone rang, and I looked down to see Dalton was calling me.

I declined the call and placed the phone in my lap. Immediately it rang again, and I silenced it before turning it to 'do not disturb'. When the driver pulled into the airport, I opened the door and slung my duffle over my shoulder, muttering a thank you before briskly walking into the airport. There were few people flying this early on a Thursday, and I walked to the counter to purchase a ticket.

"Good morning. I need a ticket to Atlanta, please. One way, first flight, if possible," I requested and looked over my shoulder to make sure I wasn't being followed.

The gate agent was a nice older lady, and she leaned in as she typed, her lips barely moving. "Are you okay?"

I turned back to see her worried eyes and felt kindness coming from her. I nodded and fought the tremble in my chin. "I found out my boyfriend lied to me about everything, and I just want to go home and forget about him."

"Honey, men are liars, and I completely understand. Let me see what I can do about getting you back home," she explained and turned her attention to the computer. "Here we go. There is one seat left, and I claimed it for you as a family emergency. The gate agent will hold the flight, but you're going to have to run to make it."

I went to hand her my credit card, but she held her hand up. "I used some of my employee miles and comped your flight. I hope you get home safe, and don't worry, sweetheart. You're young. You'll find a good man who treats you right. You just have to believe."

The tears welled in my eyes as she handed me the ticket, and she stepped out from behind the counter to hug me. Touches from strangers usually made me defensive, but she reminded me of what a grandmother should be, so I took her embrace, hugging her back.

"Thank you," I whispered, and she released me with a smile.

"Go, darling. You have ten minutes before they close the gates." She smiled at me, and I nodded before gripping my bag and taking off in a jog.

The gate was on the other side of the terminal, and I dodged early morning travelers as I ran for my escape. How did it come to this again, running from liars and trying to find my heart inside the turmoil?

The gate agent lifted her head to me as I ran up and handed her my ticket. She looked at it and me before ushering me inside the plane and shutting the door. After finding my seat, I stowed my bag at my feet and secured myself for the flight. As we taxied down the runway, I felt relief and overwhelming sadness.

He gave me something I always wanted, but it wasn't real. He showed me how to love, but it was a lie. He used me, and I would never forgive him or myself for the cowardly act.

Vowing a life of solitude would be better than the pain, I rested my head on the window and let my gaze stay locked on the horizon as thoughts of what might have been flashed like a cruel movie in my mind. Landing in Atlanta, I didn't feel any safer. As hard as I tried, I couldn't stop the thoughts from swirling in my head. As I walked away from the gate, something terrifying crossed my mind, and I stumbled over my own feet, catching myself against a pillar. A passenger tried to help me, and I flinched away from their touch as the ramifications of the terror overtook me.

What if The Community was somehow involved? Were they looking for me? Were they going to make me fulfill the promise I made to them all those years ago? Was he looking for me?

I saw a sign for the ladies' room up ahead, and I tugged my bag to my chest as I hurried down the corridor and into a stall. Locking the door, I turned my phone on, and it immediately started chiming, showing dozens of missed calls, voice mails, and texts from Dalton. As tempted as I was to read them, I couldn't trust anything he said.

The phone started to ring in my hand, and I declined the call quickly before dialing the one number I could remember. A number repeated over and over to ensure it wasn't forgotten. The number Kelly made me learn ten years ago when I ran away from everything I thought my life was going to be, and straight into the unknown.

A voice answered the phone, and I spoke a single word. "Succor."

"Are you safe?" the woman on the line asked, and I nodded as tears built in my eyes.

"Yes."

"Do you need a pick-up?"

"Yes."

"Location."

"Airport."

"Name?"

Exhaling, I picked a name far from my own. "Vengeance."

"Twenty minutes, blue SUV with a black stripe down the side."

The call disconnected, and I turned it off, remembering the protocol and moving on autopilot. I used the bathroom and washed my hands before walking back into the airport. There was a gift shop up ahead, and I reached into my duffle, pulled out the twenty-dollar bill from my wallet, and slapped it down for a hat without looking back. I tucked my wild hair into the hat and kept moving. The airport was massive, and I stayed away from the underground trains, choosing to walk from terminal to terminal until I could see the signs for passenger pick-up.

I was safe inside, and the thought of walking out alone, not knowing who or what may be looking for me, had me on edge. My eyes swung side to side as I walked, and I tried not to make eye contact with anyone. The less anyone remembered about me, the better. The bright sun was shining through the doors leading to the pick-up area, and I pushed the door open to the humid Georgia air.

Countless vehicles parked at the curb briefly with a passenger jumping out or hailing their ride, and I looked for the described vehicle. I saw a blue SUV parked down the sidewalk, farther away from the doors, and I hiked my duffle onto my shoulder and walked toward it. The black stripe down the side came into view, and I stepped to the passenger's door.

The window rolled down, and the woman behind the wheel asked. "Name?"

"Vengeance," I replied, and she pressed a button, unlocking the door.

I got inside and stowed my bag on the floorboard as she pulled into the line of traffic and merged onto the highway. She didn't speak as we traversed the interstate, and even though I didn't know who she was, I knew one thing for sure. I was safe.

Chapter 21

Skid

I woke up to the sun shining into the living room, and I listened to hear if Grace was awake. She didn't need me during the night, and I stood from the couch, stretching my sore back. I picked up my phone to check the app and saw it was dead. Silently cursing, I plugged it in and walked to the bedroom to check on Grace.

The door was closed, and I pushed it open gently, sticking my head inside. The room was dark, and I stepped inside, letting the light from the living room filter in as I stepped to the bed. She wasn't there, and I moved to the bathroom to see immediately she wasn't inside. Realizing she must be on the back porch and worried why she didn't wake me, I walked through the kitchen and opened the back door. Grace wasn't outside, and I started to panic.

Running back into the bedroom, I opened the curtains and let the room fill with light as I tore open the closet door. Her duffle bag was gone, and when I looked in the bathroom, all her personal items were missing.

"Son of a bitch," I yelled and ran to grab my phone.

It had enough charge for me to turn it on, and I snatched the plug from the wall and ran upstairs to my office. The whole house had cameras installed, and I needed to find out where she went. Sitting at my desk, I plugged the phone back in, and the screen came to life as it connected to the network.

Dialing Grace's number and putting the speaker on, I logged onto my security system and waited for it to show secure. Her phone rang once, and the call was sent to voice mail. My laptop pinged, and I quickly brought the camera to my bedroom and dialed it back until I found Grace sleeping.

Dialing her number again, it went straight to voicemail, and I knew something was wrong. Needing backup, I dialed the first person who could help.

"Skid, what's shaking, brother?" Gunner asked as my eyes stayed locked on Grace's sleeping form as I advanced the recording to figure out what happened to her and when.

"Grace is gone. I need the brothers to hit the streets and find her," I barked and could hear loud shuffling in the background.

"What do you mean she's missing? Where the fuck is she?" he asked, and I stopped the recording when I saw her sit up from the bed.

"I'm going through my cameras now, but I woke up to find her and all her stuff gone. No note, and her phone goes straight to voicemail. I need to find her now," I yelled as I watched her walk into the living room and watch me from across the room.

Her eyes were sad, and I could see the tilt in her head, her tell of contemplation.

"I'll get the brothers headed out now, but you need to call the madman. Whatever is going on isn't club business, but she's your woman, so I'm making it our business. Tell him not to cross me, and he better fix whatever he fucking broke, or so help me god." I understand his anger at Devlin but now wasn't the time.

"Just find her," I barked and hung up the phone as I watched her climb the stairs to my office.

Dialing Devlin's number, it rang twice before he answered. "Skid, how's Grace feeling today? James said she was sick yesterday."

"She's fucking gone, Devlin," I hollered as I watched her try to turn on my computer and begin to look through my desk. "Oh, fuck."

There wasn't sensitive information left lying around, so I wasn't worried about Devlin's secrets. It was mine that I feared she discovered.

"What's going on, Dalton. Talk to me," he returned forcefully as I paused the video.

"I'm linking you into my camera system," I explained, and a moment later, I could see he had a visual. Pressing play, I watched as Grace reached deep into a drawer and, with horror, saw she pulled out the envelope with Aubrey's thumb drive inside. Opening the envelope, she held up the thumb drive, and I heard Devlin yell.

"Motherfucker. How could you leave that lying around for her to find?"

"I didn't, asshole. It was behind a locked door in my office. I don't know what possessed her to come in here last night," I reasoned as the image of Grace on the camera showed her pacing the office with the drive in my laptop.

I didn't want to see, but I couldn't look away as Grace sat down behind my desk. She opened a file on the drive, and I could see the raw pain in her eyes, and the video began to play. When she threw up in the trashcan, I cursed into the room as I flipped my chair onto the floor and punched a hole in the wall behind my desk.

"Calm the fuck down and let's figure out where she went so we can find her and fix this epic fuckup," he urged with compassion in his voice.

My heart broke as we watched Grace return the drive to my desk and leave the room. I reached inside and pulled out the envelope, pissed I didn't destroy it when I had the chance. In less than ten minutes, I watched Grace pack everything she brought with her, walk past me in the living room, and out the back door.

"How did I not hear her leave?" I asked, not expecting an answer.

"You can't blame yourself, and once we find her, we'll explain everything to her. I promise, Dalton, we'll make this right," he explained, and I didn't believe him.

Grace would never forgive me for my betrayal. I should have told her more about why I came into the bar last month. Instead, I tried to win her heart and push the truth as far away from her as possible. I was selfish and didn't want to tarnish myself in her eyes. It was wrong of me, and I would spend a lifetime making up for it, if I can find her and convince her to give me a chance.

"Did you install the software on her phone so we can track it?" Devlin asked, and I collapsed onto the couch in my office.

"No. I didn't want to invade her privacy like that and thought there wouldn't be a need. Damn it!" I yelled, and Devlin's dark voice came through the phone.

"Come to the office here. It's time to use everything Callahan Cyber has to find your woman. You have my word—she will be in your arms soon."

The phone disconnected, and I rubbed my eyes, hoping to keep from tearing up. The last time I cried was the night Devlin saved Jacob, sending Sadie into Gunner's arms. If I couldn't find Grace and fix this, I feared I would live in the darkness forever.

After changing into a pair of jeans, a T-shirt, and my boots, I pulled my cut on and sent Gunner a text. He said there were a few brothers on the road early this morning, and he's checking with them to see if Grace was spotted. I hopped onto my bike and drove well over the speed limit from my cabin into Pierce Bluff. The drive that normally took twenty minutes I completed in just under thirteen.

I pulled into the underground garage and walked to the elevator. Pushing the button for the office floor, I climbed into the suffocating box and clenched my hands, needing to get rid of this nervous energy. Grace was out there alone, hurt, scared, and probably angry.

The door opened, and I stepped into the small entrance before punching my code into the secure lock. Inside, twenty monitors lined one wall, and all the windows had been blacked out, making external light or someone's ability to spy impossible. Devlin was typing away on his laptop, and I looked for James.

"He just ran upstairs to grab something, but he'll be right back," Devlin explained without missing a keystroke.

I opened my computer and asked, "How far have you gotten?"

"She ordered an Uber from the gas station just outside Portstill, and it took her to the Memphis airport."

"Fuck. She's running. Do we have eyes inside the airport?" I inquired.

The door opened, and James walked in. "Got it."

Devlin looked at me and smirked. "We do now."

James sat at his computer, and a minute later, the cameras inside the airport came to life on the screens in front of us. With the information we had on what time Uber said she arrived at the airport, James was able to find Grace being dropped off. He used our facial recognition software and let the system track her. She approached a ticket counter and glanced over her shoulder before speaking with the agent. I couldn't see where she was flying to as the agent handed her a ticket and pulled her into a hug.

"Where are you going, Grace?" I asked as she took off in a jog away from the counter.

Pain was etched on her face, and I was the cause of it. I hurt her, and I prayed I would get the chance to make it right. She may never forgive me, and I'll have to live with that, but I would let her know there was no need to run. Not from me. Not ever.

She ducked and dodged passengers as she ran through the airport, and when I saw the destination, I felt slightly better but not much.

"She's in Atlanta. Now we need to get into their system and see what her next move was," James explained as he dropped the Memphis cameras and began to enter Atlanta's. I walked to the sliding glass door and glanced at Devlin.

"I need to call Eddie. Maybe he'll know where she went."

"We'll find her."

James gave me a look over the monitor that said he wasn't going to stop until we all knew Grace was okay and it gave me some reassurance. His desire to protect Aubrey was as strong as mine to protect Grace, and it sucked we were safeguarding them from the same dead predator.

I dialed Eddie's number and put the phone to my ear as it rang. "Skid. How's my Grace doing?"

I ran my hands through my hair and sat down hard onto a chair on the covered patio. "Eddie, I fucked up, and Grace took off."

"What the hell happened? And where is Grace?" he yelled, and I exhaled, knowing whatever ass chewing or ass kicking he was going to give me, I deserved.

Not knowing how much he knew of her past, I asked, "What do you know about Grace's years in foster care?"

"Why do you want to know that?" His tone was gruff, and I hated to push, but I was going to.

"Are you aware of what she endured?"

"Are you?"

"Eddie, I don't even know where to start, so I'll just give you an overview," I stated.

"No, asshole. You're going to start at the very fucking beginning and tell me everything so I can find Grace. Now start fucking talking, Dalton," he yelled and I started from the beginning.

After a few minutes of me explaining what led up to now, I sat silently waiting for him to respond. If he wasn't on my side, I didn't stand a chance with Grace. I gave him one final truth, so he knew I was for real in the depths of my need to protect Grace.

"And I know Grace's dad was your half-brother, and you were raised separately. I know she's your niece."

"Her *father* was my half-brother," he spat through the phone. "Don't ever call him her dad. That word is poison, and he doesn't deserve the association."

"My suspicions are right, aren't they?" I muttered, and he clicked his tongue.

"It's worse than whatever you image, Skid. It took years for her to tell me, and I know for a fact, I don't know the half of it. She lived for years with someone who took her love and perverted it for his own sick pleasure. All with the guise of teaching and loving her to be better. When all he did was destroy her ability to trust her own judgment. It was warped so badly that she doesn't believe love is real. Until you, and you fucked that up beyond repair."

"Help me," I begged, my voice breaking as a tear fell down my face.

I could hear his breathing through the phone and covered my eyes from the sun as I rested my head against the back of the chair.

"I'm going to make a few phone calls, but I can't promise anything. If Grace feels the need to protect herself, she will do anything, including going underground, to achieve it."

"Please," I begged one final time and cleared my throat. "Please let me know if you find out anything, and I'll do the same."

"Take care, Dalton," Eddie responded, and the call was terminated.

Sending a quick text to Gunner to call off the search, I spoke into the air. "Fuck, fuck, fuck." Opening the door, I walked back into the freezing cold room.

I could see the program running, trying to find Grace in the heavy foot traffic inside the Atlanta airport. Devlin stood and walked to me. "I need your phone."

Curious but trusting, I unlocked the phone and handed it to him. He plugged it into his computer, and a minute later, he had the last phone call I made to Grace pulled up. This was one last one she sent to voicemail, and I had no idea what he was doing.

"Here she is," James said, and I turned away from Devlin and looked up at the monitors. "She's moving fast and damn. Did you see that? Something has her terrified, and I don't think it's you, Skid."

I could see the sudden change in her, and when she tripped into the pillar, I clenched my hands in rage. She was in and out of the bathroom in under five minutes, and we watched her speed walk through the airport, hiding herself under a hat and keeping her head down. Outside, she started looking for something, and James focused two different cameras on her as she walked to a blue SUV parked at the end of the long sidewalk.

The tag number was visible, and I stood silent as she climbed inside with an unknown woman and pulled into traffic. My chin fell to my chest, and I felt her slipping through my fingers. Turning to the nearest wall, I punched the sheetrock repeatedly, and someone grabbed me from behind, stopping my violent outburst.

My wild eyes met Devlin's, and he gripped into my shoulders as he forced me to look at him. "You need to keep your cool. I've got a track on her now, and as soon as she stops moving, I can lock onto her location. I need you to calm the fuck down and be ready to move."

"How can I let her be out there alone? She's scared, and I hurt her," I yelled, slamming my fist into my chest. "How can she forgive me?" I asked and fell to my knees, feeling my heart being ripped from my body.

James stood and joined Devlin as they helped me from the floor. I'd never been weak a day in my life, but feeling Grace's love, then losing it, was killing me. They walked me to the couch, and James kneeled in front of me.

"Dalton, I've known you going on a decade, and in that entire time, I've never seen you as settled as you are with Grace. I know your first instinct is to save the day, and countless times in the past, that's what you've done. For us. For your club. For your family. It's time you let us save you. Let us find Grace, and we'll make her understand. Your intentions have always been to protect her, and she will forgive you."

"How can you be sure?" I croaked out, shaking my head.

"Because I know love, and that woman I met yesterday in the park, she loves you. She just needs to remember you're on her side. Trauma can cloud someone's perception when they're confronted with demons from the past. It's your job now to let her speak her truth and hold her until she's whole again."

I looked to see Devlin on his computer, and when he looked at me across the room, his smile turned devious as he explained, "I know where Grace is, and I know how to get her to listen. Get ready, boys. We're heading to Atlanta."

Chapter 22

Grace

The room looked the same as I walked inside. A decade ago, I walked into the building unsure and untrusting. Today, I walked in only slightly better than before. My heart physically hurt from Dalton's betrayal, and as I moved toward the person who taught me confidence, I felt some of the pain lessen. He looked across the desk, and one side of his mouth lifted into a smile.

That was as much affection as I was going to get, and when I stopped in front of him, I suddenly felt out of place, like this wasn't where I was supposed to be. I wasn't scared and didn't fear for my safety, but I knew instantly I shouldn't have run.

His appraising eyes locked with mine as my internal debate raged on, and when the realization, I'd made a mistake fully dawned on me, he finally spoke. "Figure it out?"

Sighing, I sat down on the chair in front of his desk and nodded. "I shouldn't have run," I rationalized, and sat back in the chair.

Bringing his hand up to his chin, he rubbed the bottom contemplatively before he asked. "Then why did you?"

The images from the thumb drive played in my head, and I squeezed my eyes shut, pushing his words out of my head. "I was scared."

Leaning over the desk, Rhys softened his voice as he inquired, "What scared you, Grace? I need to know if there is a threat to you."

I shook my head, feeling the anger building in him as I explained. "There isn't a threat. I just think . . . I don't know what to think. But I know he's no threat to me."

"Grace. I don't have time to dance around, so I'm going to need you to tell me everything. Who or what has you sitting in my office? Not that I'm not happy to see you, but for you to call me after all these years, I need the whole story."

Rhys was still a mystery to me, but from the first moment I met him ten years ago, I knew he would protect me. He had money. That was obvious from the luxury house surrounded by acres of dense forest and tall gates tucked away in the northern outskirts of Atlanta. What he did, who he was, and why he saved me were never questions I asked, and he never explained.

All I knew was my friend Kelly connected me with him, and when I ran away from Kevin and Connie's, Rhys gave me a home. There was something about him that made answering the painful questions easy. After a few weeks of gently coaxing the truth from me, he broke the dam inside me, forcing the shame to the surface, then began to build me back up. He made me confront the pain and betrayal and taught me that I was manipulated by someone I should have been able to trust.

Then he encouraged me to tap into my anger.

Four months later, he helped me move onto the next chapter of my life, leading me straight to Eddie. Being back here made me feel like a failure, and I hung my head as I explained what drove me back to him.

"I met a guy back home and decided to take a chance when he asked me to go to Tennessee to meet his family. Yesterday something started scratching at an old memory, and I couldn't seem to connect all the dots." I paused, and he patiently waited for me to continue. "I snooped, which I know was wrong, but I found a thumb drive inside his desk, and when I played it, I . . . he . . ."

A single tear fell down my cheek, and I swiped it away, mad that Kevin Ringman was still haunting me. "I always worried Kevin did it to someone else and on the drive was proof. I panicked, not knowing if it was one of them or . . ."

"Grace, who's the guy?" Rhys asked, his tone menacing and dark.

"I don't want you to hurt him, Rhys. He never hurt me." I tried to make him understand, and he stood from his desk.

"No, Grace. He did hurt you by having some connection to all of that and not being honest about it. He was wrong. He should have told you from the start." There was a long pause as I thought about his statement before he asked. "Why don't you want me to hurt him?" Rhys's normally brown eyes were turning almost black, and my heart beat faster, worried for Dalton.

My voice broke when I defended, "Because I love him."

"Then, for now, I promise I won't hurt him, but I need to know who he is and why he had something so vile in his possession. I need to know why he sought you out, and then I'll determine if he needs to be dealt with."

I gripped onto his forearm as I stood from the chair. "I won't tell you anything if there's a chance you may go after him. No matter what he had possession of, I know he's a good man and not a part of all that."

Rhys looked down at my hand on his arm and brought his eyes to mine. He taught me not to back down when faced with adversity, and if that meant I had to stand up to him, then I would. No matter what, Dalton didn't deserve to be hurt. At least I didn't think he did.

"He promises," a small voice said, and I turned to see a beautiful woman with long blonde hair and bright green eyes walking into the room through a side door.

She walked up to Rhys, and the softness in his look to her told me she was someone important to him. I'd never seen him soft with anyone, me included, so to see him so pliable with her was a shock. Turning to me, the small woman stuck her hand out and introduced herself to me.

"I'm Regan. I'm Rhys's sister."

"Grace," I replied, and her eyes turned kind to me.

"He's mentioned you in the past. It's nice to finally meet you."

Rhys looked at both of us and offered a small smile as he walked around the back of his desk and sat down. Looking at me, he spoke, his words direct. "Grace, please tell me what I need to know, and I'll promise to speak with you before I do anything to your friend."

Regan leaned over and whispered to me, "I promise, his bark is worse than his bite." Turning to look at her brother, she said, "I'm going to start lunch while you talk. Grace, will you be joining us?"

Her eyes swung back to me, and I looked to Rhys for instruction. I knew I didn't need his protection from Dalton, but he was the first place I thought to come, and now I'm worried I made a mistake. He nodded, and I looked at Regan. "I'd love to join you. Thank you."

She walked to the door and gave her brother one final look before leaving us alone. I wanted to ask questions but knew it wasn't my business.

"Grace, tell me," Rhys instructed, and I leaned back in the chair, crossing my arms over my chest.

"His name is Dalton, and he's a member of the Death Hounds," I started and explained how we met, how he saved me, and everything, except the dirty parts, about our time together. Toward the end of the story, I looked up from my lap and met Rhys's deep brown eyes. He was fighting a smile, and I was confused by his sudden change in demeanor.

"Did you ever meet anyone outside of his club?"

Nodding, I replied, "I met one of his bosses yesterday. His name was James Callahan."

Rhys began to laugh and shook his head as he stood. Walking to me, he kneeled and took my hands into his. "I promise I'll get to the bottom of everything. Why don't we head over to the gym and get some mat time in before Regan finds us for lunch."

"I . . . I guess." Standing, I followed him out of the room and down the long hallway leading to the gym.

His sudden attitude change gave me whiplash as I followed him into the familiar gym. This was the room where Rhys taught me to channel my feelings into actions, ensuring no one ever took advantage of me again. Not knowing or even understanding why he was suddenly okay with everything that caused me to run, I picked up a pair of sparing gloves and looked at him.

"Let's get started. I have a feeling we will be interrupted very soon." His voice had a lilt to it, and I looked at him with confusion as I slipped the gloves on.

For the next two hours, we worked through the stances and katas that he taught me, and when I started throwing punches into the heavy bag, I began to feel like myself. I was in control again, no longer spiraling and the longer I punched, the worse I felt about abandoning Dalton without giving him the chance to explain.

Rhys had left me alone half an hour ago, and when I threw the last swing into the bag, I felt the fatigue in my arms. Flinging the gloves onto the floor, I sat down on the mat, fighting to catch my breath. A noise from over my shoulder drew my attention, and standing in the doorway was a man I'd never seen before.

He was intimidating and sexy in a way that scared me. Black hair and beard, dark eyes, and a devious smile graced his handsome face as he walked into the gym. He was wearing black military pants with a tight-fitting shirt and an empty weapons holster on his hip. If he was here, Rhys was aware and didn't think I was in danger, so I stood from the floor and pushed my sweaty hair off my face as he approached.

Stopping ten feet from me, he smiled and spoke, his voice deep and refined. "It's nice to finally put a face to the name, Grace. I'm Devlin Callahan."

Those were the last words I remember before my world turned dark, but the last thing I remember was the floor quickly approaching as I let the darkness drag me under.

"Welcome to my home, Grace," the tall man with black hair and dark brown eyes said as I walked into the house.

Kelly made all the arrangements for me to stay here, but I was still confused about where here was and who this man was. As I followed him, I hugged my small duffle to my chest and glanced left and right, looking to see if anyone else was around. A woman in a uniform pushed a cleaning cart and smiled warmly at me as we walked past her. The man nodded to her, and I forced a smile as we passed.

I ran away yesterday, leaving behind everything I was taught to want and now realized was a lie. A sick manipulation for another's sick desire, and with every step I took, I felt more stupid and naïve than the last.

"How could I have been so stupid?" I muttered, almost to myself, and the tall man turned to me with kindness in his eyes.

"You weren't stupid, you were young, and someone exploited you. There's nothing to be ashamed about. By coming here, you've already proven you're strong, and if you trust me to guide you through the next phase, I promise, I'll give you all the weapons you need never to fall prey to someone again." I looked up at him through tears. "Do you trust me, Grace?"

I didn't know him, but Kelly trusted him, so I would too. She's the only person who knew what happened and she's the only person who ever liked me, for me. Not for what I could do for them.

"I guess," I replied, and he nodded.

"That's all I need for now. Follow me."

There was a woman waiting when we got to a small bedroom on the second floor. She appeared to be in her late fifties or older, and she walked up to me with a smile. "I'm Mariella, and I'm going to help you get comfortable."

The man waited at the doorway and explained. "Mariella will take care of all your needs until you feel ready to talk. You're safe now, Grace. Please make yourself at home."

With those words, he left, and I looked at the kind woman for guidance. She took me by the hand and walked me to the bed. I sat down, and she took my duffle from me, setting it on the bed beside me.

"Who is he?" I asked, not expecting an answer.

"His name is Rhys Weston, and he's going to help you," she explained.

"How do you know he can help me?" I asked, and she stood from the bed.

Just as she reached the doorway, she turned to look at me. "He's a good man. Trust him, Grace."

She left me alone, and for the next three days, I had meals and snacks delivered to my room, but I didn't step foot out of it. I felt safe inside, but on the morning of the fourth day, Rhys knocked on the door.

"Are you ready to get started?"

Those words were my redemption, my salvation, and my future rolled together, and I wouldn't pass up the opportunity he was offering.

I blinked, seeing Rhys's familiar office as I woke up. Not sure what happened, I tried to push up from my position on the couch, only to have Rhys enter my field of vision. "Are you okay, Grace?"

Nodding, I sat up and felt my head swimming as I tried to remember what made me pass out. Visions of a dark man dressed in black flooded my brain, and I swung my gaze around the room, seeing we were alone.

"I must have imagined him," I said. "How did I get here?"

"Grace, honey. I think it's time we talked."

"Are you mad at me?" I asked and felt my chin tremble.

Rhys and Mariella had saved me all those years ago and if I'd somehow done something to upset them. I wanted to fix it.

"Why would I be mad at you? You've done nothing wrong." I shrugged and went to stand when Rhys placed his hand on my shoulder, encouraging me to stay seated. He squatted in front of me and took my hands into his. "I need you to do me a favor. Can you do that?"

"Of course. What's the favor?" I asked, and his gaze glanced over my shoulder before returning to mine.

"I need you to trust me the same way you did when you came here all those years ago. I need you to know I'd kill anyone who tried to hurt you. Do you believe that?"

"Yes."

"Then let that trust be at the front of your mind, okay?" he asked, and I nodded, biting into my lip with worry.

A door opening behind me made me want to turn, and Rhys kept his hands in mine and whispered, "Trust."

Footsteps sounded behind me, and I kept my eyes locked on Rhys as whoever it was entered the room from the rear. As they approached, I could hear someone growl, and chills erupted across my body as I waited for them to walk closer. As the footsteps ceased, I closed my eyes briefly, and when I opened them, Dalton was standing behind Rhys with his arms crossed over his chest and a glare directed at him.

His blue eyes lifted from Rhys's hold on me, and when I met his gaze, I felt the tears building. He smiled at me and spoke softly, "Hey, baby. I've been so worried about you."

"What . . . how did you find me?"

Rhys stood from in front of me and mouthed 'trust' as he walked around the desk.

Chapter 23

Skid

The entire flight to Atlanta, my knee bounced with nervous energy. Devlin had a charted plane waiting at the airport and within an hour and a half of him locating Grace, we were in the air. The flight was less than two hours, and the only thing he would explain about where Grace was is to say, "She's safe with a friend, and he'll help make everything right."

James had a hard glare in his eyes as he worked on his computer, and when I asked what was bothering him, he shook his head and said nothing. I was getting pissed and I sent a text to Gunner.

Me: I'm in the air to get Grace.

Gunner: Do you need us to provide backup? I can have six brothers on the road in fifteen minutes and they can be there in less than four hours.

Me: Hold off until I survey the situation. Devlin says it's under control, but I worry his need for revenge may be greater than what's best for Grace.

Gunner: I can't believe I'm about to say this but trust the madman. If I'm wrong, I'll kick my own ass, but I think he has control of whatever he's walking you into.

Me: I fucking hope so or I'll kill him myself.

Gunner: Keep in touch.

"How can you be sure your friend is going to help us? No disrespect, but you two don't have many friends, and I don't know whatever bullshit you have going on to cause Grace pain," I asked as we began our dissent into Atlanta.

"Because the only reason he's alive and living the life he has is because of James," Devlin explained, and his brother snapped his green eyes to him, glaring a hole in the side of his head.

Devlin shook off the silent threat, and I could feel the tension rolling off them both. Whoever was with Grace must be more to them than a friend, and I'm starting to think I may need to have Gunner send the boys. That way, when this shitshow goes sideways, I can get Grace safely away from whatever war these two idiots may start.

The plane landed, and we taxied to a private hanger along the far side of the runway. An SUV was waiting for us, and Devlin got behind the wheel as I climbed into the passenger's seat and James set up in the back with his laptop open. I could hear him clicking away on the keyboard as Devlin followed the GPS instructions to Grace's location.

The closer we got, the more my nerves grew. I feared she would shut down before she gave me a chance to explain, and I worried she might never forgive me. I would grovel, and I've never begged for anything, just to have another chance with her. To make things right and to have the life I promised her. She's my old lady, and I want her by my side.

The silence in the car was pissing me off, and as we crept through traffic on the interstate, I turned to the back seat and looked at James. He lifted his eyes to me, and I turned my attention to Devlin in the driver's seat. He glanced at me as he drove, and I cleared my throat.

"I vowed a life for a life to you all those years ago for saving Jacob, and I'd like to think we're friends." Devlin nodded, and I looked at James, whose eyes had softened to a degree. "I love Grace. If I can get her to listen to me and she can find a way to forgive me, I'm done with all this secret shit. I need to be able to give her the life she deserves, and I can't do that if I'm always in the dark, looking for boogeymen and bad guys." James raised his eyebrows with a smile, and I continued. "You two provided me with more than I could have ever asked for, and you ensured my family's future. For that, I say thank you. But after today, I'm out. I want to make Grace my old lady, and I plan to spend every day of the rest of my life with her on the back of my bike, giving her wings to fly."

"Well, damn. Dalton grew up," James remarked, and Devlin cut his eyes to me as he switched lanes.

"I can't think of a better way to spend your life than with a good woman's love. I'd never ask you to stay in the dark, Dalton. Grace makes you happy, and I'd never stand in the way of that." His remark choked me up a little, and I swallowed the emotion as we got off the interstate.

The area around us was wealthy from all indications, and the houses were bigger the further we drove. After a few minutes, large gates and tall fences became the normal as James closed his laptop before leaning between the two front seats.

"There's no way Callahan Cyber would be half as good as it is today if it wasn't for you. You've been the closest confidant Devlin and I've had over the years, and with the help of your brothers, you've protected our families like they were your own. There's nothing more I want than to see you happy," James explained as Devlin pulled the vehicle into a driveway and stopped at a guarded building. "And you're part owner in the company, so it's not like you need to work anyways."

I cut my eyes to a laughing Devlin as James sat back with a satisfied smile on his face. What the fuck is he talking about? Shelving that question, I turned my attention to the driver's open window as a guard with a sidearm walked up to the SUV.

"Are you gentlemen lost?" he asked, and Devlin's lips lifted in a smirk.

"Tell Rhys, Devlin Callahan is calling in his favor."

The guard walked to the small building and picked up a phone. He looked at us while he spoke into the receiver, and I wanted to jump out to make him open the gate. Grace was close, and the longer he took, the shorter my fuse became. I was about to yell through the window when the guard nodded and hung up the phone. He walked back and leaned into the window.

"Drive through and park in front of the main house. Someone will meet you."

Turning, he pressed a button, and Devlin drove through the opening gate. Looking around, I saw the winding driveway was surrounded by thick groves of trees. A house grew larger the closer we got, and when I saw the mansion in front of me, I looked at Devlin.

"How do you know this Rhys fella?"

He put the car in park and turned off the ignition as he spoke. "A few years ago, I helped locate his sister. She was a part of that trafficking case we helped the government with. Her brother had been looking for her, and it was the software the three of us designed that helped locate her. He owes us a favor."

A large man with black hair and dark brown eyes stepped out of the opening door, and when he crossed his arms over his chest, I asked, "Are you sure he knows he owes you a favor?"

James chuckled menacingly as he opened the door. "He does now."

The three of us got out of the car as Rhys walked down the stairs and stopped in front of us. His eyes were cold and dead, and I wondered how the fuck Grace ended up here with him. Who was she to him?

"I was wondering how long it would take you to show up at my doorstep," he said, and his eyes cut to me.

I stood tall with my arms crossed over my chest, ready and willing to fight this huge man if it meant I could get to Grace. He tilted his head to the side, and I saw a brief glimpse of Grace in the movement. Stepping up to me, Devlin and James watched from the side as he pressed closer to me. I clenched my fists and flared my nostrils as I exhaled, waiting to throw down.

"I've got one question for you, Dalton, and honesty is best with me." He raised his eyebrows, and I mimicked him, waiting for his question. "Are you in any way connected to what Grace found on that drive last night?"

I closed my eyes briefly and prayed I didn't strangle him. Opening my eyes, I stepped closer until our noses almost touched as I barked. "The only thing I'm guilty of is not telling her the whole truth when I met her, but to answer your question. No, I'm in no way connected to that vile shit, other than to try and find the nasty fuckers who hurt those two girls so I can kill them. Now where the fuck is Grace?"

My voice raised, and he gave me an evil smile as he stepped back from me. "Grace is inside, and I think it's time we all had a talk. Follow me."

Rhys glanced at James, whose jaw was clenched, and he shook his head. The three of us followed him up the stairs and into the house. The welcomed air conditioner stifled the oppressive heat outside as we followed him down a hallway. The sound of someone beating a punching bag sounded into the hallway as we walked past a closed door, and Rhys stopped to open a door at the end, lifting his arm to usher us inside.

I walked in first and swung my eyes around the room, seeing we were alone. Devlin walked in next, followed by Rhys, and last was James, who stood at the back of the room with his watchful gaze locked on the mystery man sitting behind a large desk. I took a seat in front of him, and Devlin sat next to me as Rhys leaned back into his chair.

"Someone needs to tell me what caused Grace to run to me, thinking they were after her again."

I sat forward quickly and looked at a confused Devlin before turning my eyes back to Rhys.

"Who are they?" I asked, and he leaned his forearms onto the desk, steepling his hands.

"What do you know?" His tone was inquisitive and angry, and I was getting sick of all the secrets.

Standing, I pushed my closed fists onto the table and leaned over him, letting him know he didn't intimidate me. "I know some sick fucker hurt not only my woman but another little girl, and if he wasn't already dead, I'd show him what real pain is."

"That was you, wasn't it?" Devlin asked, and my head snapped to him.

Rhys stood from his chair and chuckled. "Why, Devlin, are you accusing me of causing that asshole and his sick fucking wife to burn to death on the interstate, trapped in their wrecked car, knowing the painful death that awaits them? What kind of a man do you think I am?"

"I know what kind of man you are, Rhys. We're family after all," James remarked, and I couldn't take any more secrets.

"Family? Fires? Them? Will one of you assholes tell me what the fuck is going on and where Grace is, or I swear to everything I care about, I'll shoot every one of you," I yelled, and Devlin stood from his chair, placing a hand on my shoulder.

"Rhys and James are cousins. And we can talk about that later. Right now, I'd like to talk to Grace and see if I can get this whole misunderstanding worked out," Devlin remarked, but I shook my head, knocking off his grip on my shoulder.

"Fuck that. She doesn't know you and James scared the fuck out of her yesterday. I need to see her," I said and swung my eyes to Rhys.

He shook his head and explained, "Dalton, is it? Or do you prefer Skid?"

"I don't give a fuck what you call me as long as you take me to Grace."

He sat on the edge of the desk, and I crossed my arms, widening my stance as he exhaled. "Ten years ago, I was getting out of the Army and looking to make my mark on the world. My family had been torn apart when I was a kid," his eyes cut to James, who grunted before he continued, "and I was trying to pick up the scattered pieces. My sister was twelve years younger than me and had been put into a different foster home. It was through that weak connection that I met Grace. My sister, Regan, and Grace's friend, Kelly, were roommates in one of the group homes, and when Kelly needed help, she reached out to me looking to hide Grace."

I sat down in the chair, the picture starting to take shape as I listened. "Grace was so lost when she came here, and I worked with her for months, me and a therapist, to figure out exactly how much damage that fucker caused. When she was strong enough, I helped her find her way to Eddie."

"Her uncle," I interjected, and he nodded. "How did you make that connection?"

"My cousin isn't the only hacker in the family," Rhys joked, and James shook his head with a sadness coming from him. "Anyways, I contacted Eddie, and he was ready to provide her with a safe place to land when she was ready. She was doing fine until you walked in the door, so explain to me how you ended up in Alabama, looking for Grace."

"I saw the thumb drive, hoping to give some justice to another little girl. When I discovered he was dead." My gaze met Rhys's and he danced with delight at the mention of the Ringmans' death. "Something about it didn't seem right. No way that kind of thing happens, and she be the only one, so I started digging. One sixteen-year-old girl who went from happy to gone almost overnight, and something told me he got to her too. Months later, I found Grace on one of our cameras using our facial recognition software, and I saw something in her eyes I recognized. Pain, shame, regret. I went to the bar to see if she was okay, to make sure she wasn't trapped in her pain, and I fell in love with her."

"Why didn't you tell her what led you to her?"

"And say what exactly?" James cut in and walked across the room. "Hi, I found a thumb drive of your foster father raping a little girl and I want to know if it happened to you too. She would have shut down and cut him off."

Rhys scratched his head and lifted a shoulder. "I can see that. Now, what are you going to do to make her understand."

Devlin spoke first. "I'm going to talk to her and explain a few things. Then, we can braid each other's hair for all I care."

Rhys stood from his seat, and I watched as Devlin followed him to the door. "Don't fuck this up."

He nodded and walked out of the room, leaving James and me alone in Rhys's large office. I looked at James, who was still standing at the rear of the room, and asked, "So, that asshole is your cousin?"

"Unfortunately. When it was time for Marco to pick his payment, he flipped a coin and I was the unwilling choice. Rhys and I were close growing up, but it was only after Marco was dead that I was able to reach out to him. I found out his mother had Regan, and Rhys did everything he could to see her, only to have the state keep them separated. I made sure to write to Regan through the years, hoping to foster a relationship between them, and when she disappeared four years ago, shortly before her twentieth birthday, he came to us for help. He's an asshole, but his intentions are good."

James walked across the room and sat down next to me as my eyes stayed on the door Devlin and Rhys walked out of, hoping they would return with Grace quickly. A few anxious minutes later, the door opened and Devlin walked in with Grace in his arms, passed out. I scrambled to him and took her from his arms, carefully carrying her to the couch and placing her down.

Kneeling in front of her, I pushed some damp hair from her forehead and whispered, "I'm here, Grace. Please wake up."

Rhys grasped my shoulder, and I looked up at him. "Let me, please. She's vulnerable and scared."

I reluctantly stood back from the couch and watched as he kneeled in front of her. She tried to sit up, and he stopped her, speaking quietly to her as she looked around. James pushed the door to the room closed as Rhys met my gaze. I walked around the couch, and when Grace saw me, her eyes filled with tears.

I kneeled in front of her and said, "Hey, baby. I've been so worried about you."

"What . . . how did you find me?"

The sadness in her voice killed me, and I gently took her hands into mine, kissing the backs of both as I promised, "I'll always find you, Grace. You're mine, remember?"

Chapter 24

Grace

I looked down at my lap, letting the tears fall behind my curtain of hair as Dalton held onto my hands. He lifted my face to his and brushed the tears from my cheeks as he whispered, "I'm so sorry, Grace. Please forgive me. I never meant to hurt you."

I looked at Rhys over Dalton's shoulder, seeing the dark-haired man who I now know to be Devlin Callahan standing with him. Confused why they were here, I looked at Dalton and asked, "Can someone please tell me what's going on?"

"I think we need to be someplace more comfortable. Would that be okay, Grace?" Rhys asked, and I nodded.

Dalton offered his hand to me, and I stood, trying to pull my grip from his. He linked his fingers with mine as we walked out of Rhys's office and down the hall to the sunroom and a part of me felt better to have his hand in mine. The rest was curious how he found me. There was a large table under an umbrella, and I sat down as the four men pulled out their seats. Rhys sat across from me, and Dalton was on my right.

James sat at the end of the table, silently watching everything unfold, and I ripped my gaze from him, feeling like he could see every painful moment of my life. Devlin sat to the left of Rhys, across from Dalton and the men kept looking at each other with a worried expression passing between them.

Clearing my throat, I started, "Who's going to tell me what's going on?" I removed my hand from Dalton's and crossed my arms over my chest as I tilted my head, appraising them. None of them made a move to speak, and I stood, pushing my chair back. "Fuck this. I'm going to pack, then I'll be out of all your lives in a few minutes. Thanks for the enlightening conversation."

I made one step away from the table when James spoke, his voice low and his words filled with painful anger. "My sister, Aubrey, is the little girl on the thumb drive, and I'm sorry you ever had to see it."

I collapsed into the chair and my mouth fell open as I looked at him. "Why did it even exist? And why didn't you tell me about it?" I asked, turning my last question to Dalton.

182

His blue eyes cast down before meeting mine, and he exhaled before speaking. "I never meant for you to ever see it."

"Would everyone stop saying that. Seeing it wasn't as painful as living through what I know you're all aware of. So, someone tell me the truth."

Devlin cleared his throat and I turned my attention to him. "Ten years ago, I discovered my wife, as a teenage girl, was being abused by her adoptive parents. When I went to save her, I found her adoptive father watching . . ." He swallowed deeply and looked back at me, lowering his voice as he explained, "He was watching Aubrey's rape, and I killed him for not only what he did to my wife, but what I saw on the TV."

I could see the rage and anger in his eyes, and I felt Dalton take my hand as Devlin continued. "That sent me on a path to find the little girl being hurt. When I did, I killed her father and his whore of a girlfriend, who instigated Aubrey's introduction to . . . him."

"You saved her," I remarked, but he shook his head.

"I didn't, but that's not my story to tell. What none of us knew was Aubrey made a copy of what Tiffany, the whore, was recording, hoping to use it for leverage. To whom and for what, we'll never know, but I tried to save Aubrey from any more pain."

"You did," James remarked and cleared his throat.

"She fell in love with my friend, Hayden, and when she finally told us what happened, she gave us the thumb drive." Dalton picked up the story, and I turned to him, catching Rhys's eyes as Dalton spoke. "I didn't want Devlin or James to watch it, knowing it would cause them pain. So, I did, and then I discovered that . . . he and his wife were dead." Dalton glanced up at Rhys before looking at me. "I never intended to hurt you, but I felt in my soul he had hurt another girl. I looked everywhere for you, needing to see you were okay with my own eyes, and when I saw you, I fell head over heels for you."

"Why keep it a secret?" I asked with pain bleeding through my words. I never wanted anyone to know, and now a table full of people are aware of what I let happen.

"They didn't want to hurt you by asking, I'm sure. How did you figure out your gut was right, Dalton?" Rhys asked, and I wanted to strangle him with my bare hands for pushing the issue.

"Your nightmare," he whispered, and I looked down at my lap, feeling the heat creep up my face, knowing he certainly knew.

I stood from the chair and began to pace as the four men watched me with worried expressions. Swinging my gaze to them all, I inquired, "So, every one of you thinks you know what happened to me because of what Aubrey dealt with? No offense to your sister, James."

James, Dalton, and Devlin all nodded, and I shook my head in disgust. Looking at Rhys, he raised his eyebrows and nodded, giving me the go-ahead to let the anger free.

"What a bunch of egotistical assholes. You think she and I lived through the same thing? You have no fucking clue what I lived with," I spat and pointed at them all. "You want all the juicy details? Fine. I'll tell you everything, and you can run along, knowing you saved your sister from the monster all those years ago."

"Grace," Dalton started to say as he went to stand, and I walked to him and pushed him into the chair.

His worried eyes met mine, but I couldn't acknowledge his pain when mine was too raw. I felt exposed and was letting my anger guide me. Walking to the head of the table, I kept my gaze on Rhys briefly, and he closed his eyes, knowing what was about to be said. When his dark orbs met my watery ones, I let the truth fall from my lips.

"All I ever wanted was someone to love me." I looked at Dalton and shook my head with a sad laugh. "When I was twelve years old, Kevin Ringman took me camping. It was something that we did as 'a family' a few times a year, and this trip, Connie was sick and didn't go. During the trip, he played on my vulnerability, on my need for love, and twisted my emotions into his fantasy. He drugged me and asked if I wanted him to be my daddy. I was young, stupid, and naïve, so I said yes."

Devlin went to speak, and I held up my hand. "You wanted to know, so sit still and shut up while I tell you." I was pissed, more pissed than I'd ever been, and I was letting every painful word, every lie, every manipulation out. "A few weeks later, he took me to a party where I was the guest of honor. A nice woman told me how special I was to Kevin and how he could be my daddy, if I was willing to make a promise. I did, and that night, he raped me in front of five men, taking my innocence from me while I thanked him for loving me."

Scoffing, I began to pace at the head of the table while the memories fell from my lips. "For four years, he made me feel special, promising this was what daddies did to teach their daughters to be good wives and mothers. He was showing his love to me and getting me ready for my life. I was grateful he cared enough to teach me and kept his secret, always looking for stolen moments with him." Shaking my head, I tried to dislodge the memories, and I could see the worry on all the men's faces as I pushed ahead. "A month before my sixteenth birthday, he started to distance himself more from me, and I heard him talk about your sister, in passing. I assumed, like he had explained, that I was getting ready to make my final commitment to The Community, and he was going to help another little girl find a daddy."

Dalton's eyes stayed locked on me, and I could see love looking back. I hoped he still felt the same when it was all said and done, but for now, I had to trust. James held his head in his hands, listening to my painful tale, Devlin was grinding his teeth as he listened, and Rhys was showing pride at my strength.

"Kelly saw something that I never wanted her to see, and she explained how it was wrong. I didn't know, and the shame filled me, still fills me, knowing how dumb I was. I willingly let a predator take advantage of me, just for some scraps of his perceived love. Jesus, I was stupid."

Dalton stood from the chair and met me at the head of the table. Taking my hands into his, he looked me in the eyes and spoke. "You're not stupid, Grace. You're braver than you can imagine, and you're stronger than you give yourself credit for."

"Keep believing that, Dalton," I replied and took my hands from him, wrapping them around my waist. "I told the people who should have been able to help, but they didn't believe me, so I ran. Kelly helped me find Rhys, and he facilitated me finding my way."

Dalton gently grasped my shoulders and said, "Grace, you had the strength to start over. Alone at sixteen with no guidance or network to fall back on. You alone, pushed those demons to the side and found a life that made you happy. I can't imagine what you lived through, but I know this for sure. You beat him. You're still standing, and he's gone, never to hurt another person again."

"But did I beat him? I don't even understand how real love is supposed to look. I'm pathetic," I muttered, turning away, and felt Dalton grip lightly onto my shoulders, bringing my gaze up to his.

"You want to know what real love looks like? Look at me. At us. We're as real as love gets and I'll be damned if I'm going to let that fucker take up any more space in your head. I love you, Grace. Please give me the chance to show up, not with words, but with actions how much you mean to me and how I treasure every second with you." His voice was hard, and I could see the pain in his blue eyes.

Pain for me. Pain for us. I stared up at him and wanted to believe him. I looked at my shoulders where his hands still rested and raised my eyebrow at him, silently requesting him to remove them. Hurt lashed across his face as he released me, and I turned to the table, needing to finish this once and for all.

I knew Dalton loved me, but it would take time for my heart and brain to catch up. Eddie always told me when I found someone who loved me completely, I would be able to tell them the whole truth. Dalton was that person, I just wished I could have been the one to tell him, instead of him knowing before he met me.

He sat down, and I joined him, taking his hand into mine and smiling at him. He returned the smile and kissed the back of my hand before I turned to the table.

"What else do you want to know? Because once I say this, I'll never talk about it again." Turning to James, I explained, "Except privately with Aubrey, if she wants to, that is." My voice lowered, unsure of the sudden offer.

"I think she may appreciate that, but know, none of us, or our wives either, will ever judge you for what you survived. The women in our lives are fighters and have survived some of the worst life can throw at them. When Skid said, you're strong, believe him, Grace. You are the bravest woman I've ever met."

I wiped a tear from my cheek and replied, "Thank you. Even if I don't feel strong."

"Then I'll be strong for you until you're able to be strong for yourself. That's what a man does for his old lady," Dalton explained, and I met his watery gaze.

Rhys spoke, and I looked at my friend. "Grace, let's finish this so you can get started living your life. I think you have a good man by your side who, correct me if I'm wrong, will kill anyone who ever tries to hurt you again."

Dalton said, "I'll send them straight to hell."

"Then it's time. Tell them," Rhys instructed, and I cleared my throat before starting.

"They call themselves The Community, and their sole purpose is to train young girls to follow 'their God-given path.'" Devlin looked confused, so I backed up. "It is a group of men and their brainwashed wives. They prey on vulnerable young girls, promising them a 'daddy's love' and twisting them into pliant, subservient . . . sex slaves. When the girl turns sixteen, the process of finding them a husband starts. I went to one wedding between a sixteen-year-old girl and a forty-three-year-old man."

"So, the wives are aware of what the men are doing with young girls?" Devlin asked, and I looked at Dalton before responding.

My eyes cast down, and he lifted my face, whispering, "Don't be ashamed, Grace. After today, you'll never have to think about any of this ever again. Please tell him. I promise nothing will change how I feel about you." Leaning closer, he pecked me softly on the cheek and spoke. "Nothing."

I met his soft blue eyes and turned to Devlin. "There was one time when Connie walked in, and I panicked, worried she would be angry and send me away. I was terrified of not having that love he showed me and tried to get him to stop. She walked up to the bed, and he leaned over to kiss her as he was . . . she said, and I quote, 'Is she doing a good job, Daddy? Does she make you happy?' He said yes, and she petted my head, whispering, 'Good, girl,' before she left with the other foster kids for the weekend."

"Fucking bitch," James snarled, and Devlin leaned forward.

"Tell me about The Community. Do you remember any of their names? Where they lived?"

"They lived all over central Missouri, and when I ran away, there were eleven that I knew of. I have no idea now."

"Would you recognize any of them if you saw a picture?" James asked, and I nodded.

"I can tell you one of their names, but that's only because the girl he was ... teaching... let it slip one night while we were changing. It was one of the few times there was more than one ... daughter at a gathering. Usually, our daddies liked to show us off one at a time, so he could get all the praise. In reality, he wanted everyone to watch him as he ... taught her. They're sick and need to be stopped, but I don't know if I'll be any help." I lowered my voice, guilt filling me. "I should have tried harder to get the other girls' help. How many more were hurt because I didn't speak up? I could have saved them, saved your sister," I said, turning to James.

He looked at me and expressed, "You were a child who didn't deserve what you lived through. You don't get to carry guilt over what someone else did. You tried to speak up, and the system failed you. I promise, I'll find every member of The Community and when I do, that will be their last day alive."

I could hear the sincerity in his threat, and I smiled sadly before releasing Dalton's hand and standing from the chair. Looking at the men sitting around the table, I asked, "Do you have any other questions because I'm going to find a quiet corner and try to forget about all of this."

Rhys spoke, and I looked at the man who gave me hope when I thought there was none. "I think you need to call Eddie and let him know you're okay. He called and made me promise to have contact with him."

I walked around the table, and Rhys stood pulling me into a deep hug. I wrapped my arms around his waist and heard Dalton grumble behind me. Looking up, I commented, "I'm sorry I brought all this to your doorstep again."

"I'm glad you came, Grace. You brought my family back to me, and it makes me laugh at how small the world is."

Shaking my head, I let him go and was met halfway around the table by Dalton. He wrapped his arms around me, and I rested my face against his chest, feeling his strong heart beating against my cheek. Sighing, I realized how much weight was off my shoulders after telling him. I was always worried about him leaving or judging me, but knowing he wasn't going anywhere, I finally felt his words pierce through the concrete surrounding my heart.

"Why don't you find Regan and tell her to come see the family before you run back to Tennessee," Rhys suggested, and I looked up at Dalton.

"Would you come with me?" I didn't want to be alone, even though I knew there were things he needed to discuss with his bosses.

"I've got no place else to be but by your side." He took my hand into his, and as we walked away from the table, he muttered, "I officially resigned from Callahan Cyber. I'm all yours, Grace."

Chapter 25

Skid

Hearing the whole truth of Grace's past, I wanted to dig Kevin and Connie Ringman up so I could kill them again. They took the innocent love of a child and let their perversions twist it into something depraved and disgusting. Knowing there were still members out there possibly hurting other young girls, filled me with rage. Trying to shake off the anger, I followed Grace into the house.

A young woman with blonde hair and green eyes appeared from the kitchen with a tray of sandwiches. "Hey, Grace. I was just coming to find you." She looked at me with wide eyes and muttered, "I didn't know we had company, or I would have made more."

"It's no problem, Regan. Rhys asked for me to find you. He's in the sunroom with your cousin, James, and wanted you to come say hi," Grace replied, and Regan smiled brilliantly into the room.

"I'll take these to them and come back to make you something, if that's okay?" I could tell she was eager to see James but was still being polite.

"I'm not hungry. Are you, Grace?" She shook her head, and I looked back at the small woman who I know lived over two years in misery. "We'll occupy ourselves if you want to go see James."

"Thanks," she excitedly replied and walked quickly down the hall with the tray of sandwiches.

"Is there some place you'd be comfortable talking?" I asked, and she looked up at me with worry.

"Have you changed your mind?" she faltered, and I cupped her face with my hands.

"I love you, Grace. Until the sun burns out and the stars fall from the skies, I'll love you. Never question that, and don't think that anything you told me changes that, either."

Her blue eyes met mine and she pushed onto her tiptoes. I leaned over, meeting her in the middle as her lips pressed against mine. She was raw and vulnerable, and I wouldn't push her, but feeling her soft lips against mine had my cock growing in my pants. It was the wrong time for it, and I tilted my pelvis away, not wanting to make her uncomfortable.

She pulled back from the kiss and asked, "Where do we go from here?"

"Home, baby. We go home, and tomorrow, we decide what future we want to have," I responded and wrapped my arms around her.

She stepped closer, resting her hand over my heart as she questioned, "Just like that?"

"Just like that. Do you believe I love you, Grace?" She nodded, and I silently exhaled. "Do you love me?"

My heart beat faster, waiting on her reply. "With everything in my heart."

"Then we figure out the rest later. That's all we have to focus on now." I kissed her again and whispered, "That and making you my old lady."

She smiled sadly and inquired, "What about Eddie?"

"Eddie is welcome anytime, and if you would feel better living closer to him, we can move. Whatever you want, Grace."

I didn't want to be away from my club, but I would if it meant she was truly happy. The Death Hounds were my family and a part of my blood, but Grace owned my entire heart, and my future was in her hands.

"I don't want you to move away from your family. I just want to make sure Eddie stays a part of my life. He's been the closest thing to family I've ever had," she stated, and I felt it was time to clear the air completely.

Taking her by the hand, I led her to the closest chairs and sat her down. She looked worried, and I suggested, "Why don't you call him."

She pulled her phone from her back pocket and turned it on. A minute later, when all the missed calls, texts, and voicemails alerted, she dialed his number and put the phone to her ear. She smiled as tears filled her eyes. "I'm fine," she said, speaking into the phone. "He's right here. Yes. Okay." Pulling the phone away from her ear, she pressed the speaker icon, and Eddie's voice filtered through the phone.

"I see you met Rhys, Dalton." His voice was hard, but there was a hint of laughter under the anger.

"He's a real peach," I replied, and Grace chuckled, making me smile for the first time today.

"Grace, have you told him everything?" Eddie asked, and Grace nodded. "He knows it all."

"Dalton, are we going to have any more issues with secrets?" Eddie asked, and it was my turn to laugh.

"That's funny, coming from you. Tell her, Eddie. She's strong enough to handle it, and she doesn't deserve any more deception," I answered, and she cut her worried eyes to me.

"Deception? Eddie's never lied to me." Withdrawing her hand from mine, she leaned back defensively.

Clearing his throat through the phone, Eddie spoke, and I could see the emotions overtaking Grace as she listened to him explain. "I haven't lied to you, but I have kept something from you, Grace. Please understand I didn't want to cause you any pain after those years, and then after time, I was afraid you would be madder for me waiting, so I just kept my mouth shut."

"What?"

"Your father was my half-brother. When you were six, I tried to adopt you from foster care, but the state wouldn't let a single, active-duty soldier be responsible for a young girl. It was only after Rhys contacted me, a few days after you showed up, that I realized I could have a part in your life and never have to burden you with the truth."

"Why didn't you tell me all those years ago?" she asked, her voice breaking as she began to cry.

"You were so hurt, and I didn't want you to ever think I'd manipulated you like they did. I just wanted to be around you, however you would have me."

I could hear him crying through the phone, and I pulled Grace to my chest as her tears fell. Looking up at me, she smiled. "Dalton, I'd like you to meet Uncle Eddie."

I laughed and replied, "It's nice to meet you, Uncle Eddie."

Eddie laughed, and I kissed her on the temple before leaving the two of them to speak alone for a few minutes while I checked on Devlin and James. I was ready to get Grace home, so she could truly put the past behind her, but I knew the Callahans. They were going to dig through every one of those fuckers' lives until they had every name. With Rhys helping them, I had no doubt they would find them all and save any girls still being brainwashed by their sickness.

When I got to the sunroom, Regan was busy talking to James at the table, and I looked for Devlin and Rhys. "They went into Rhys's office," James remarked with a rare smile and turned back to an animated Regan.

I left them to talk and walked back through the house to Rhys's office. The door was open, and I walked in to see the two men leaning over a laptop on the coffee table, pointing at the screen. They looked up at me as I sat down in a chair across them and waited for an update. I might not be an active part of what they were planning, but if there was to be a reckoning, the Death Hounds were going to get their piece of vengeance.

"She's talking to Eddie, and then I want to get her home. She's had a long night, and I want her in my bed when she finally crashes," I said, and they both leaned back to observe me.

"Are you going to be able to handle what's to come?" Devlin asked, and I grew curious at his unspoken meaning.

"What's coming?" I asked, and he shrugged.

"Could be nothing. Could be something, and until I have a better understanding of timing and participants, I don't want to speak prematurely," Devlin replied, and Rhys looked on without speaking.

His silent treatment toward me was pissing me off, and I leaned forward, resting my forearms on my knees as I maintained eye contact with him. "Do you have a problem with me, Rhys?"

He shook his head and said, "I generally don't like anyone, but seeing how you treat that beautiful young woman, I have to say, you're not so bad."

"Then why the attitude?"

"He's a moody dickhead, that's why," James stated as he walked into the office with Grace and Regan in tow.

The two women were smiling as they walked in, and it was good to see Grace with happiness on her face instead of the fear and shame that I saw when she ran from me. She walked in front of me, and I tugged her by the wrist, causing her to fall into my lap. She smiled at me and snuggled into my chest as Regan took a seat next to me.

"I invited Regan to come to Portstill for a few weeks to meet Amaya and . . ." James cleared his throat and said, "We'd love for you to join us."

Rhys gave James a shit-eating grin and sat back in his chair. Devlin shook his head at the two men and looked at me. "The plane will be ready in an hour to take us home. Grace, I need to ask one more thing of you, and I promise, it will never be mentioned again."

I didn't want to discuss it anymore, but I knew what he wanted without him saying. She stood from my lap and walked to the desk before taking a pen from the cup and writing something down on a piece of paper. Folding it, she reached her small hand out and dropped it into Devlin's open palm.

"The name you're looking for is on that, and from this point forward, the only time I'll discuss this is to verify only." She looked at me and nodded at me to follow before she pulled Regan into a hug and walked out of the office.

"It's over for Grace, Devlin. She deserves peace of mind and to put this behind her. Find them and send them to hell where they belong, but never ask anything of her again—any of you. Or I swear, I'll rain fire down on all of you. Are we clear?"

Regan smiled at me, and I extended my hand to her. "It was nice to meet you, Regan. I hope to see you when you come for a visit. Rhys, no offense and thank you for taking care of Grace, but I hope never to see you again."

With that, I walked out of the office to James's laughter and found Grace waiting for me down the hall. She looked up at me as I walked to her and squealed when I lifted her into the air and hugged her to me.

"We need to leave soon. Do you have everything ready?" I asked, and she shook her head. Placing her on her feet, I linked my hand with hers and said, "Lead the way."

Her small duffle bag was resting on a bed in the back of the house, and I looked around the room as she pushed a few pieces of clothes into the bag. There were pictures on the dresser, and when I picked one up, I saw a young Grace with a younger Rhys. She was smiling up at him, and part of me wanted to walk back into his office and punch him in his face.

She walked up to me as I set the frame back on the dresser. "That was the day I finally beat him in the gym."

"That explains his scowl," I remarked, and she chuckled.

She led me through the large house and into a gym across from the now-closed office door. I could hear James, Devlin, and Rhys speaking behind the door as Grace walked into the gym. I followed and saw large mats, hanging bags, and various training weapons on the wall. She was picking up a towel from the floor and returning a few of the weapons to the wall when I walked up behind her and pulled her back into my front.

Leaning against my chest, she rested her head as I wrapped my arms around her stomach. "So, this is where your ability to knock someone out comes from? I think I may need to see you in action, you know, just to see what you're capable of."

"She'll kick your ass and smile while she does it," Rhys remarked as he walked in with Devlin and James.

"You're just mad I beat you," Grace joked and stepped away from me.

"Once. You beat me once," Rhys replied, and Grace wiggled her eyebrows.

"Once is all it takes."

He walked up to her, and I stood my ground as she turned her attention to him. Brushing a piece of hair behind her ear, he asked softly, "Are you going to be okay, Grace?" His dead eyes cut to me and then back to her. She nodded, and he leaned over, kissing her cheek, and then stepping back.

"Dalton, take care of her," he instructed.

"With my life," I replied and scooped her into my arms.

We walked to the front door, and I looked back over my shoulder as we got to the SUV waiting for us. Regan was standing next to Rhys with her head leaned onto his arm as we climbed into the vehicle. James was up front with Devlin, and I had Grace on my lap in the backseat. The drive was quiet, and I needed to know what James meant earlier.

As we pulled into the airport and turned toward the hangers, I inquired. "What did you mean by your statement earlier, James?"

Grace looked at me with confusion as Devlin stopped the car and turned off the ignition. They pivoted in their seats, looking at us in the back as James explained. "When we sold the software, we had your name put on the ownership documents. You own thirty percent of the company."

He opened the door, got out of the vehicle, and climbed the stairs to the private plane Devlin charted without another word. Grace sat next to me with her eyes wide and her mouth open at James's declaration.

"After everything you've done for us over the last ten years, you couldn't think we wouldn't include you in the business. He meant what he said. We wouldn't be what we are without you," Devlin remarked and left Grace and me alone in the vehicle as he got onto the plane.

"What are they talking about?" she asked, unsure, and I kissed her until we were both fighting for breath.

"It means whatever you want in this world, you've got," I explained, and she brought her hand to my bearded cheek.

"All I want is you."

Bringing our foreheads together, I whispered, "You've got me forever, Grace." Looking deeply into her eyes, I said, "I love you."

Her blue eyes glistened with unshed tears as she replied, "I love you."

She smiled at me, and I got out of the SUV and offered her my hand. She hopped down, and I escorted her to the waiting plane. Climbing the stairs, she walked through the doorway and gasped when she saw the luxurious plane.

Devlin and James were huddled together in the four seats that faced each other, both with laptops open as they worked. Grace glanced at them and walked down the aisle to the couch on the side wall of the plane. Sitting down, she wiggled into the soft leather seat and sighed contently. I plopped down next to her and wrapped my arm around her shoulder, feeling her snuggle into my chest.

The entire flight home, Grace was secure in my arms, and as we touched down in Memphis, I knew today was the first day of the rest of our lives. I vowed that I would make up for every painful moment she experienced and give her a life filled with joy and happiness.

Devlin gave me a look as the plane taxied into the hanger, and I saw the monster inside him pushing to the surface. When vengeance needs a reckoning, the Callahans were more than ready to oblige. One thing they forgot, though.

Grace was mine, and the Death Hounds will have their pound of flesh. One way or another.

Chapter 26

Grace

The entire drive from Memphis to Portstill, Dalton kept his arm around my shoulder and his other hand covering mine. It was almost like he had to touch me to make sure I was real and not going anywhere. I never expected Dalton to show up looking for me at Rhys's and to find out James was Rhys's cousin was mind-boggling.

Devlin drove, and James was busy on his computer, typing away and mumbling to Devlin as the miles passed. I knew they were investigating The Community and looking into the name I gave them, but I didn't want to know what they found. It may sound like I was sticking my head into the sand and ignoring everything, but it took me years to not worry and look over my shoulder, so I refused to look back.

My future was sitting next to me, and with Dalton by my side, I never had to worry if his love was a manipulation. The sign for the Portstill city limits was up ahead, and I pressed up to whisper into Dalton's ear.

"Can we go straight home, or do you need to work?"

"Home, baby. This isn't my business anymore," he explained, and I smiled as I rested my head against his chest.

Devlin pulled into the underground parking garage of one of the buildings across from Pierce Lake, and I looked up when I heard him mutter, "Damn it."

Parked inside were three Death Hounds, and Dalton sat up with a smile to see who was waiting for us. Devlin parked the car, and I saw Gunner get off his bike and walk toward the vehicle. Dalton opened the door and clasped hands with his President as Devlin and James left the vehicle. Claw stood to the side, observing everything.

The third brother was standing too far away for me to see his name, but I wasn't scared as I climbed out of the back seat. Dalton wrapped his arm around me as we all gathered on the passenger side of the SUV.

"Grace, it's good to see you. Are you okay?" Gunner asked, and I nodded.

"Yes, thank you. I'm sorry if I caused anyone problems," I said, and the tall man smiled down at me.

"If Skid was my old man, I'd need to take off from time to time myself." He chuckled and everyone joined him, releasing some of the stress building.

"I want to get Grace home," Dalton said, and Devlin and James stepped closer.

Ever the quiet one, James stood and watched as Devlin spoke to Gunner. "I need to speak with you about some business. Can you talk now, or would tomorrow be better?"

"I want to escort Grace and Skid home, but why don't you come by the clubhouse tomorrow and we can talk," Gunner replied, and Devlin nodded once and extended his hand to the men.

They all shook hands, and then Devlin turned to me. "Grace, it was such an honor to meet you. Elise and I would love to have you and Skid over for dinner soon."

"That would be nice," I admitted. "I'll make dessert."

"I look forward to it," he replied before he and James turned, leaving me with the Death Hounds.

Dalton looked down at me and smiled. "Are you ready to go home?"

I felt the tears building, and I blinked rapidly as I answered, "Home sounds nice."

"I'll lead. Jackal can bring up the back," Gunner stated, and Dalton helped me to his bike.

After stowing my duffle in the saddlebag, he helped me onto the back and climbed onto the front. I wrapped my arms around his waist and hugged myself tightly to him. He fell in line with the other brothers as we pulled out of the garage. Driving through Portstill, a few of the citizens stuck their heads out, waving at the club as we drove through the main street on the way to Portstill.

The road leading out of Pierce Bluff was smooth, and I got lost in thoughts of our future. There were no more secrets between Dalton and me, and I felt freer than ever before. We were getting closer to his cabin, and I lifted my arms from around his waist and leaned back, feeling the wind pushing against me. The stress and worry bled from me as Dalton placed his hand on my knee while he drove down the road. I'm sure I looked ridiculous to Claw and Jackal, but when Dalton sped up, I knew he understood.

When I saw his road up ahead, I placed my arms back around him and kissed the back of his cut, right over the skull in the middle of his Death Hounds logo. This beautiful man, hardened by life and situation, found me when I was lost and saved me from a life of loneliness. Seeing his cabin come into view down the long tree-covered driveway made me emotional.

As the bikes pulled into the front of the cabin, I felt tears building in my eyes, realizing this was my home. A real home with real love by a man who would move earth to make me happy. I never thought it would happen for me. I guarded my heart and lived a life of solitude, afraid someone would see how broken and confused I was.

Dalton saw me and refused to let me stay buried in shame and regret. His love brought me to life, and as the bikes turned off, casting us into momentary silence, I gripped onto Dalton tighter. He turned in my arms and glanced over his shoulder to see tears falling down my cheeks, wetting the back of his cut.

He brought his hands to my arms and asked, "Grace, baby, what's wrong?"

I released my hold on him, and he stood from the bike, bringing one hand to my cheek and stepping close. I swiped at the tears as the other three Death Hounds stood by, watching but not invading the moment. A smile broke out on my face, and I looked up at Dalton. His blue eyes appraised me, and I brought my hand to his cheek as I explained.

"Nothing's wrong. In fact, everything's right."

"Then why are you crying?" His thumb brushed across my cheek, and I took a stuttering breath.

"I just realized. This . . . you . . . I'm home," I tried to explain, the overwhelming relief too much to take as I cried.

Dalton closed his eyes briefly, and when his gaze caught mine, I could see them glistening as he smiled down at me. "You're home, Grace."

I hugged myself to his chest, and he cleared his throat before speaking. "Let's get you inside and into a warm bath. Then I'll get you something to relax while we decide on food. Does that sound okay?"

I nodded and pushed back, wiping the errant tears still falling. He helped me from the bike, and I turned to see Gunner watching with a huge smile on his face. The other two men appeared uncomfortable, with Claw looking away as he rubbed the back of his neck, and Jackal scrubbing his boot across the dirt.

"Would you like to come inside?" I asked them, and Gunner stepped forward.

"Thanks, darlin'. We're going to head out but make sure you stop by and see Sadie in a few days. She's been worried about you," Gunner explained, and I looked down briefly before meeting his intimidating gaze.

"I'm sorry to make everyone worry."

He leaned over and placed a chaste kiss on my cheek before he replied. "That's what families do, but next time, talk to Dalton before you run. I've known him for ten years, and he is the best man I've ever met. He'll never hurt you, and if he does, I'll hold him while you beat him up."

"She doesn't need you to hold me. She can beat me on her own, from what I've heard," Dalton said, and Gunner pulled a face, showing he was impressed.

"I'll pay you to beat up Skid," Claw replied, and I shrugged with a smile.

"I could never hurt my old man."

Dalton scooped me into his arms, and I shrieked as the Death Hounds chuckled. "On that note, I'm taking my old lady inside. Thanks for the escort."

I looked over Dalton's shoulder as he carried me up the stairs, and Gunner winked at me before pulling on a pair of sunglasses and cranking his bike. Dalton punched a code into the panel by the door and the door unlocked before he carried me inside and kicked the door shut with his foot.

He placed me on my feet in the living room, and I looked up at him. His blue eyes were filled with love, real true love, and I couldn't help myself. Wrapping my arms around his waist, I pulled myself closer to him, feeling his warmth against me. He pulled me tighter to him and kissed me on top of the head.

"Let me get you settled and fed," he suggested, and my stomach growled.

I released him and stepped back. Smiling, I linked my hand with his and tugged him toward the bedroom. In the far corner, opposite the king-size bed, was a large tub in front of a window. The view was of beautiful trees and flowering bushes, and it was stunning.

Turning to Dalton, I asked, "Would you like to join me for a bath?"

He brought his lips to mine and kissed me, letting me feel his length pressed against my stomach. I flexed my hips into him, and he groaned before breaking the connection and resting his forehead against mine.

"I know you've had a stressful few days, and I want to give you time. Let me take care of you, and if you still want me afterward, I'll give you all you can handle and then some."

"Don't . . . don't you want me?" I asked, unsure why he wouldn't want naked tub time with me.

He grabbed my hand and brought it to the front of his pants, wrapping it around his hardness, and squeezed my hand. I could feel his want, his need, and I looked up at him, seeing the fire in his eyes. "Do you feel how hard I am for you? How much I want you? I will never not want you, but I need to take care of you first. Shower, smoke, food," he squeezed my hand around his length again, "then, I'll make you come so hard, you'll pass out and sleep until tomorrow. Will you let me take care of you?"

My breathing accelerated, and I swallowed thickly before whispering, "Yes."

He released my hand and brought his to the back of my head, pulling my lips to his and kissing me until I didn't know which way was up. Stepping back, he winked at me and left me breathless in the room as he turned on the water to fill the giant tub. After testing the temp, he walked back to me and asked, "Do you need help getting into the tub?"

I shook my head, and he kissed my cheek. "I'll be right back."

He walked out of the room with a swagger in his hips as I stared at his tight ass. Smiling to myself, I felt my kiss swollen lips and giggled. I slipped my shoes and socks off, placing them to the side before I reached down and pulled my shirt off. My bra, pants, and panties followed next, and I stepped up to the tub, testing the temperature.

It was warm and inviting, so I stepped over the side and sank down in the quickly rising water. Moaning into the room, I felt the knots working out of my back from the last days' worth of tension. Closing my eyes, I relaxed into the water and waited for Dalton to return.

"Fuck, you're beautiful," he said, and I opened my eyes to see him sitting on the edge of the tub, looking at my naked body under the water. He reached over and turned the water off as steam rose into the room. "I thought this might make your bath better," he suggested and pulled out a joint.

"You think of everything," I said and smiled at him.

"I'll try, but if I fuck something up, please, Grace. Don't run from me again."

I sat up and placed my wet hand on his knee. "I'm sorry. I never meant to leave, but it was all too much, and I let my fear win. I promise, I'll only run to you, never away."

He kissed me, brushing his tongue against mine, and I sighed when he pulled away. He pulled up a chair and spoke softly, "Lean back."

Following his instructions, I settled into the water as he lit the joint and inhaled, getting the end glowing before bringing it to my lips. I took a draw off it and watched as he carefully pampered me. When we were half finished, he snubbed it out and grabbed a washrag from the cabinet.

Wetting the rag, he poured some bath gel on it and encouraged me to sit up. I rested my chest on my propped-up knees as he washed my back and arms. Sitting back, he cleaned my chest, keeping his eyes on mine and never pushing past the soft care he was giving me.

"I'll let you . . ." He blushed, and I took the rag from him and washed the rest of me quickly.

Grabbing some shampoo from the edge, I wet my hair and washed it, rinsing it in the water and sitting up to wipe the droplets from my eyes. I was relaxed and happy as Dalton extended a towel between his two spread arms. Stepping out of the tub onto the bathmat, I smiled when he wrapped the towel around me and lifted my damp body against his chest.

"I can walk, Dalton." I chuckled as he carried me to the bed and gently placed me down.

"I know you can, but that doesn't mean you have to. I like having you in my arms," he admitted, and I blushed. "Let me get you something to wear until I can take you shopping tomorrow."

He grabbed a Death Hounds T-shirt from a drawer and lifted a pair of boxers. "Would this work?"

"The shirt will be enough, unless you're expecting company."

He closed the drawer and walked to me, handing me the shirt. "No company. Just you and me, babe."

I stood from the bed and kept my eyes on him as I let the towel fall to the floor at my feet. His gaze turned heated, and he licked his lips as I pulled the shirt over my head, hiding my nudity from him. I could see his hard length pressing against his jeans, and I wanted to touch him, to feel him.

Somehow sensing my need, he took my hand and kissed it with a smile on his lips. "Food next, darlin.'"

He guided me out of the bedroom and into the kitchen. Picking me up, he placed me on the cold counter and stepped between my legs. "I have burgers and fries on the way unless you want something else."

My stomach grumbled again, and I shook my head, replying, "Burgers sound perfect."

He pecked me on the lips and explained, "I'm going to take a quick shower. Do you need anything?"

I shook my head, and he helped me off the counter before jogging through the living room into the bedroom. I could hear the shower turn on as I sat on the couch and picked up the TV remote. I wasn't much for television, preferring to engross myself in books, but until I could get back to my place in Alabama, I'd have to settle for what was available.

Some mindless show about nothing was on when I heard the shower turn off. Watching the doorway, I waited for Dalton to reappear when a knock sounded on the front door.

"Food's here," I shouted, and Dalton yelled back.

"I'll be right there."

There was no need for him to rush into the room when I was right there, so I grabbed a blanket from the couch and wrapped it around myself, not wanting to be indecent. I stood and walked around the couch to the door just as Dalton appeared from the bedroom.

"I've got it, Grace. It's one of the prospects."

I shrugged and returned to the couch as he walked to the door and opened it. "Hey, man. I didn't know you were back already. I want you to come in and meet Grace."

I glanced over my shoulder as Skid stood in the doorway, and when he began to turn toward me, I stood from the couch and checked I was covered before facing the door. A tall man with a blond mohawk and beard walked inside, and something about him caused warning bells to go off in my head.

He had gauged ears and was covered in tattoos. His fingers, hands, arms, neck, some of his face, and the sides of his head were covered in bright ornamentation and black and white pieces of art.

The man lifted his green eyes to me, and terror filled me from the inside out. I took a step back as he walked over, and Dalton turned to speak to me, only I couldn't hear anything he was saying. The man looked at me with curiosity as my feet pushed me away from him. Dalton appeared in my line of sight, blocking the stranger from me, and he took ahold of my face, saying something to me until I finally focused on him.

"Grace, baby. What's wrong? Needles, call Doc," Dalton rattled quickly and stroked my cheeks, whispering that I was okay and safe.

I didn't know what it was about the man, Needles, that scared me so deeply, and I looked from him to Dalton before muttering, "I'm sorry."

Running into the bedroom, I slammed the door and sank down to my ass, fear and panic overwhelming me. I've never met him, but I knew him. I just couldn't remember how. A knock sounded against the door as Dalton's worried voice filtered into the room.

"Grace, I sent him away. Please open the door. It's okay, baby. Please open up."

I slid to the side and opened the door. Dalton rushed in and fell on his knees next to me as he checked me for injury. "Grace, what's wrong. You have to talk to me. What did he do?"

"I don't know. I've never met him, but . . ." Confusion was winning, and I felt terrible for the way I acted.

Dalton must be embarrassed over how I treated his brother. "I'm . . . I'm sorry."

"Please don't apologize. I need you to talk to me. Tell me what's going on."

I brought my eyes to him and whispered, "I know him, I just don't remember how."

"Needles? You know him?" I nodded, and he continued, "But you've never met him?" I shook my head, feeling like I was missing something.

"Did he hurt you?" Dalton asked, his nostrils flaring and his eyes turning to slits.

"No. I feel like I'm going crazy, but I swear, I know him . . . somehow."

He helped me from the floor and asked, "Do you feel up to eating?"

"Yeah," I replied, and he tugged me into the kitchen while I ran through where I might have crossed paths with a heavily tattooed biker.

Someone as distinctive as him isn't the type of person you forget where you met them, so it was bothering me not to remember. Dalton and I sat at the table in the kitchen, and he watched me like a hawk as I kept pushing the memories, hoping to figure it out.

The sun was setting when we finished with dinner. Dalton walked me to the back porch and pulled me onto his lap as we sat on the oversized chair and watched the stars push into the sky. The warmth of his body and the exhaustion of the last two days won over my need to remember, or my desire for Dalton, and I fell asleep against his chest, happy that I was finally home.

Chapter 27

Skid

Grace fell asleep in my arms, and I kept watching her, afraid she would have a nightmare. Seeing her so scared of Needles, hearing the panic and uncertainty in her voice, had the anger inside me growing.

When she ran off from him earlier, I looked at him and asked, "What the hell was that all about?"

"I don't know, man. I'm sorry if I scared your old lady," he muttered and handed me our dinner before walking outside.

I heard his bike crank as I ran to check on Grace. Seeing her so scared had me rethinking my decision to stay out of digging into her past. She snuggled into my chest, and I slowly stood with her in my arms and carried her into the bedroom. Not wanting to wake her, I used my bare foot to push the covers so I could lay her down.

When I went to put her on the bed, she clung to me, even in her sleep. She whimpered, and I kissed her forehead. "You're safe, Grace."

She finally relaxed in my arms, and I placed her onto the bed, gently covering her with the blanket. She looked agitated in her sleep, and I didn't want to leave her alone for long. Glancing one more time at her, I ran upstairs and unlocked my office door. My laptop sat on the desk, and I grabbed it before relocking the office and running back downstairs.

Grace was rolled onto her side, facing my side of the bed, and I quickly walked around and got under the covers. Sitting up, I opened my computer and gently stroked her hair while I waited for it to connect. A ping sounded into the room, and I looked at Grace to make sure I wasn't disturbing her as I began to search.

I'd been going through the list of people Devlin and James collected from the cult when a message popped up on the screen.

Devlin: I thought you were done with this.

Me: Something strange happened with Grace tonight and I've got to get to the bottom of it.

Devlin: What happened?

Me: She saw Needles and freaked out, saying she never met him but she knew him.

Devlin: What did he say?

Me: He's as confused as I was but didn't know what freaked her out.

Devlin: I think you may need to be at the meeting with Gunner in the morning. Can you get free?

Me: What's going on?

Devlin: I'll see you in the morning.

"Fucker," I muttered and shook my head, knowing that asshole knew something.

Grace pushed closer to me in her sleep, and I closed my laptop and placed it on the nightstand next to the bed. Snuggling into the covers, I lifted my arm above Grace's head, and a few minutes later, her head was on my chest and her arm across my bare stomach.

It took forever to fall asleep as visions of my sweet Grace filled my head. I could see a young girl, yearning for love and being taken advantage of by a group of faceless people that morphed into her running for her life, scared and looking over her shoulder.

Sometime in the middle of the night, I woke up to a small hand wrapped around my hardened shaft and blinked my eyes to wake up. "Grace, baby, what are you doing?" I asked, and she gripped my shaft tighter, forcing a small moan from me.

"I'm showing my old man how much I love him," she replied and pumped her hand up and down a few times.

She kissed my chest, and I looked down at her as she brought her blue eyes to mine. "You don't have to do that."

She sat up and straddled my pelvis, tucking her small feet along my legs as she leaned over and whispered against my lips, "I want to."

Lifting my ass, I pushed my shorts down as Grace pulled her shirt off, exposing her pert breasts to the room. I sat up, feeling her wet pussy rubbing my shaft and kissed her, pulling her body closer to mine. She reached between us and lifted her hips to align my cock with her perfect pussy.

Her eyes were locked with mine as she sank down, engulfing me in her tight, wet perfection, and I closed my eyes as the pleasure overtook me. Looking back at her, I saw her tilt her head back, exposing her neck to me as she lifted herself, leaving only the head inside, then slowly lowering back down.

Kissing her neck, I rocked my hips in time with hers, letting her take the lead when all I wanted to do was power fuck her, erasing all the bad from her mind. She gripped onto my shoulders as I dragged my lips up her neck and nibbled on her ear.

"Oh, fuck," she moaned and bounced faster, swallowing my cock as she sought her release.

"That's it, baby. Ride my cock," I urged, lying back and thrusting up into her.

"Dalton," she groaned, and her pussy contracted around my shaft.

I pinched her nipples and watched as she threw her head back and her movements faltered. Gripping onto her hips, I jacked her up and down as she came, her body trembling on top of me as she reached her peak.

"Grace, fuck, yes," I moaned and worked my hips faster, finding my release as she shook and convulsed on my cock.

She collapsed on top of me, and I hugged her closer to my body as we panted into the room, trying to catch our breath. Grace turned her head, letting her unfocused eyes find mine as she whispered, "I love you, Dalton."

Lifting her chin, I kissed her and replied, "I love you, Grace."

She smiled and rolled to the side of me as I tugged her back to my chest and pulled her closer. I heard her breathing even out, and in that peaceful moment of holding her in my arms, I silently promised her that no matter what, I would slay every single fucker who ever thought it was okay to do to another child what was done to her.

Even if it meant staying in the darkness where the monsters lurked, allowing the craving for blood to consume me.

The sun shining into the room woke me, and I felt Grace snuggle closer. I wanted to spend all day with her, satisfying whatever need she had, but I had to contact Gunner and let him know I was coming to Devlin's meeting. I reached for my phone and sent him a text, knowing he still got up at five every morning.

Me: I'll be there when you talk to Devlin. Will fill you in when I get there.

A few minutes later, my phone dinged and I lifted it to see his response.

Gunner: Needles told me what happened last night. Any ideas what set her off?

Me: None, but I'll figure it out.

Gunner: And then what?

He knew I would get as bloody as necessary to protect Grace, even if it meant battling a brother. I didn't want to jump to a conclusion. Needles had been a friend since I was a kid hanging around the club with Uncle Mick. He was a few years older than me, but he was always a good guy. When he left after his dad, Torch, died, it was years before I saw him again. I would never assume he did anything to hurt Grace or any other woman, just by the way he treats women.

Shaking my head, not understanding what the fuck was happening, I responded.

Me: I'll blow up that bridge when I cross it.

I placed the phone back down and pulled a naked Grace closer to me, happy to wake up with her in my arms. I fell back asleep with Grace tucked against me, and when I woke up, I knew I was alone in the bed. Touching her side, I could feel her warmth and knew she hadn't been up long.

I slipped from the bed and pulled on my shorts before finding a shirt. Walking into the living room, I saw Grace sitting at the kitchen island with a steaming cup of coffee in her hands. I walked up, and she glanced over her shoulder with a smile as I kissed her on the cheek.

"Good morning, beautiful. Did you sleep well?" I asked, and she nodded with a yawn.

"I slept great. How about you?" she inquired as I poured myself a cup of coffee and leaned against the counter as I took a swallow.

"Best night's sleep I've had in a while," I joked, and she blushed, ducking her head in embarrassment.

I walked to her and met her eyes with mine as I wiggled my eyebrows as I said, "You can wake me up like that anytime you want."

I stood there, smiling at her like a goofy bastard, when my phone rang, interrupting our moment. I looked at the display and saw my sister was calling. Answering the phone, I smiled at Grace as I spoke, "Good morning, Sadie."

"Good morning, little brother. I want to steal Grace from you today and take her shopping. You're paying, so when can you be here?"

I covered the phone and silently thanked my sister for keeping Grace occupied while I met with Gunner and Devlin. "Sadie wants to take you shopping today. Are you up for it?"

She cast her eyes down and whispered, "I don't have the money to go shopping right now. Maybe after I find a job."

I uncovered the phone and spoke to Sadie. "We'll be there in an hour."

Hanging up the phone, I walked in front of Grace and lifted her gaze to mine. "Grace, you don't have to get a job, and you never have to worry about money again. It's my job to take care of you, and I intend to spoil you. Please, let Sadie take you shopping today with my credit card."

"You don't have to do that," she muttered, and I brought my lips to hers.

Keeping the kiss simple, I pecked her on the mouth and replied, "You're my old lady, and it's my job to make sure you have everything you need or want in this life. Let Sadie get you started until we can get back to Alabama to pack your stuff. Please."

"Only if you're sure."

I smiled and took her by the hand. "Let's get ready, and we can stop by the omelet house on the way to the compound."

We got dressed, and Grace pulled her wild hair into a curly pile on top of her head. I led her out to the garage and helped her into the truck, knowing we would need it to bring back whatever she bought today. After turning my cut around, I got behind the wheel and drove into Portstill, passing the compound and pulling into the omelet house.

We walked inside as Jackal was finishing up his breakfast at one of the tables in the back. He was in charge of the armory and ran the club's gun shop in town. He was a pissed-off biker, but when he looked up and saw Grace, he gave her a rare smile as she sat down across from him. His scowl returned when he saw me, and I rolled my eyes at him.

"Good morning, Grace. I don't think we got properly introduced yesterday. I'm Adam, but the brothers call me Jackal," he said as the waitress brought two cups of coffee for Grace and me and cleared his dishes from the table.

Grace looked at me, then turned back to him. "Do you prefer Adam or Jackal?"

"Whichever you prefer, pretty lady." He slid from the booth and slapped me on the shoulder. "I'll see you soon."

Jackal walked to the register and nodded at us before slapping some bills down and walking out. He patched in three years ago, and in that time, he turned our mediocre gun business into one of the most sought-after stores in Tennessee. His attitude left a lot to be desired, but no one expected chatty bikers, so I was used to it.

"He seems nice," Grace said as the waitress walked up to take our order.

I choked back a laugh as we ordered, and when the waitress left, I responded, "No one has ever described Jackal as nice."

"So, do I call them by their club names or their real names?"

"Some prefer their club names, and others don't have a preference. The best thing to do is call them what they introduce themselves as, and if you get confused, just say 'hey you'. They'll answer."

"I just don't want to embarrass you. It's bad enough I freaked out over Needles last night."

The waitress placed our food down and refilled our coffee before leaving us alone. I took her statement as an opening and casually asked, "Do you still not remember how you know him?"

She took a bite and shook her head. I waited as she lifted her coffee cup to wash it down before she spoke. "It was probably the stress of everything yesterday because I'm certain I've never met him before. He's . . . memorable at a glance."

I wanted to believe her, but I saw the look of terror in her eyes yesterday. He did too, and that's why he left so quickly. Needles would never hurt a woman, and seeing Grace so upset had him backing away to calm her.

"That's probably it," I remarked as we finished our breakfast.

The waitress stopped by, and I asked for the check. "Your friend covered it already."

I shrugged, and we left the diner, driving straight to the compound. A new prospect was at the gate and he hustled to the truck. "Skid. Ma'am," he remarked before opening the gate and giving us access to the compound.

Devlin's black SUV was parked along the side of the clubhouse, so I pulled my truck next to it. Sadie walked out and started toward the truck when I turned to Grace, handing her my credit card. "I want you to go crazy."

"I'll get what I need, but I won't be stupid about it."

I grasped her by the back of the neck and pulled her to me. Her eyes grew wide as I kissed her, licking the seam of her lips until she opened. Our tongues dueled, and she moaned into my mouth as she surrendered to me. When I felt she was sufficiently pliant, I pulled back and said, "Have fun, baby. Spend lots."

Sadie knocked on the window at Grace's side, and she turned to see my sister waving like an idiot. The door opened, and Sadie rambled, "I was thinking we could go to the mall in Nashville, or if you'd prefer, there are some great outlet stores in Lincolnville."

Grace climbed down from her seat, and I met her at the back of the truck. Pecking her on the lips, I whispered, "Love you."

"Ditto," she replied, and I lightly popped her butt as she giggled and walked away with Sadie.

I watched her walk beside the clubhouse and down the path to Sadie and Gunner's house before I turned and walked into the clubhouse. It was early, and most of the brothers were either at their jobs or still passed out from last night. A few were nursing coffees, looking like death warmed over, and I bypassed them all and headed straight for Gunner's office.

The door was closed, and I knocked, waiting for an invitation. His office was private, and no one entered except for Sadie, without permission, and even then, she knew to use caution when he was holed up behind closed doors.

"Enter," Gunner yelled, and I opened the door to find him, Devlin, James, and Claw already gathered around the table.

Devlin sat at one end and Gunner at the other, while James and Claw sat to each man's right. Closing the door behind me, I took a seat in the middle. My two worlds collided from time to time, but this was the first time we actually collaborated, and it gave me hope that Gunner would knock the chip off his shoulder where Devlin was concerned.

"How's Grace this morning?" Gunner asked, and everyone turned their attention to me.

"She's blaming her freak-out yesterday on . . . the earlier events of the day," I delicately stated, refusing to divulge any of her secrets.

It was enough Devlin and James knew, but in turn, I knew their women's secrets and had seen them at their worst.

"I know something is going on, and I know the basics, so you don't have to give too much information, but we need to understand what's happening," Gunner insisted. I shook my head, knowing I would have to explain a few things that weren't mine to share.

I exhaled and looked to the Callahans for strength before I turned to my brother-in-law and one of my closest friends to explain.

"What I'm about to tell you, and understand I'm not telling you everything, does not leave this room. You can never discuss it with anyone, not even Sadie." Gunner's eyes grew wide, but he nodded his agreement. Claw sat quietly, and I saw him acknowledge my request before I continued. "Grace was brainwashed by a cult when she was in foster care. They taught her that . . . fuck . . . they taught her how to be a good wife and mother, starting at age twelve. The foster parents were a member of something called The Community, and Grace said they basically trained her to be a sex slave for him, until he found her a husband."

"Are you fucking serious?' Claw asked.

"Unfortunately, it's so much more than what I just told you. She ran away at sixteen and has been fighting guilt and shame for years."

"That's so fucked up," Gunner grumbled, and I could see anger radiating off him.

"What does that have to do with last night?" Claw injected, "No offense, but I don't see Needles being a member of a sex cult, so what got Grace so upset?"

"She thinks it was the culmination of a stressful day, but I could see real fear in her eyes when she saw him. It was instinct," I explained, and Devlin opened his laptop. "For the record, I do not think he has anything to do with them, but something's off."

"I may have some answers, and they might not be the ones you want to hear," James said, and I lifted my gaze to him.

"Are you accusing one of my brothers of hurting a woman? I know we're outlaws, and some of our dealings are outside the rules, but hurting a woman is against what we stand for. So, you better have some proof to back up your accusations," Claw barked, and I held up my hand to calm him down.

"James isn't accusing anyone of anything. He's just telling us what he uncovered. Give him a chance to explain before you get pissed off," I returned and raised my voice. "Grace is my woman, and if I can stay calm, so can you."

Gunner smirked, and Claw sat back, crossing his arms over his meaty chest as Devlin turned his computer so we could see the screen. James stood and pointed at the screen to a picture.

"This is Prescott Baker. He's an investment banker in Springfield, Missouri, and is Needles's former stepfather. He was married to his mother when your former president died, and a then fourteen-year-old Needles, or Monroe, as he was called then, was forced to live with them." James continued as another picture appeared and Prescott's slid to the corner of the background. "Prescott had lots of business organizations he was a member of, so I tried to connect him to Kevin Ringman, Grace's foster father. I spent hours yesterday looking through Prescott's life, and I finally found the connection."

A third picture appeared, and we leaned forward as Devlin stood and began to speak. "This is how we connected Prescott, Kevin, and the name Grace gave me, Matthew Wilhelm. Matthew and Kevin went to middle school together and stayed friends through college, often going on vacations together. Prescott and Matthew are first cousins and closer than brothers. The three of them joined a club a little over fifteen years ago called The Community for Family Values and Education."

The picture was of eleven men, all appearing to be around the same age, with one older man who stood in the center. They all wore black robes that covered their hands and rested on top of their feet. The older man looked familiar, and I looked at Devlin.

"Who's the old man in the center?"

"That's Baldwin Granger, Connie Ringman's uncle."

"Fuck. Are you telling me this man somehow convinced eleven men to become pedophiles and then used his niece in his sick game?"

"What I'm telling you is there are eight of them still alive, and I plan to go after each one. Starting with Monroe's former stepfather," Devlin responded, hatred pouring from him.

"Needles deserves to know what's about to happen," Claw remarked, and James shook his head.

"I hacked into Prescott's life last night, and it seems he made arrangements with Kevin for when it was time to find Grace a husband. They planned to marry her off to Needles, only he left and came back to the club before they could make their move."

"What?" I yelled, pushing back from the table. "How is that possible?"

"Each member must promise to teach the next generation. Prescott promised a son, only he couldn't deliver. It seems like some of them fostered kids and others adopted, but they spared their blood children from their sick game."

"I swear to God, I'll kill that fucker. How could he be a part of all that and act like everything is fine," I said. Gunner stood up from the table and walked in front of me, placing his hands on my shoulders.

"Do you think Needles knew about those assholes' plans?" I shook my head. "Do you trust him?" I nodded, so he went on. "I heard a few things about what he lived through during those years. It changed him, and when he came back to the club, he was more reserved, more attentive. Smokey told me years ago that if someone ever pushed Needles too far, he'd bury them where they stood. Not once has he ever done anything to make me think negatively about him, so I believe he deserves to be told part of what's going on so he can decide if he wants his retribution."

"I agree with Gunner. Nothing about him shows he was aware of what they were doing, but some of the records we found indicated he survived some pretty horrific shit." James reasoned, "He may want to handle Prescott himself, and if that's his choice, I personally believe he should get it." I sat down, pulling my hair and wanting to scream. This shit never ends.

Chapter 28

Grace

Sadie and I went to the outlet mall in Lincolnville, and she dragged me from store to store, insisting Dalton would want me to have an entire wardrobe. I didn't like shopping, but spending time with her was fun. Kelly, and a few other girls I lost touch with years ago, were the only women I'd ever spent time with. Being around Sadie, I realized what I'd missed out on all those years.

A friend.

"So, what did my stupid brother do to upset you?" Sadie asked as we sat down at a table in the food court with too many bags.

"It wasn't him. It was just some crap from my past that I thought was buried." I kept my response vague, hoping she wouldn't push too hard.

Sadie was beautiful with the same piercing blue eyes as Dalton, and I was comfortable around her. She had tattoos up and down her arms, and I envied her ability to be herself. I always hid, not wanting to stand out, and I started thinking about getting some ink.

"Can I tell you something personal?" she inquired as we ate our slices of pizza.

I shrugged, not sure what she was going to share. "If you want to."

She pulled her lips together and exhaled a deep breath before leaning closer to me and lowering her voice. "When I was fifteen, I was attacked on the street." I gasped, and she smiled sadly, shaking her head. "I survived, and for years, I hid what happened, not wanting people to look at me with disgust or pity."

"I can understand that," I mumbled, and she nodded.

"I can see in your eyes that you do, and I'll never ask you what you survived. But know this. You are not alone, and the anchor you carry with you, dragging you back into the painful memories, isn't so heavy if you share the load."

She took a sip of her drink, and I looked down briefly before meeting her eyes. They gave me the same comfort as when I looked into Dalton's, and I whispered, "I was taken advantage of by my foster father for four years, and he . . . brainwashed me into thinking it was okay."

It was the simplest truth I could say, and amazingly, it felt good to admit it. She reached her hand out and touched mine, grounding me as I felt another piece of the shame fall away. The pain wasn't as severe, and I hoped, with time, I could move past it all and not look back.

"I'm sorry you lived through that but look at how strong you are now. You survived, and that's all any of us can ask for," she explained as we gathered our bags and threw our empty plates away.

"Does it get easier?" I asked as we left the mall and walked to her vehicle.

She opened the trunk, and we shoved the countless bags of clothes and personal items into it before she replied. "Time can lessen a wound, but it's always there, just under the surface. The memories will fade but still linger deep in your mind. What you survived shaped you, but it doesn't have to define you. Be the person you want to be, Grace, and let the past stay where it is. Behind you."

We got into the car, and as she pulled into traffic, I looked over at her. "You're pretty amazing. You know that, right?"

She giggled, and I joined her as she said, "I try to tell Dalton and Jacob how awesome I am, but they still don't see it."

On the drive back, we talked about club life, and she filled me in on the troublesome upbringing she and her siblings existed in, and how the Death Hounds saved her. Dalton saved me, and I was grateful for the woman sitting next to me who raised him to be such an honorable man.

As we drove through Portstill, she pointed out a few of the businesses that the club owned, telling me a little about each but not going into too much detail. Dalton explained the club business wasn't my business and I understood there would be secrets he had to keep that didn't affect me. I could live with that if he was honest with me and told me so.

Stopping at a red light, she pointed to the opposite corner. "That's Needles's tattoo studio. He's got six artists under him and only does custom work. Mostly it's for the club, but he has a few private clients that he still does work for."

Hearing his name didn't scare me as much as it did when I saw him, and I pushed, needing to know a little more about him so I could figure out where I knew him from. "Did he do any of yours because they are beautiful."

She rolled her arms to show the tattooed sleeves and smiled as the light turned green. "He's the only person Kade trusts to do my ink. Monroe, that's his real name, by the way, helped me cover some scars a few years ago, and from there, I was hooked."

At the mention of his name, the memory flooded back to me.

"This is your future husband, Grace. His name is Monroe," Daddy said and handed me a picture.

The blond-haired man with haunting green eyes looked nice, and I smiled up at Daddy. "When do I get to meet him?"

I didn't want a husband, but it wasn't my choice. Daddy explained it was time for me to be a wife and mother, and he was going to help another girl named Aubrey. She didn't have a daddy, and he said he had enough love to share with her. I didn't want to share him, but I couldn't say no.

"He's out of town for a few months, but when he returns, his father will let me know," Daddy explained as I followed him down the hallway.

"Does he know about me?" I asked as we entered the room, and he closed the door behind us.

"He's aware of his expectation, just like you are. Don't worry, my saving Grace. Daddy's not going to make you marry a bad man."

"Thank you, Daddy," I replied, feeling sick as he sat on the bed and lowered the zipper on his pants.

"Is that how Daddy taught you to say thank you?"

I snapped my eyes to Sadie, and she looked at me with worry. We were parked in the lot of a grocery store, and I turned my head to look out of the front window. I needed to see Dalton but didn't want to scare his sister any more than I'm sure I already did.

"Grace, are you okay? You turned white as a sheet, and you zoned out there for a minute," she inquired with concern in her voice.

Clearing my throat, I tried to explain. "I'm sorry. I didn't mean to scare you. I'm okay, I promise."

She didn't seem convinced as she muttered, "Only if you're sure."

Nodding, I offered her a smile, and she pulled back onto the road but kept glancing at me as we drove the last few miles to the Death Hounds clubhouse. The gate opened, and she parked the truck next to Dalton's.

"I had fun today," I said as she turned the truck off and swiveled in her seat to look at me.

"I'm not sure what has you bothered, but if you ever need to talk, I'm always here for you."

We got out of the truck, and I saw Gunner and Dalton walking out of the clubhouse, headed toward us. I looked at Sadie and whispered, "Please don't tell him. I will, just . . . not right now."

Remembering the interaction with Kevin, I feared the ramifications of my memories. If Needles . . . *Monroe* . . . was involved with The Community, why was he here? Why was he a Death Hound? The Community carried themselves like they were above the rest of society. Good clothes, the right house, and hand-picked friends were just a few of the expectations, and he fit nowhere into the mold.

"It looks like you took my advice and spent lots." Dalton chuckled as he walked up and hugged me to him.

"I tried," I replied, and he tilted his head to look down at me.

His blue eyes peered at me, and he looked over my shoulder to Gunner and Sadie. "Can you move her bags to my truck? I want to show her something in my cabin before we head home."

Sadie giggled. "I bet you want to show her something."

I looked confused as he linked hands with mine and urged me to follow him. Waving to Sadie and Gunner, I said, "Thank you," as Dalton tugged me away from them.

When we got far enough from the building that no one was around, Dalton asked as we kept walking. "What happened? I can see it in your eyes something upset you. Was it my sister? She means well, but she's nosy as fuck."

"Sadie's great," I affirmed as we climbed the stairs to his cabin at the compound.

He unlocked the door and placed his hand on my lower back, ushering me inside before he closed the door. Sitting me on the couch, he joined me and took my hands into his. "Then what's going on?"

Chewing on my lip, I looked at him and knew he needed the truth. Or at least what I was told. I couldn't trust what anyone from The Community told me, and I was still trying to come to terms with that.

"I remembered how I know Needles," I started, and his blue eyes narrowed as I spoke. "I never met him, but Kevin showed me a picture of him, telling me he was going to be my husband. It was when . . . when he first mentioned Aubrey and how it was my time to fulfill my promise."

Tension rolled off him as he quietly asked, "But you never actually met him?"

"No. I was told he was out of town, and his father was making arrangements for him to return so we could get married and honor our promise. I ran away a few weeks later and hadn't thought about him since." I paused and looked at Dalton through a watery gaze. "It was his eyes I remember. They were haunting, and I could see sadness staring back at me."

"Devlin uncovered some things this morning, and I was going to meet with Needles to discuss them this afternoon. I can tell you that in no way do I think he was involved or even aware of what they planned for him. As soon as he could, he came back to Portstill from his mother's house and patched into the club," Dalton explained.

"Why wouldn't he stay with his parents?"

"His dad was Torch, the club president over fifteen years ago. Needles lived here on the compound from the day he came home from the hospital, but when his pops died in an accident, his mother reappeared and practically dragged him out of here. That's all I know, but I swear to you, I don't think he's a part of any of this."

"Can I . . . can I talk to him?" I asked, and Dalton squeezed my hand.

"You don't have to do that, baby. It's my job to protect you," he said, and I shook my head.

"If he's not a part of all of it, then I have nothing to worry about. He's your friend and brother, and I want to put this behind us. Please, I promise I won't cause any problems."

Dalton leaned over and kissed me with his hands on my cheeks. "You're so brave, Grace. Yeah, I'll let you come with me, Gunner, and Devlin, but if at any time it gets too much, we will leave. Agreed?"

Pecking him on the lips, I responded, "Agreed. Now take me home so I can show you what I spent your money on."

He laughed and scooped me up from the couch. Spinning me around inside the small living room, I wrapped my arms around his neck and knew, deep down, no matter what, he would always protect me. Dalton's love was healing me, and together, we were complete.

A few hours later, I was on the back of Dalton's bike with my arms securely wrapped around his waist. We were headed to Monroe's shop to speak with him, and I was nervous. Not for me, but for him. If he was another unwilling participant in The Community's sick beliefs, he was as much of a survivor as I was.

We pulled into a back alley behind his shop, and Dalton parked next to two other bikes before he turned his bike off. A black SUV was already parked, and I exhaled deeply as we walked into the shop.

Needles sat in a chair against the back wall, and when he saw me walk inside, his eyes grew wide. Devlin and Gunner sat on a couch next to him and turned their gazes to us. Dalton placed his hand on my lower back and urged me inside, giving me strength.

"I wasn't expecting you, Grace. It's nice to see you," Devlin remarked and cut his eyes to Dalton.

I looked between the four men and could feel the anger and tension rolling off all of them. I was the reason this was happening, even indirectly, so I sat down and smoothed my hand over the imaginary wrinkles in my new jeans.

"I'm sorry to interrupt your meeting, but I felt it was important to be here to support Monroe," I explained and sat down on a couch across from Devlin.

Dalton sat next to me, closer to Monroe, and took my hand into his. Monroe kept looking at me and finally spoke, his deep voice calm as he asked, "Do I know you, Grace?"

I glanced to Dalton and then turned to face Monroe as I explained. "You don't know me, and I don't know you, but we know of each other. At least I do."

"I don't understand what the fuck is going on. Can someone tell me and stop side-stepping all these secrets?" he uttered loudly, and Gunner looked at me.

He gave me a nod, and Dalton squeezed my hand as I began. "I'm the woman you were promised to by The Community."

His eyes grew wide, and he pushed back from his chair to stand. Dalton leaned forward, and we watched as Monroe paced the floor, muttering to himself. Devlin's hard eyes appraised the situation, and Gunner looked worried as he sat silent.

"I swear to God, I didn't know about any of it until a few years ago, when my mother finally divorced that sick piece of shit. Goddamn it!" he yelled, and I flinched at the raw pain and anger in his voice. "I knew he was a demented motherfucker, but this shit takes the cake."

Monroe turned and looked at me with pain evident in his green eyes. "Grace, I promise I wasn't a part of any of it. I didn't even know about you or any of their plans for us. I swear on my cut, I didn't know."

His voice was painfully angry, and I stood from the couch and stepped around an observant Dalton. Monroe stood still as I approached, and he glanced at the men behind me as I looked up at him. His eyes cast down at me with worry, and I smiled sadly.

"I believe you. I don't blame you, so please don't blame yourself. We were kids who got caught up in some . . . disturbing events, and I just wanted you to know I hold no bad feelings for you." I looked over my shoulder at a smiling Dalton, and I turned back to Monroe. "In fact, I think we should be friends." His eyes grew wide, and he opened and closed his mouth as I continued. "I don't know about you, but I don't have many friends and could use all that would have me. Can we do that, Monroe? Can we be friends?"

"You're pretty unique. Do you know that?" he asked, and I shrugged.

"I just want to put all this behind us, and the best way I see to do that is to take the sting out of the memories." Leaning closer, I lowered my voice and explained, "Think about how pissed off they would be to know we're friends. It would negate everything they tried to teach us, and we could prove to them we're stronger than they are."

"Skid?" he asked, and Dalton stood to join us as Gunner and Devlin looked on.

"I have no problem with my old lady and you being friends. As long as you understand she can kick your ass, we're all good."

"Really?" Monroe asked, and I chuckled.

"Maybe," I replied, and the room broke out into laughter.

"Now that everything's settled, Skid, you and Grace can head out. I have a few questions for Needles, and then, I promise, it will all be over," Devlin reasoned, and I looked up at my new friend.

I hugged him before he could stop me, and he went stiff, patting me awkwardly on the back until I released him. Dalton shook his head and pulled me to him, wrapping his arm around my neck. "That's the last hug, friend," he taunted and led me out of the tattoo shop.

I climbed onto the back of his bike, and we pulled away from Monroe's shop. Having my arms wrapped around Dalton, feeling his love, and knowing there were no more monsters to slay, gave me hope that our future would be as happy as we wanted it to be.

As we pulled into the front of the cabin, I smiled to myself, knowing that I found someone who could love me through all the pain and regret I had lived years with. He pushed the solitude away and saved me from my nightmare. My life was darkness and silence, and now, it was happiness and light.

With love, could you ask for anything more?

Chapter 29

Skid

Two weeks later

I pulled my black gloves on and twisted my neck, popping the kinks out and getting ready for destruction. The information Needles gave Devlin was invaluable and as we walked through the woods leading to the large house tucked off the road, I knew this was the end. Devlin, James, Gunner, Needles, Jackal, and I silently traversed through the trees, and when we approached the side yard, we all stopped.

"Do you have eyes inside the house?" I asked James, who had his cell phone in his hand.

"Inside and out," he replied and looked down at the device.

Prescott was hosting a Community party tonight, and we arrived before the guests. The sun was already set, and I looked at Needles, seeing the tremor in his hands. The story he told me last week when we got drunk at the lake physically made me sick. I don't know how he survived what Prescott and his mother put him through, and I still don't understand how he could have anything to do with that vile woman.

She turned a blind eye to it all, just for the money and prestige that came with being Prescott's wife. Something caused her to divorce him a few years ago, and since then, she's depended on Needles for support.

The six of us watched the house, monitoring who came and went for almost half an hour before the camera picked up a little red-haired girl walking into the party with her small hand in that of a much older man. I closed my eyes briefly, needing a moment to push aside the disgust at what they planned for her.

"Let's move," Devlin urged, and we took off, staying in the shadows until we got to the back door.

There were fewer cameras on the back of the house, and we used that as our entryway. Gunner popped the lock and silently pushed the door open to reveal a mudroom off the kitchen. Noises from behind the door in front of us were muffled, but I could hear someone speaking about the little girl.

"Are you excited for tonight?" a man asked, and another chuckled.

"I've been ready for tonight. Is everything in order?" the second voice inquired, and I looked at Needles.

His eyes were practically slits as he stepped forward and whispered, "Let's end this shit once and for all."

James pressed a few buttons on his phone and replied, "Cameras are covered. Let's finish this."

His desire to avenge Aubrey and my desire to avenge Grace was nothing compared to Needles's need to rip these assholes apart. He wanted to attack them head on, but we had to play our cards right and protect not only the club but any innocents involved. If we went nuts, like he wanted, we would all end up in prison, and I refuse to be away from Grace, locked in a cage.

We all grabbed our weapons then readied ourselves for the battle ahead. Eight men inside were all that stood between The Community and annihilation. And one innocent little girl.

Devlin nodded to us and silently opened the door to the kitchen. He stepped inside, and I followed behind him, seeing the room empty. James looked at his phone and pointed to the left. "That way."

Moving through the kitchen, we listened for anyone outside the door before Devlin pushed it open, revealing a large dining room. James nodded to the right, and we walked to the door, hearing voices coming through.

"Is she ready to be brought in?" a man asked. While another replied, "I'll send for her."

"Kill them all and protect the girl," Gunner whispered, and we all exhaled.

Jackal stepped up, kicking the door with his big black boot, and we filed into the room, catching the seven perverts off guard. I swung my eyes around and didn't see the girl. "James. Innocent."

He nodded and moved to the other door in the room, listening for approaching footsteps.

"Who the hell are you?" Prescott yelled, and Needles walked up from the rear and stood with his eyes locked on the man. "Monroe? What the hell are you doing here? You walked away from your chance years ago."

He picked up his weapon and aimed it at Prescott before announcing, "I never asked for a chance."

With the silencer on the gun, it barely made a sound into the room as he pulled the trigger, dropping Prescott to the floor with a bleeding hole in the head. A few of the other men screamed and tried to run, only to be met with a fist, a knife, or a bullet to the head. Their noise was going to alert whoever was in the house with the girl, and I slapped my hand over another man's mouth to silence him.

Pulling him to me, I menacingly whispered, "This is for every little girl you sick fuckers hurt." My knife came down onto his chest, punching into his heart as he gurgled behind my hand. "I hope you burn for eternity, you degenerate piece of shit."

He flailed for a minute before his arms dropped to his side, then I released him with a thud onto the floor. There was one man pressed against a bookshelf with his hand out, begging Devlin for mercy.

"Mercy won't be found here. The devil demands his payment," he stated as he shot the man. First in the crotch, then in the head.

The seven men were dead or dying on the floor as James watched from the second doorway. He held his hand up and muttered, "Stop."

We all froze as he looked at his camera and pressed his finger to his closed lips, then stepped to the side of the doorway. We watched as the door opened and a beautiful little girl walked in, blinking her eyes heavily as she was led into the room by the last man who needed to die.

When she stepped into the room, James snatched the man up by his collar and slapped a hand over his mouth to stop his screaming. The little girl looked up at James, and he glanced over at us for help. She went to turn her head to us, but Needles ran across the room and scooped her up, pressing her face into his chest and leaving with her safely in his arms. She didn't need to see all the blood or what was going to happen to the last member of The Community.

We dug and dug for the last two weeks, tapping into emails and phone calls until we verified every last member. They never grew in size, and from all accounts, the little girl here tonight was the last one with them. Hopefully, we saved her before they could hurt her, and I glanced into the hallway to see Needles kneeling in front of her to check her out.

"What is this about?" the old man asked, and I recognized him as Baldwin Granger, the leader of The Community.

"Well, if it isn't the ringmaster of this shitshow," I taunted as James released him, pushing him into the room.

He looked around, seeing all his proteges dead on the floor, and tears flooded his eyes. I stepped closer, knowing his sickness was what hurt my Grace, and I wanted to look into his eyes as he died.

"Do I know you?" he asked with snot running down his face.

Wiping his nose on his sleeve, he collapsed to the floor onto his knees, and I squatted in front of him. Lifting his chin with the tip of my knife, I looked at him as I explained, "Grace sends her regards and wishes you the best when you finally get to hell. She hopes you burn for what you did."

Swiping the blade, I watched blood flow from his gashed open chin as he yelled for help. I gripped into his white hair and brought his face to mine. "I bet all the little girls you hurt begged for help too."

"I . . . they . . ." he stumbled over his words, and I looked over my shoulder at Devlin, Gunner, James, and Jackal.

"Do you have any questions for him?" Everyone shook their head as they watched, and with slow precision, I began to cut into his face.

Slice after slice, I watched as his eyes rolled back in his head, and he slowly and painfully started to slip away. Tossing him onto his back, I kneeled next to him, and with a single thrust, brought the knife down in between his eyes. He flailed like a fish out of water for a moment before he fell silent, and it was over.

I stood and looked at the four men still in the room and glanced out to see Needles holding the little girl close to him.

"What's the exit plan?" I asked, and Jackal stepped forward with a demented smile.

He pulled a lighter from his pocket and lit the flame, explaining, "Electrical fire."

"Handle it. Let's get the girl out of here and figure out what to do with her," Gunner suggested, and I whistled for Needles.

His cut was over the little girl's head as he carried her inside, and I guessed her age to be ten, maybe eleven. I shook my head as his worried eyes met mine, and as he got closer to me, I whispered, "We'll make sure she's okay."

I could tell he wasn't sure, but he nodded as he walked out the house and back into the woods. With Devlin's government connections, we wouldn't have any blowback from tonight, but I worried about her and where she would end up.

Leaving Jackal to handle his business, the rest of us followed Needles outside and traversed the small grove of trees until we came to our two vehicles parked on the edge of the wood line. Needles placed the girl in the back seat and closed the door softly before turning back to us.

He ran his hand through his blond hair and looked exhausted as he asked, "What do we do with her? She's terrified."

"I'll call Sadie and see if she can sleep with us tonight until Devlin figures out who she is and where she belongs," Gunner offered just as a large explosion rocked us.

A huge fireball rolled into the sky, heating us through the trees as a laughing Jackal ran through the woods toward us. His face was filled with joy as he leaned over, catching his breath from laughter.

"Noodles, where are you?" a small voice sounded from the SUV, and Needles turned to the door, opening it quickly.

The girl looked up at him with tears in her green eyes, and I could see the heartbreak on Needles's face at her pain. He took her by the hand and offered her kind words, then she shocked us all when she launched herself out of the backseat and latched around his neck with her small arms.

He turned his tearful gaze to us and mouthed, 'Help me.'

She stayed attached to him the entire ride home, and when we got to the compound, he tried to hand her to Sadie, only to have the little girl scream, "Please, Noodles, don't let me go!"

Everyone's heart broke for her, so for the night, Needles settled into the recliner in Gunner and Sadie's house, holding the little girl in his arms, ensuring she was safe.

When I got home, Grace was waiting for me. She knew where we were going and was worried. When I unlocked the door, she immediately wrapped her arms around my waist, and I felt her tears wetting my shirt as she cried.

Knowing how much pain she'd experienced for so long, I didn't tell her about the little girl that night. I picked her up and carried her to the shower with me, needing to get the stench of death off me but unable to let her out of my arms.

Grace was the bravest and strongest woman I'd ever met. She lived through the worst betrayal and hid herself, afraid of people's lies regarding love. She made herself strong, and I was the lucky bastard that got to call her mine.

She settled into my chest that night, wrapped in my arms, and I knew, no matter what, we would always have happiness. After living in silence after the dark nightmare, the only place to go was up.

Epilogue

Grace

Two weeks later

Last week, I'd finally gotten the nerve to meet with Aubrey. She and I sat on Dalton's back porch while he and Hayden gave us time alone. It was the hardest thing I've ever done, and when she pulled me into a bruising hug and whispered, "It's not your fault." I broke down crying.

Aubrey amazed me with her ability to put her pain in the past. She took something that could have been devastating and turned it into strength. I didn't go into detail about The Community and what their plans were, and I didn't tell her that last week, they were all destroyed for their sick perversions.

I could see us being good friends since she and her friends are so close to Dalton, but there was a small part of me that still felt guilt over what happened to her. Dalton reminded me that I had nothing to do with what she endured, but I still felt like I was to blame. I agreed to start seeing a counselor about everything, and I hoped they could help me get past the last hurdle.

This morning, Dalton woke me up with his head between my legs and a smile on his face as he brought me to climax. He was attentive to my needs and always seemed to know when I needed his strong arms around me or an earth-shattering orgasm. After he and I found release together, he pulled me against his chest and asked if I wanted to go to a Death Hounds party. After the last one, I was afraid of how the brothers would look at me, but when they started calling me Rocky, I laughed, knowing I'd found a family.

The party was in full swing, with music playing over the speakers around the compound and food lining tables under the picnic pavilion. I was visiting with Sadie and a few of the other old ladies when the music suddenly stopped. Looking up, I saw Dalton walking toward me with something draped over his arm.

When he was in front of me, I looked up at him with a smile and noticed everyone was watching us intently.

"Grace, since the moment I laid eyes on you, I knew you were mine. Tonight, in front of my brothers and my friends . . ." He paused and looked off to the side. I followed his line of sight and saw Devlin, Elise, James, Amaya, Hayden, and Aubrey standing in the distance with huge smiles on their faces. Dalton turned back to me, lifted the leather cut up, and turned it so I could see the back. "I give you this cut, declaring to the world that you're my old lady. I want to ride with you through life's ups and downs, and I vow to make sure you have the wind to lift your wings and fly."

Tears streamed down my face as he looked at me expectantly. I nodded, and he spun his finger to encourage me to turn around. He slid the cut over my shoulders and spun me around as the Death Hounds and our friends cheered. His tattooed hands cupped my face, and he kissed me until I felt my knees wobble.

The group surrounded us and offered their congratulations as the music cranked back up and the alcohol began to flow. It was a raucous party, and I was surprised to see Devlin and the rest were still here. I thought for sure they would have left, but the Death Hounds were showing them hospitality as everyone visited and laughed.

Dalton was talking with Devlin when Sadie sat next to me and nudged me with her shoulder. "Welcome to the family."

I tucked a lock of hair behind my ear and ran my hands down the smooth leather vest. "You did an excellent job raising him and Jacob, just in case they never said thanks."

I met Jacob shortly after coming back from Atlanta, and he was just as handsome and charming as his brother. You could see they all had different fathers, but they all had the same striking blue eyes that seemed to pierce into your soul.

"I don't know about an excellent job, but I did what I had to do, and I'd do it again if needed." Sadie was shy about compliments, but I wanted her to know how important she was to her brothers.

"It looks like he wants to eat you alive." She chuckled as Dalton approached us.

Realizing the club wasn't shy about sex and all that came with it, I shrugged with a smile. "Maybe."

Just as Dalton stepped up to us, she muttered, "Starving is more like it."

He leaned over and kissed his sister on the cheek, and turned to me. "Feel like taking a walk?"

I looked at a giggling Sadie and saw Gunner walking up to us. Turning back to Dalton, I replied, "That sounds like fun."

He took my hand into his, and just as we started to walk away, Gunner shouted, "Remember, there are kids at Piper's cabin."

Dalton looked over his shoulder and threw up two fingers as we walked through the crowd of Death Hounds. Passing through the clubhouse, we walked farther away from the party until the music was barely audible. We were past the small cabins and not quite to the large houses where some of the married brothers lived when Dalton spun me around to face him.

His thumb caressed the line of my jaw as he whispered, "I need you, Grace."

I wrapped my arms over his shoulders and linked my hands together. "Then take me."

His stiff length was pressing against his jeans, and I rubbed my pelvis against him, needing him just as much. He walked me backward until my back rested against the trunk of a large tree, brought his lips to mine, and kissed me until I was squirming against him. I could feel him smile against my lips as his hand moved from my waist, slowly pushing my shirt up until his hand was cupping my breast.

Nibbling down my neck, I whimpered, and he whispered, "Don't worry. I've got you, darlin.'"

His hand inched down until he reached the button of my jeans, and with a flick of his fingers, they were open. Lowering my zipper, he pushed his hand into the front and flicked my needy clit with his thick fingers, forcing my hips to chase them. I was soaked and he groaned when he pushed into my wet pussy.

"Fuck. You need it bad, don't you?" he asked, and I nodded, reaching out and opening his jeans.

Dalton began to kiss down my chest, biting through my bra into my nipple and working my jeans and panties down my legs as he lowered himself onto his knees in front of me. I looked down at him, and his hypnotic blue eyes met mine. This powerful man, who was respected and feared by many, was kneeling at my feet, waiting to show me unimaginable pleasures, and I asked myself silently, how did I get so lucky?

"I love you," I whispered.

He smiled before replying, "I love you too."

He pressed his face into my center and swiped his tongue through my wet folds. My knees nearly buckled as he flicked and sucked my clit, pushing me closer and closer to release. I gripped into his hair as he lifted one leg over his shoulder and pushed two thick fingers into me.

Faster and faster, he pumped his fingers into me as my orgasm pushed closer to the surface. A well-placed bite on my clit had me erupting into euphoria, and Dalton grabbed onto my hips to keep me from falling as I shook through muffled moans.

When he rang the last drop from me, he stood, and his beard was drenched with my juices. He ran his hand down his beard and licked the palm of his hand as his heated eyes locked onto mine. I went to lower to my knees when he stopped me.

"I need to be inside you," he clarified and stepped closer to me.

His hard cock was peeking out of his pants, and I grasped the shaft and pumped my hand a few times. He took my hand and brought it up to his lips, kissing my wrist. Dalton reached under my thighs and lifted me, placing my back against the trunk of the tree as he let the head of his cock brush against my wet lips.

"Please," I begged, and he lowered me as he pushed his hips up, filling me with his enormous shaft.

His head came to rest against my shoulder as he pumped his hips, working deeper into me until our pelvises were pushed together. Dalton brought his gaze back to me as he worked himself faster and harder into me. I bounced against the tree and gripped into his shoulders as our panted moans filled the air.

"Oh . . . oh, fuck," I muttered as I felt his curls rubbing my clit, pulling me into another orgasm.

"Fuck, yes, Grace. Show your old man how much you like being fucked. Come on my cock," he urged and slammed his mouth to mine.

I moaned and whimpered as stars lit up behind my eyes. Electricity shot through me, and every nerve ending fired, forcing my body to convulse and twitch as he fucked me faster. Slapping skin echoed around us, and I dug my nails into his cut as he slammed his hips into mine, finding his own release.

He hugged me closer to him, and I felt his heart beating strong against my chest as we caught our breath. Pulling back, he smiled at me and pecked me on the nose. Biting my lip, I smiled at him as he retracted his still hard shaft from me and gently placed me onto unsteady feet. I could feel him slipping from me as he helped me redress.

After we had our clothes back on, he took me by the hand and led me back to the clubhouse. The party was still in full swing, and when we exited the clubhouse to the front where everyone was, another round of cheers erupted. I hid my face in his arm, and he wrapped it around me and whispered, "Don't hide, darlin'. You have nothing to be ashamed about."

I looked up at him and acknowledged, "I know."

We smiled like fools at each other as we rejoined the gathering. Dalton went to speak with James as I visited with Elise, Aubrey, and Amaya. Devlin was nearby, speaking with Gunner, and Hayden was practically glued to Aubrey's side.

Monroe was standing off to the side of the party, watching but not engaging, and I worried about him. We were becoming friends, and he'd designed a beautiful tattoo for me that we had planned to do next week. There were times he would call and check on me, asking if I'd heard about Iris, the little girl they saved from The Community party.

He told me about her bad dreams and how difficult it was when he had to turn her over to the state. There was no record of her, and a name was all she knew about herself. I feared how long they had brainwashed her, but he said she never showed inappropriate actions toward him, so I believed she might have been spared the worst of their manipulations.

"I'll be right back," I said to the group, and they nodded as I stepped away and walked to Monroe.

He smiled sadly at me and finished off his beer as I sat down in a chair next to him.

"How are you doing?" I inquired, and he leaned back, sighing.

"I wish Callahan had some information on Iris, but he said they're still waiting on her DNA results."

I pursed my lips and made eye contact with a watchful Dalton. He smiled and nodded to me before turning back to his conversation. We all knew

Monroe was struggling with what happened, and his worry about Iris was honorable.

"Have you seen her?" I asked, but he shook his head and leaned over, resting his forearms on his knees.

"They said until they can figure out who she belongs to, it would be more confusing to her to have me around." His voice was filled with anger, and I could see the pain across his face. Meeting Iris and having her attach to him so quickly was taking a toll on him.

"I call bullshit, but you know the state does things their own way."

I sat with him as the party raged on and silently watched the group. They were an unexpected group of men who found each other, creating a dysfunctional family that loved deeply and protected without mercy. To the outside world, they were outlaws. To me, they were family.

I patted Monroe on the back and told him, "I'm going to get another beer. Do you want one?"

He nodded. "Thanks, Grace."

As I walked across the yard to the coolers, Dalton met me and linked his hand with mine. "Is he okay?" he asked, and I shook my head.

"He's struggling with Iris and worrying about what's going to happen to her."

"Devlin said he'll have some information tomorrow. The tests are back, and he's running them through the system, so maybe he can discover something about her to help us figure out how she got with them and who her family is."

I looked up at him and whispered, "If her family gave her to them, they don't deserve her back."

"I agree, darlin'. Devlin will get it worked out. I promise."

I could see that he was trying to make me feel better but didn't believe his own words. We were all worried about Iris and who she was going to end up with. A strange thought popped into my head, and as hard as I tried to shake it off, it would leave me. I tugged Dalton by the hand, and he looked down at me with worry.

"I think we should foster Iris until things can get worked out. Do you think that's possible?"

"Why would you want to do that?" He wasn't being mean, just curious.

"I know what it's like not to have anyone, and if I can help her with what-ever she lived through, maybe it would make things better for her."

He grasped the back of my head and brought his lips to mine, kissing me until I fought for breath. "You're a good woman, Grace. And yes, I think that's something we can get arranged."

I wanted to do something to make up for my years of silence. After living my life hidden in the darkness, fighting nightmares and the crippling pain of my past, I'd finally found peace within the light. If helping Iris find her way and possibly giving Monroe some peace of mind was something I could do, then I would.

Because that's what family is for.

Thank you for reading Skid: Death Hounds MC #2. If you enjoyed the book, please consider leaving a review. Something as simple as I liked it/ I didn't like it helps indie authors immensely. While this is the end of the original Embattled Dreams storyline, there is more Darkness coming. Nee-dles: Death Hounds MC #3 will be available April 2022 and will reunite the Death Hounds and the Callahan's for more bloodshed and vengeance.

Sign up for my newsletter to get early release information, cover reveals, and giveaway opportunities.

https://authorhjmarshall.com/newsletter/

Continue reading for an excerpt of Embracing My Nightmare where all the Darkness began. Meet Devlin Callahan, the madman of the Flats, and discover how far a man would go for the woman he loves.

The End . . . for now
Important Information

If you or someone you know is a victim of abuse or sexual assault, please reach out for help. Call your local police, emergency responders, or contact one of the following.

National Center for Missing and Exploited Children
1-800-THE-LOST (1-800-843-5678)
www.missingkids.com[1]
National Child Abuse Hotline
1-800-4-A-CHILD (1-800-422-4453)
www.childhelp.org[2]
RAINN National Sexual Assault Telephone Hotline
1-800-656-HOPE (4673)
www.rainn.org[3]
National Foster Care and Adoption
1-800-394-3366
www.childwelfare.gov[4]

---

1.   http://www.missingkids.com/

2.   http://www.childhelp.org/

3.   http://www.rainn.org/

4.   http://www.childwelfare.gov/

About the Author

H.J. Marshall began her love of reading and writing at an early age and has always dreamed of being a writer full-time. A nomadic youth exposed her to different perspectives of life, community, and culture, resulting in a lifelong love of food, music, and history. When she is not writing, she enjoys the music of all generations and genres, writing full-time, and living in her quiet cabin in the woods. Currently landlocked, H.J. dreams of her beach house, salty air, and a life filled with laughter.

HJ's Hellions Readers Group[1]
Amazon: https://amzn.to/2RVvPfv
Instagram: https://bit.ly/37dn7Rr
Goodreads: https://bit.ly/37WTL7Q
BookBub: https://bit.ly/2uiCTd7
Facebook Author Page: https://bit.ly/2SiH0hc
Facebook Readers Group: https://bit.ly/2vHXGXT
Newsletter: https://authorhjmarshall.com/newsletter/
Website: https://www.authorhjmarshall.com

---

1.   https://bit.ly/2vHXGXT

Embracing My Nightmare

Prologue
Elise

Horrid screams pierced through the thick veil of sleep I was swimming in, pushing the monsters back into the recesses of my mind. I tried to fight my way through the darkness and back into the light, fearful that whatever was causing the screams was worse than the demons who chased me when I slept.

My father, Roger, had forced the pill down my throat with a strong grip on my neck as he poured the water into my mouth, making me choke as he yelled at me. His fingers dug into the tender skin as I swallowed the bitter pill, and I knew I would have bruises from his brutality tomorrow. I had become good at hiding the evidence of their abuse, but I feared these injuries may be the worst ones yet, and that was saying quite a bit.

My mother, Sally, watched him, shaking her head at me in disgust while they waited for the pill to take effect. Roger held me to my small bed by the throat, his eyes wandering over me, making my stomach lurch as I noticed the lust in his gaze. It took little time before I was dragged into the dark world of sleep, teetering on the edge of awake and unconscious, fearful of what tonight would bring.

Lately, Roger had become more brutal with his punishments and his eyes had lingered too long on my developing figure. Yesterday, he had 'accidentally' walked in while I was showering, and I knew deep down that he was about to subject me to a worse punishment than ever before.

My sixteenth birthday was last week, and they had locked me in my room, reminding me I wasn't special and didn't deserve a party or even a present to open. I had grown accustomed to their cruelty, but their words still stung my heart like a poisonous arrow. I locked my feelings away and dreamed that one day, someone would love me for the person I was and not try to change me for their own needs and desires.

They reminded me daily that they had adopted me, screamed at me that I should be more grateful that they had taken me off the streets and into their loving home. *Loving home, my ass.* I lived every day of the last six years maneuvering through the landmines they set for me. Harsh words and hard fists had been my daily routine since I could remember. I never understood why they hated me so much or why they had adopted me if they didn't want kids.

It was bad enough someone left me at a church when I was five years old. The pastor's wife found me filthy, starved, and crying for someone who never came back. After no one claimed me, I went into the foster care system and after five years of rotating homes, Sally and Roger Hutchins adopted me. They kept the name the state assigned to me, and they never attempted to bond with me. I was always a burden to them, and I never knew why.

I could hear angry voices shouting from the other room, but as hard as I tried, I couldn't shake the tomb of sleep that had encased me. I was lucid to what was happening but couldn't move more than a twitch. They had drugged me before, but nothing to this effect. I knew whatever was happening in the other room, I was powerless to stop it or to protect myself.

I didn't know if I would stop what sounded like my 'parents' being beaten, even if I was able to. They had treated their two dogs better than they had treated me, and some days, the only food I got was the meals the school served. I learned years ago to hide a small part of my lunch, just in case they decided I was too much of a burden and starved me for days.

"Please, don't hurt him," Sally pleaded with the unknown person who was with them. "He's all I've got in this world."

"WHAT ABOUT HER?" the man's voice bellowed, startling me, and for the first time, I truly feared for my life.

The timbre in his voice was dark and deadly, and I felt the goosebumps on my skin as the sound of flesh hitting flesh filtered into my small bedroom. My head swayed as I forced my eyes open, blinking as the harsh sounds filled my room. Someone had shoved my twin bed against the far wall, and as my blurry vision started to clear, I could hear Sally's sobs.

"You promised you would care for her, to protect her, and love her. And what did you two do? You neglected her, you beat her, and you starved her." The stranger's voice sounded hollow and deadly as he questioned her.

Thud.

Thud.

Thud.

"You were paid well to take care of her and you failed. How could you do that to her?" I felt my heavy legs begin to move, the pinpricks of feeling starting to ease down my limbs, causing me to twitch with pain. The bed squeaked and I forced my limbs to still, afraid whoever was causing all the commotion would come to see if I was awake.

"Please. We never wanted this. Never wanted her." Her cries echoed into my bare room, and I felt the last little piece of my heart shatter. I was aware they never wanted me, but to hear someone had paid them to take care of me and that they didn't care enough to even try, had tears falling down my cheeks, soaking the pillow under my head. "We were forced to take her, and she's nothing but a little whore, strutting around the house, trying to catch his eye. She's a dirty slut who deserves . . ."

Her scream pierced the last of the fog I was trapped in as Roger's grunts sounded over the attacker's roar. Sally pleaded and begged for the man to stop, and finally, the thuds ceased, and the only sounds were heavy breathing and her broken sobs.

The rusty bed frame groaned slightly as I moved, trying to get the blood back into my limbs. My head was swimming and my vision was hazy from the drugs they had forced on me, but I needed to see whoever was causing my tormentors pain. I needed to know who was avenging me, the unwanted girl.

I tried to lower my arms but found they had been bound to the bed with soft silk. My heart thumped loudly in my chest as the drug fog threatened to take me under again. The low voice of the unknown man drifted through the room, but my brain was too hazy to understand the words he was uttering to my 'mother'.

Fuck her and her bastard husband for what they had put me through. I hoped, whoever he was, that he made them suffer. I hoped it was painful and drawn out before they met their makers. The fresh pain of their abuse was clear on my emaciated body. I should have forgiveness for them, but having spent a life unloved and unwanted, I had hardened the last of my heart to survive.

"You want me to do what?" she screeched and my head snapped to the door at the fear coming from her.

"You heard me, you stupid bitch. Either you do it or I will, and I promise, I won't be merciful. I promise to make you suffer for everything you did to her. Now choose," he yelled, and I tried to draw myself into a tight ball on my bed.

I was covered with a light sheet and there was slack in my restraints but not enough for me to free myself. I was stuck between nightmares with no place to go, forced to be the silent witness to whatever danger Roger and Sally had brought to themselves. I silently prayed that sleep would take me back under to avoid whatever fate awaited me, but with each passing second, I became more alert.

The cocking of a gun stilled me in my bed and my body trembled. Was I going to be next after he was finished with them? Was tonight the night I would finally die in the hell I had existed in for so long?

"CHOOSE!" the man bellowed, and I turned my head into the pillow, hoping to silence the begging and pleading coming from Sally.

"I-I-I c-c-can't," she cried, and the gunshot echoed into the room, making me jump as my ears rang, muffling the screams coming from Roger.

"You killed her, you son of a bitch," Roger wheezed out with a cough, and the anger and terror in his voice scared me to my core. "How could you kill her? After everything we did for Elise! For you!"

"You did nothing for her, you selfish bastard. You lied to me and I warned you to never try to double-cross me. I thought out of everyone, I could trust you to keep your word. You're a depraved man, Roger. Too bad Sally beat you before she killed you. Sad, she felt the only way out was suicide."

"Please, don't. Don't!" Roger screamed as the gun sounded again.

The silence stretched out, and I was shivering from panic as the door opened. Slamming my eyes shut, I hoped it would be over soon and I could finally be free from the horror my life had been. He walked slowly across the room, and as hard as I tried, I couldn't hide my trembling.

The bed dipped as he sat next to me and I squeezed my eyes closed and waited. Softly, a hand brushed the hair off my face, and with a gentle stroke, he ran his finger down my cheek. He leaned in and whispered into my ear, "You're safe now. They can't hurt you anymore."

My eyes opened slowly, and the bright lights shining through the door shadowed him. I could tell he was a large man, but the only thing I could make out was his jet-black hair that framed his face. His intoxicating scent enveloped me—a woodsy scent mixed with the bitter smell of copper.

Recognizing the smell as blood, their blood, I tugged on the restraints, trying to move away from him. His hand flexed on his lap and he reached out to touch my face again. I tilted my head away and whimpered. With an audible exhale, he placed his hand back on his lap and stared at me.

"Please don't hurt me," I pleaded on a whisper.

His gaze moved to the bruises running up and down my arms and wrapping around my neck. A low rumble rose from deep in his chest. "I could never hurt you, Elise. I should have been here sooner. I'm sorry it took me so long."

He stood from the bed and the absence of him next to me caused a pain to lance through my heart. How could someone who just killed my 'parents' cause such a reaction in me? What was wrong with me that my first real sign of attraction was to the person who just murdered two people? For me.

"I don't understand. Who are you? Why were you looking for me? Why did you kill them?" My eyes grew wide, and I didn't know if he would punish me for seeing him or for asking questions that I didn't want the answers to. My breathing became erratic, and he moved closer to the door.

"Calm down, little lamb. Someone will be here soon to untie you. When they arrive, tell them that Roger drugged you, tied you to the bed, and you woke up when you heard the gunshots. You don't know who shot who, but you heard the gun go off twice. Tell them everything that has happened to you, but I ask one thing."

"I'll do whatever you want. You saved me from them," I reasoned, hoping to dissuade his anger. He groaned low before clearing his voice.

"Never mention me to anyone. *Ever*. I wasn't here, and you never saw me. It's safer for you. Promise me, lamb." His deep voice cascaded over me and I nodded.

His eyes shone a deep blue briefly, the reflecting light cascading into the small room as he observed me. "Say it."

"I promise," I whispered.

I meant every word. I would never tell a soul about the man who saved me from the misery I had existed in for so long. Who would believe me anyway? I wasn't special. I was just me.

He turned to leave, and with his back to me, he spoke his final words with a marked promise. "Live your life, lamb. Experience the world, make friends, but remember one thing. You belong to me. I'll be back for you when you least expect it. When that day comes, be prepared. I won't take no for an answer."

I felt his warning down to the depths of my soul and I knew that our next encounter would be the changing point in my life. Whoever my savior was, he had just become my new nightmare.

Made in the USA
Middletown, DE
27 January 2023